THE KING'S OUTLAWS

HIGHLAND WARLORD

Bestselling & Multi-Award Winning Author

AMY JARECKI

PUBLISHER'S NOTE: This is a work of fiction. Names, characters, places, and incidents either are the product of the author's imagination or are used fictitiously. Any resemblance to actual persons, living or dead, business establishments, events, or locales is entirely coincidental.

Edited by: Scott Moreland

Book Cover Design by: Dar Albert

Published by Oliver-Heber Books

0 9 8 7 6 5 4 3 2 1

FOREWORD

The King's Outlaws is a romantic series based upon the heroes who supported Robert the Bruce during his rise to greatness. It was an era of brutal unrest, which is often misunderstood. The following foreword summarizes the political climate and historical events leading up to the opening of Chapter One.

A great deal is unknown about Robert the Bruce's early life. It is a fact that the Bruce Clan had divided loyalties because of their land holdings on either side of the Scottish/English border as was the case with many noble families. However, Robert the Bruce's actions even as a young man demonstrated a leaning of patriotism for his beloved Scotland. He was a loyal son, a dedicated father, and a nobleman caught amid the turmoil of his time.

Robert the Bruce was only eleven years of age when King Alexander III died in March of 1286. Indeed, Robert would have still been a lad at his father's table when in 1290 he received news of the death of Alexander's only heir, the Maid of Norway. With no clear successor, Edward I of England, who was also Alexander's father-in-law, was invited by Scottish magnates to select the next king. Several families stepped forward as competitors for the crown, but those with the strongest claims were the Balliols and the Bruces. Edward, who later earned the moniker, "Hammer of the Scots", immediately seized the opportunity to declare himself suzerain, or overlord of Scotland. The Bruces were considered too powerful for Edward's interests and, thus, in November of 1292 he selected the weaker competitor, John Balliol, as king.

Afterward, to protect his family's claim to the throne, in 1295 Robert de Brus, 6th Lord of Annandale, resigned the earldom of Carrick to his eldest son, Robert the Bruce, now a twenty-one-year-old man.

During Balliol's four-year reign, Edward required the Scottish king to repeatedly submit to humiliating subjugation. In 1296, Balliol retaliated, was defeated, and eventually sent into exile in France. Of course, Edward saw fit to retaliate and flex his muscle against the Scots. Most memorable in this rising was the sack of Berwick in the spring of 1296 where, for three days, Edward's army slaughtered men, women, and children in one of the most savage acts of war ever committed. Further rubbing salt into the wound, at Wark the Scottish nobles, including the elder Bruce and his son, were required to sign the Ragman Roll declaring fealty to Edward, after which, the patriarch of the Bruce Clan decided to withdraw from the political scene. No matter what the new Earl of Carrick felt or how much he desired revenge, Robert was bound by a familial duty to obey his father.

But he eventually acted on his conscience. On the 7th of July1297, Robert the Bruce took part in a failed rising at Irvine. As a result, he was nearly forced to surrender his daughter, Marjorie, to Edward. But when Robert refused, three sureties were accepted on his behalf, that of Bishop Wishart, the Stewart, and Sir Alexander Lindsay. Needless to say, Bruce then came under a great deal of English scrutiny. Also in 1297, William Wallace joined forces with Andrew de Moray and defeated the English at the Battle of Stirling Bridge. In June of 1298, Wallace was retained as Guardian of Scotland and, as legend has it, was knighted by the Earl of Carrick. This act was a key indication that the Bruces, as with many nobles, had finally endured enough of Edward's tyranny and had begun subtle activities to support the Scottish cause.

When Wallace left for the Continent to seek help from the pope, it is important to note that Robert the Bruce was appointed guardian along with Bishop Lamberton, and John Comyn, nephew of John Balliol (yet another contender for the throne). Bruce and Comyn did not get along, possibly because of Robert's radical leanings toward independence, but his fervor ended up seeing him edged out of the guardianship.

By 1300, there was once again one Guardian of Scotland, Sir John de Soules. At this time, Edward was still conducting raids into Scotland and, in 1301 after skirmishes led by Robert the Bruce, Edward captured Turnberry, Robert's ancestral castle. In a political ploy to regain his lands, he surrendered in January of 1302, six months before his twenty-eighth birthday. With the restoration of his estates, he was hamstringed by the determination to stay alive and stay free. It is said the ensuing years were the most difficult of his life. He was called upon many times to act in the service of Edward and prove his loyalty. But Bruce wasn't entirely convincing. For example, when Edward asked Robert to supply siege engines for the 1304 attack on Stirling Castle, Bruce complied, sending the trebuchets without an essential component which rendered them useless.

Following the death of his father and the execution of William Wallace, Bruce became more daring in his pursuit of the throne. He propositioned John Comyn (the only other viable contender for the crown at this time) and asked John to choose one of two alternatives—either John reign as king and grant Robert all his lands and possessions, or Robert assume the throne, granting John the likewise property rights. John accepted the second proposition which was formalized by sealed indentures and oaths of good faith.

But Comyn immediately broke his oath by writing to Edward and revealing Robert's "treasonous" acts. Robert the Bruce was then summoned to London where he was presented with the evidence and told he would be put to death. Assisted by the Earl of Gloucester, Robert immediately fled back to Scotland and arranged a rendezvous with John Comyn at the Church of the Grey Friars in Dumfries. On the 10th of February 1306, the two men were unable to reconcile, Robert wanted to avoid violence but as their quarrel escalated, he stabbed Comyn, an act that gravely disturbed the future king. With haste, he rode to Glasgow, made a confession to Bishop Wishart, and received absolution for his sin.

Now, time was of the essence. There could be no more waiting. Bruce and his retinue raced for Scone, the traditional place of inauguration. Many supporters joined him on his ride northward, including James Douglas, a man who had ample cause to hate the English clear to his very soul.

I

SCOTLAND, 23 MARCH 1306. THE ROAD TO SCONE.

The orange glow of dawn skimmed tufts of striated clouds in the eastern sky. But James Douglas hardly noticed. Neither did he pay heed to the icy breeze cutting through his mail and the quilted weave of the aketon beneath. Even the chausses covering his thighs were stiff from the cold. Surely the skies threatened a late snow, though James preferred to be nowhere else this day.

From a ridge overlooking the Glasgow road, he sat atop a fine palfry, his breaths billowing a steamy grey. If only the horse were his and not a loan from Bishop Lamberton. But these were dark times and the name of Douglas had all but been smote from the nobility. One day, James intended to own a herd of gallant warhorses. Just as his father had before the wars.

Intently, he watched the road for movement. At last, his chance had come. And no matter how hot his impatient blood thrummed through his loins, he vowed to maintain his vigil and remain patient. Soon he would right the wrongs against his father and regain his lands.

And the time was nigh.

At last, a robust contender had come forward to claim the throne of Scotland, a man with cods enough to pull together this great nation and send the English back across the border once and for all. And James fully intended to be at the center of the maelstrom.

After daylight had spread across the glen, a flicker of metal caught James' eye first, followed by the white blaze on the nose of a bay horse. He counted thirty riders creeping through the trees with a wagon and sentry in diamond formation at the rear. Not an impressive number for a king or even an earl, for that matter, but perhaps the small retinue would not attract as much attention as an army of five hundred or more.

Before he picked up his reins, James closed his eyes and turned his face to the heavens. *Dear God, I am not gifted with the silken eloquence of a holy man, but in my hour of need, please grant me the words to convey the strength of my fealty and the depth of my desire to ride at this man's side.*

Taking an earnest breath, he cued the palfry down the incline and onto the road while the approach of horses thundered from around the bend. James dropped his reins and raised his hands, driving his mount with his knees.

At fifty paces, the retinue came into view. James grinned at the sight of Robert the Bruce in the lead—he would have assumed no less. By his reputation, the contender was no coward. And what a sight to behold. Clearly a warrior, Bruce presented an imposing image, his armor immaculate, a surcoat emblazoned with the rampant lion, a cloak of black, his shoulders broad. And to add to the picture, the nostrils of his enormous steed flared.

The men flanking Bruce drew their swords. "Halt!" bellowed one.

James relaxed his knees and let his horse amble to a stop. "James Douglas, son of William, Lord of Douglas, come to pledge my fealty to a worthy man who would be king."

"The lad's father surrendered at Berwick," growled the man on the right.

A shot of ire flared up James' neck, but he bit his tongue. Damnation, he was no lad.

The Bruce brushed his beard with gauntleted fingers. "I kent his father well. Lord Douglas surrendered the burgh and his life in good faith, intending to spare those within his garrison."

The man-at-arms smirked. "Little good that did."

Grinding his molars, James slid from his horse. Now was not the time to debate the errs of his da. "I was but ten years of age when my father died in the Tower, his lands given to Clifford by a foreign king. *My* lands. *My* birthright."

"I, too, have lost much at the hand of the usurper." The Bruce urged his mount forward, though one of the men-at-arms followed. "Tell me, what news brought you to this place on this day at this time?"

James dropped to his knee and bowed his head. "My liege, since my father left this world, I have been an apprentice to Bishop Lamberton. Upon receiving your missive, he urged me to ride ahead and pledge my sword."

"I don't trust him," growled the man-at-arms.

"Wheesht, Neil." The Bruce dismounted, handed the naysayer his reins, and returned his attention to James. "You must forgive my brother. He is only looking out for my welfare."

Giving a nod, James eyed the man before he returned his attention to His Lordship. "Very well. Though judging by his girth, I can easily best him in a battle of swords."

"Strong words from an unproven pup. Perhaps a match can be arranged." Bruce sauntered forward, cocking his head to one side. "Your beard is thick, though your face is that of an unblemished canvas. Pray tell, what is your age?"

As a sharp spike roiled in his gut, James clenched his fists. "I am a man of one and twenty, trained to wield a sword. I've not been bested by any knight in Lamberton's court."

"Indeed? And your claim can be substantiated by the bishop?"

"It can." James rose. "I—"

"Watch yourself," warned Neil.

The Bruce sliced his palm through the air but kept his eyes on James and one hand on the hilt of his sword. "Clearly, you were aware that I am headed for Scone. Why did you not wait to approach me there?"

Again demonstrating his vassalage, James spread his hands to his sides, though he didn't kneel this time. "When news was received of Comyn's death by *your* hand and the absolution granted to you by Bishop Wishart in Glasgow, I felt you needed my sword now whilst you are most vulnerable."

"I assure you, my vulnerability will endure for months, possibly years to come."

"Aye, until the English are expunged from Scotland once and for all."

"I appreciate your verve, Douglas. Tell me, have you earned your spurs?"

"Not as of yet. I rather hoped being knighted would be an honor bestowed by my king."

Chuckling, the Bruce turned toward his men. "Did you hear that? I'm liking this young man more by the moment." He then placed a hand on James' shoulder. "I should enjoy witnessing this sword of yours in action."

"If I ride at your side, I pray to God you will see it raised often against our foe."

"Then come." The Bruce turned up his palm to catch a snowflake. "We have tarried here long enough."

"If you squeeze your hands any tighter, your fingers will fall off," said Coira in a sharp and stilted whisper.

Ailish arched an eyebrow and leveled her gaze upon her overly protective lady's maid. Well, at one time, Coira had been Ailish's nursemaid, but that didn't allay the fact that Ailish was entrusted with the leadership of her clan and had been for quite some time. "My hands are fine."

Her anxiety ratcheted up a notch as she watched yet another man exit the chamber in Scone Abbey where Robert the Bruce was hearing supplications. This morning, the vestibule had been packed shoulder to shoulder with men. Now, aside from the two women, the hall was completely empty. "I should be next."

Ailish sat forward when the steward stepped through the door and headed across the floor without even giving her a glance. She immediately sprang to her feet. "I beg your pardon, m'lord, but I have waited this entire day for an audience with His Grace."

The man stopped, a deep frown furrowing his brow. "And you are?"

"Lady Ailish Maxwell." She gestured to the scroll in his fist. "I signed my name to the roll just like everyone else. It is of grave import that I see His Grace at once."

"You must not refer to *His Lordship* as His Grace until after the crowning this eve." Huffing, the steward unrolled the vellum. "Must I warn you that women have no place within these walls?"

"Is there a problem?" asked a man, his voice resounding from the doorway. He was tall, broad shouldered, and the look in his eyes was as sharp as a well-honed dirk. If Ailish had ever set eyes upon any king before, this would be he.

Bless the saints!

She hastened forward, stopped before the man, and dipped into a deep curtsey, bowing her head. "I am Lady Ailish, daughter of Johann Maxwell, Earl of Caerlaverock and I have come to pledge fealty in my brother's stead." She pulled her ruby pendant out from under her bodice. "This was my mother's. It is all I have to prove I am Johann Maxwell's daughter."

"You simply must hear her, m'lord," said Coira bustling to Ailish's side. "M'lady took a great risk to be meet with you."

Ailish gave the maid a purse-lipped leer. As the eldest Maxwell, she could stand up for herself.

Robert the Bruce examined the necklace. "It is a fine piece, indeed." He stepped back, pushed open the door, and gestured inside. "Is that so?"

"It is." Ailish held up her palm, telling Coira to stay put, then stepped into the chamber. "I've come to support you as king and lay claim to Maxwell lands."

He skirted behind a table and sat in an enormous chair, steepling his fingers against his lips. "You said your brother is still alive?"

Ailish clasped her hands tightly to allay their trembling. "Harris—he is only nine years of age, but Earl of Caerlaverock and chieftain of Clan Maxwell all the same. I would have brought him with me, had it been safe to do so. But I do not trust my uncle. If he learns Harris still lives, I ken in my bones, he'll try to kill the lad."

"Ah, yes, it is all coming back to me now. Edward sacked Caerlaverock in the year of our Lord thirteen hundred. I recall at the time, Herbert's rise to the earldom was cause for unease."

"The man is vile. He dishonors the Maxwell Clan as well as the title of earl. He joined with Edward in the attack on my home. After days of pummeling the castle with siege engines, captured my father and hung him from the bailey walls."

His Lordship closed his eyes, a pinch forming between his brows. "Did Longshanks not have the castle surrounded? How were you and your brother saved?"

"Before Edward's army breached our walls, Da commanded our cleric to spirit me as well as my brother and sister out the Firth of Solway in a skiff. Harris was but three years of age at the time and Florrie just five. My father's last words to me were to protect the lad with my life. And I am happy to report Harris, the true Earl of Caerlaverock, is securely hidden behind the walls of Lincluden Priory."

The Bruce sat back. "The nunnery?"

She stood a bit taller and squared her shoulders. "I believe it the best place to hide him from my uncle. Please, Herbert mustn't ken the lad still lives."

"Understood, m'lady. Rest assured your secret is safe with me. And in time, I will make certain this matter is resolved. There is nothing more important than the preservation of Scotland's own."

Ailish released a sigh as if she'd been holding her breath for ages. "Bless you, Your Gr—*uh*...Your Lordship. When I received news of your coronation, I kent you would be the answer to my prayers"

"I commend your courage." The Bruce ran his fingers over his ring's enormous ruby. "When the time is right, all of Scotland will be liberated. With the news that Caerlaverock's heir has survived, the charter lands will be restored in your brother's name."

"Oh, I cannot tell you how much your words have made my heart soar."

"I must caution you." Lord Bruce's eyebrow quipped as he held up his finger. "The English presently occupy over half of Scotland's border. The task of reclaiming them will be long and arduous. But make no bones about it, I have committed my life to this task."

Ailish had never heard more uplifting news. "As have I. Tell me what I must do. I can act as a messenger or spy. Anything..."

"The best place for you is behind the priory's walls with your kin."

Ailish bit her bottom lip. Those walls were ever so suffocating—not that she didn't appreciate the nuns who'd taken her in. It was just she'd been hiding behind the grey stone barbican for six years. If only there was something more she could do to help. She wanted her uncle out of her home so badly, she would gladly pick up a sword and face them herself if she could.

"You came all this way to bring news of your brother's existence. Tell me, why did you not send a missive?"

"And miss the coronation? Moreover, miss a chance to represent Clan Maxwell and pledge our fealty?" Ailish clasped her fists over her heart. "In no way would I allow such a momentous event to pass without the representation of my kin."

"I admire your spirit," he said, drumming his fingers on the wooden armrests. "Tell me, did the nuns send a retinue to accompany you?"

"The nuns?" she asked, doing her best not to laugh aloud. "Alas, they are quite poor and there is but one old guard at the priory, and I assure you he is too valuable to the order to accompany me."

Lord Bruce blinked, his mouth dropping open. "You came to Scone alone?"

"With my lady's maid." Ailish inclined her head toward the door. "The outspoken woman in the vestibule."

"Are you jesting? The kingdom is riddled with our enemies. You could have been captured—molested, or worse."

The tips of Ailish's ears burned. Aye, she knew of the dangers, but this day was far too important not to take the risk. "We dressed in nun's habits and shared a mule."

"Good Lord, your story grows more precarious with your every word."

"I beg your pardon, m'lord but are you not happy that I have come?"

"Nay, it is not my happiness I am concerned with, but your wellbeing." His expression changed, making a wee bit of unease roil in her stomach. "You, lass, are a noble daughter of an earl. A match must be made with your hand, and safe passage to return your person securely behind Lincluden's walls is of dire importance."

Ailish gulped. "I see," she said, half-dazed. In no way had she come to Scone to find a *match*. Her duty was to represent Harris, and that was what she intended to do. Surely, His Lordship wouldn't see fit to find her a husband before her brother came of age and was securely returned to Maxwell lands.

"I will speak to the steward and ensure he is aware you will pledge fealty on behalf of your brother on the morrow. By that time, I will have appointed someone to accompany you behind the priory walls where I expect you to remain until the wars have abated."

Bowing her head, she curtseyed. There were a great many things on His Lordship's mind. She doubted he'd give a second thought to her marriage prospects—at least for the time being. "Thank you, m'lord. I am in your debt."

The Bruce rose and moved toward the door. "Come, 'tis time to prepare for the ceremony. Are you looking forward to the feast?"

"Och aye, I am. I have not enjoyed a moment of merriment since the day my father passed."

"Wonderful." He rested his hand on the latch. "And where might you be staying?"

"The monks gave us sanctuary in the nave of the Church of the Holy Trinity."

"I suppose 'tis the best place for an unwed lass as long as your lady's maid never leaves your side."

"I assure you, Coira wouldn't dream of leaving me to my own devices."

"Good," he replied, opening the door. "Then at least you should remain dry and well looked after."

Ailish agreed, though sleeping on the stone floor had given her aches and pains she'd never felt before. Still, Bruce had been correct when he'd said it wasn't safe to be alone. She'd come across more than one merrymaker in his cups who had made an indecent comment or two. Honestly, if Ailish hadn't been there to meet the man who would be crowned king this eve, she'd still be wearing a nun's habit at this very moment.

In the vestibule, Coira stood expectantly wringing her hands, though there was no sign of the steward.

His Lordship bowed. "If you will excuse me, my brother is engaging in a sparring match I cannot miss."

"Sparring, Your Lordship?" asked Coira.

"A young nobleman, bent on proving his worth. The tourney should be entertaining if you stand at a distance. And knowing Neil's prowess with a blade, I doubt the challenger will last longer than a moment or two."

Ailish and her lady's maid followed him outside until the Bruce pushed into a mob of people who instantly surrounded him. She stood on tiptoes and strained to catch sight of the contenders, but the view was blocked by the backs of countless men.

Coira took her hand and gestured up Moot Hill where a small gathering of women had assembled. "Let us join the others there. 'Tis a mite safer, though I'll say it is no proper sport for a young lady."

Ailish pulled her hand away and moved beside the woman. "In these times, I feel it is important to observe and understand the qualities that distinguish a good swordsman from bad. Especially for those of us who are entrusted with the protection of clan and kin."

"Aye, but you were a wee lass of fourteen when you fled to the sanctity of the abbey. I ken you're aware the world is a violent place, but it is ever so dangerous for a young woman like you. Especially one with your beauty."

"You sound as if you're siding with Lord Bruce."

"Siding?" Coira asked, her tone annoyingly curious. "What did he say?"

"He was quite surprised to hear that Harris had survived the siege," Ailish explained, emphasizing the reason why they'd traveled all this way. "As we'd hoped, he agreed to uphold my brother's rights to Caerlaverock when Scotland sheds the shackles placed upon us by Edward Plantagenet."

"Praises be. I would have thought no less. You haven't spent the past six years ignoring your own needs and schooling your siblings for naught. What I want to know is what did His Lordship say about *you*?"

Ailish gulped. "Me?"

"Your prospects. Surely he realized you are of marriageable age."

"The Earl of Carrack has far more important things on his mind than my present state of spinsterhood," Ailish said, doing her best to avoid Coira's interrogation. After all, the Bruce had not mentioned whether or not he had a suitor in mind. "Besides, as long as Uncle Herbert controls the Maxwell purse strings, I have no dowry."

"For now. But you just said he sides with your plight."

"He does, but he also said it will take time to drive the English out of Scotland. I'm not about to hold my breath."

"Humph." Coira turned her attention to the ring. "Oh, my, have a look at the contenders. The dark one is quite braw."

As Ailish followed her maid's line of sight, she covered her gasp with her hand. Good heavens, Coira had definitely not exaggerated. "'Tis Lord Neil Bruce and an unproven knight," she managed to squeak.

Aye, there were two men in the ring, but the younger was most imposing.

Most imposing.

He was even taller than His Lordship, his shoulders broader, his beard blacker. And though he was a young man, the look in his eyes was as determined and fierce as a well-trained falcon. Ailish couldn't recall ever setting eyes on a man who took her breath away, but there she stood, weak-kneed. She slid her palm to her chest, pressing to allay her sudden lightheadedness.

"The challenger is James Douglas, son of the Lord of Douglas," said a woman from behind.

The name needled at the back of Ailish's mind but she couldn't place it. Did her father not entertain a Sir Douglas? Did he hail from Galloway as did she?

Douglas.

A vague memory. Of course! She snapped her fingers. The challenger's father had dined at Caerlaverock. Ailish even remembered serving him wine with her own hand. And that meant their fathers must have been allies.

As she returned her attention to the ring, Robert the Bruce chopped his hand between the opponents and bellowed, “Spar!”

With a hiss of metal, both men drew their swords, sidestepping as they circled. And by the glint of malice in their eyes, it appeared to be no friendly bout.

With a feral bellow, Douglas lunged forward, his strike deflected by the older man. Though he was smaller, Lord Neil proved to be fast and agile. Their swords clanged in a blur of deadly strikes and near-misses.

While the crowd roared, Ailish clenched her fists beneath her chin, squeezing her elbows at her sides. “Must they be so vicious?”

Coira chuckled. “It would hardly be a sparring match if they exchanged pleasantries afore each attack.”

Ailish’s body jolted with every single strike. She hissed and bared her teeth as Douglas advanced, hacking his blade and showing no mercy. Goodness, Robert Bruce had been wrong about the newcomer. The pair were well-matched. But just when it seemed as if the younger man would win, Lord Neil spun, aiming for Douglas’ knees.

Ailish cringed, barely able to look, positive the poor man would be crippled for life. As the blade was about to connect with sinew and bone, James Douglas countered with a mighty upswing, the clash of metal on metal almost deafening. With his follow-through, the hilt wrenched from Lord Neil’s hand, sending the sword end-over-end through the air.

The crowd erupted with applause as the Bruce grabbed the young man’s hand, raised it above their heads, and proclaimed him the victor.

Clapping, Ailish smiled, her heart thundering beneath her heavy woolen gown. Time slowed as Douglas looked her way, his eyes boring through her as if he were indeed gifted the honed sight of a falcon.

Her breath stopped.

The young man bowed her way right before he was swarmed by the crowd.

"My heavens, that was quite a match," said Coira.

"Mm hmm," Ailish agreed, still unable to pull her gaze from the top of the man's head of wild black hair, which was easy to spot because he was taller than all the others.

"I suppose neither of us have seen men spar for some time. Was it too shocking? Did the fight bring back fearful memories?"

Shaking her head, Ailish regarded at her lady's maid and blinked. "Not at all," she said, a bit breathless, her limbs feeling feather-light as if she might be floating. "Though the match was far more vigorous than I expected."

"I most certainly agree." Coira tugged Ailish's elbow. "Come, let us find a corner in the nave where I can help you prepare for the coronation."

2

In a private chamber above the abbey's vestibule, James raised the thick chasuble over Bishop Lamberton's head. "I'm looking forward to the feast after the ceremony."

The old man shrugged into the garment, his face appearing through the neck hole with a disapproving pinch as if he'd just swallowed a bitter tonic. "The festivities should be the last thing on your mind. You may have won this day's sparring match, but you are not yet in Robert's confidence. Never forget he alone is the conduit for reclaiming your lands."

James moved behind the bishop with the stole and draped it over his shoulders, ensuring the cross settled exactly in the center of his nape. "I am keenly aware that my fate lies in His Lordship's hands and I'm doing everything I can to earn his favor. And it hasn't been easy to gain his ear. He was sequestered in the abbey hearing supplications all day."

"Aye." Lamberton faced him. "But remember your actions speak louder than words. Stay close to him. Remain attentive. And most of all, do not allow your mind to be addled by the ladies."

"I will not." James waggled his eyebrows. "Though there's nothing wrong with a wee peek now and again."

The bishop smoothed his hands down the stole. "You are an insufferable lad. Pay heed to what I say or you'll rue your actions for the rest of your days."

"Yes, m'lord, I was merely jesting. No one thirsts for vengeance as much as I. As always, I shall maintain a close vigil as we discussed."

"Excellent. I did not use my influence to see you assigned to Bruce's guard for naught."

James retrieved the bishop's miter and held it out. "'Tis an honor I shall not take for granted."

"Bless you, my son." After situating the headdress in place, Lamberton placed his meaty hand on James' shoulder. "The order of the ceremony has been decided. As we discussed, you will stand guard. Once the Bruce has been crowned, you will be among those called forward. Earning your spurs will be your greatest honor."

James' heart swelled. He'd been waiting for this moment his entire life. At long last, he would be knighted. And, God willing, by the hand of a Scottish king. For far too long, he'd been a landless outcast, biding his time, mulling about on the fringes of the nobility.

Well, no longer.

After he attended to the bishop's robes, James made his way to the top of Moot Hill, following the pathway of light radiating from dozens of iron torches impaled in the ground and burning with heady peat. He moved to his position of honor, where he stood shoulder-to-shoulder with eleven other candidates for knighthood, forming an arc around the hallowed place where Scottish kings had been crowned for centuries. He'd met a few of these men. They were all sons of chieftains and earls—Arthur Campbell and Robert Boyd were both solid Scots—men James was proud to call friends.

And everyone knew Boyd had once served as squire to the great William Wallace. But he wasn't a lad anymore. Indeed, the candidate from Kilmarnock had nearly grown as tall and as broad as James.

Resting his hands on the pommel of his sword, he assessed the others who stood with him, those fortunate men who would be knighted this eve in the Bruce's initial act of kingship. Most were in their prime as was James but, aside from Boyd, none came close to his height or girth. How many of them had lost their fathers in the wars? Boyd had for certain, but James wondered if the others had been tucked safely behind the walls of their father's fortresses.

If only he had a fortress.

His blood boiled as he clenched his fingers around his pommel. *Soon.*

With a herald from a line of trumpeters, the crowd parted, making a pathway for the procession. Led by a cross bearer, Bishops Wishart and Lamberton processed up the hill, their regal robes surreal as the velvet flickered with the slight breeze.

James gave Lamberton a nod as the bishop took his place.

A spark from a torch caught James' eye. As his gaze shifted toward the light, his breath stopped. Highlighted by the yellow flames, the same lass he'd seen after the sparring match stared directly at him. She was bonny, to be sure. Fine boned, small in stature, and even though it was night, her eyes reminded him of a cat...or of crystals sparkling in candlelight. She wore her tresses unbound, with a ribbon of gold plaited across her crown—a maid. The corner of his mouth twitched up, for only maidens wore their hair uncovered.

James nudged Boyd with his elbow. "Do ye ken who that is?" he whispered.

"The lass in blue?"

"Nay, the lovely on the far right, wearing gold."

Robert snorted. "Och, they're all lovely."

James turned his head, pretending to peer over his shoulder. "Have ye been too long without a woman?"

His friend snorted. "Most likely not as long as you, ye monk."

"Och, I may be a bishop's apprentice, but I assure you I've taken no vows of chastity."

As Lamberton turned with a frown, James pursed his lips. Aye, this was no time for idle chat. Besides, Boyd had been right on one count. There were a parcel of bonny women attending this eve, all in their finery. Moreover, James had far more important things on his mind than lusting after a lass.

But there is no harm in looking regardless of what the bishop says.

He shifted his gaze back to the beauty and grinned.

God save his faltering knees, the wee lassie smiled back. His stomach fluttered as if a hummingbird had taken flight. But the moment passed quickly and she glanced downward, covering her dainty lips with her fingers as if embarrassed.

James squared his shoulders as Robert the Bruce processed through the crowd and took his place upon the throne of Scone. The crowd fell silent as Lamberton began the Litany of Saints.

Scanning the faces of the assembly, James did his best not to glance toward the bonny lass again. Presently, he was there for one reason—to protect the king. With the breeze, torches danced, their flickers of light making some the elders appear cadaverous. A man at the back observed the proceedings from beneath a hood, the curve of his mouth grim, his eyes shaded. Was this one of the monks from Scone Abbey? Was he a spy? Whatever his purpose, he was someone to be watched.

As the chanting continued, James was unable to resist stealing a glimpse of the lass with the sable hair. She seemed to glow with rapture and clasped her hands over her heart as Robert took his sacred vows. Her face ethereal, her eyes glistened and sparkled with the same hope filling James' heart. From whence had she come? What hardships had she endured throughout the past decade of war?

James' view of the lass was blocked when the Countess of Buchan stepped forward holding a gilt crown. The monumental importance of the moment reflected in her proud smile as she raised it above the Earl of Carrick's head. "I crown thee Robert

Bruce, King of Scots; son of Robert Bruce; son of Robert Bruce; son of Robert Bruce; son of David, Earl of Huntington; son of Henry, Earl of Warrenne; son of David, King of Scots! With this diadem held sovereign over all Scottish subjects, may you do everything in your power to cause Law, Justice, and Mercy to be executed in all of your judgments."

"Hear, hear," James whispered under his breath as he watched the man with the hood take his leave.

After the blessing, the king stood from his throne and launched into an oration, swearing his life to the liberation and freedom of all of Scotland. After the applause abated, Lamberton gave him a bejeweled sword and Robert thrust it above his head. "In my first act as king, I shall knight these noble sons of Scotland."

James watched as every last one of the candidates were called forward and kneeled before the new king. When finally he was left standing alone, he bit the inside of his cheek and shot a nervous glance to Lamberton.

The old bishop ignored him, holding up the scroll with the list of names. "Come forward James Douglas, son of Sir William Douglas, Lord of Douglas."

James released a long breath as murmurs from the crowd swelled through the darkness. Aye, they all knew the stories of his father's demise and how Da had met his end in the torture chamber of the Tower of London. Untrue rumors had spread, but make no bones about it, Edward had ruined James' da and the Lord of Douglas had paid in blood.

And one day, I'll have my due.

James boldly marched forward and kneeled. Time slowed as he bowed his head, the king's voice resounding around him. The sword touched his left shoulder and then his right. As his chest swelled, he prayed his parents were looking down from heaven with pride. The glint of new silver spurs flashed in the corner of his eye, but when James looked up, a flash of metal of a different sort made his blood run cold.

"Nooooooo!" he bellowed. In one motion, he sprang to his feet, wrenching the sword from the king's hands. His Grace reached for his dirk as the hooded man's battle axe hissed through the air, aimed to sever Robert the Bruce's head.

Gnashing his teeth, James countered with all his might, blocking with an upward strike. As the weapons connected, the axe flew from the assailant's hands. With the fire of rage racing through James' blood, he shoved the king aside, wedging himself between his liege and the assassin. Before his next blink, he plunged the sword through the blackguard's heart. The man's hood fell back, his eyes stunned as he toppled backward, his lips moving with soundless curses.

James hovered over the fiend and yanked the blade from his chest. With blood dripping from the weapon, he turned and faced at least a dozen swords drawn and ready to smite him where he stood. He quickly bowed his head and presented the hilt of the royal sword to his king. "Forgive me, Your Grace."

"Stand down," growled the Bruce, motioning for the knights to lower their weapons. "Smart of you to choose the sword already unsheathed, Douglas."

James agreed, though he wouldn't boast about it.

The king spread his arms. "To commend this act of bravery, Douglas' first act of knighthood will be to stand guard over the royal retinue at the high table this eve."

"You honor me," James said as the crowd applauded.

Clapping him on the shoulder, His Grace lowered his voice. "I need you to escort a woman to Lincluden Priory. 'Tis of grave importance that she arrives safely. Afterward, you will amass an army in the borderlands. We must recruit every man able to bear arms."

"And my lands?"

"By rights, you are the Lord of Douglas, Sir James," he said. "The lands are yours. 'Tis only a matter of how and when you take them and upon that point we must be agreed."

James again bowed. How much longer would he need to wait?

Damnation, he wanted to ride straight to West Lothian and immediately start amassing his army. Take some woman to a nunnery? Doing so was a bloody waste of time. Why not assign some monks to the task? Scone Abbey certainly had enough undernourished men to assemble a retinue. Hell, they spent half the day at worship, any number of them would jump at the chance to go on a journey, especially if it meant rubbing elbows with an entire priory full of nuns.

Lamberton shook James' hand. "God is with you, my son."

"Perhaps," he said a bit too gruffly. Aye, he needed to exercise patience, but God had not seen fit to gift him with such a virtue.

When James next looked to the crowd, King Bruce and the guests were already heading for the great hall inside the walls of Scone Abbey. He started after them, craning his neck and searching for the sable-haired lass. Alas, she was nowhere to be seen.

THE REWARD FOR THIS EVENING'S HEROISM WAS THE HONOR OF foregoing the festivities, keeping vigil behind the king and acting as his man-at-arms. But James wasn't the only one. Boyd had been granted the honor as well, most likely because they were the two largest knights, and Robert the Bruce's coronation hadn't even ended before an attempt was made on his life.

As the scent of roasted meat wafted through the hall, James couldn't decide whose stomach was growling the loudest. Most likely Boyd's. Certainly, James wouldn't own to any weakness.

His needs mattered not when he was assigned such an important task.

An honor.

And he'd starve amongst a hundred succulent legs of lamb if it pleased the king. He'd ignore the laughter filling the hall. He'd ignore the music and the dancing. He'd even ignore the sable-haired lass sitting with a woman wearing a nun's habit at the table near the far wall.

Lamberton was right as the elderly bishop oft was—James had no time for women. Perhaps he'd been billeted to accompany a female southward, but he'd perform his duty posthaste and then amass his army. In truth, the assignment was but a small pain in the arse. His clansmen were to the south, just not as near the border as Lincluden.

"You're twitching like a tick on a sow's arse," Boyd growled in his ear.

James snorted. If anyone could give a good rib it was the man on his right. "Och, a deaf mute would be on edge with the floor-shaking rumbles coming from your cavernous maw," he countered out of the corner of his mouth.

"Aye," Boyd surprisingly agreed. "I missed my nooning and was still riding for Scone come dawn. Haven't slept in two days, either."

"'Tis amazing you were able to bow your head and receive your spurs without falling on the Bruce's feet."

"I wouldn't have missed this day for a king's fortune."

"Nor I."

"'Twas a bloody gallant act of bravery I witnessed this eve." Boyd snickered. "Had you not run the bastard through, I might have thought you'd staged it."

"Never." The corner of James' mouth ticked up. "And thanks for the compliment."

"Just let me have a swing the next time. I could stand to be in the king's good graces."

"Now you're dreaming."

Boyd gave James a prod with his elbow, but when Lamberton snapped his fingers, they both jolted back into their roles of expressionless henchmen. At least James felt a bit more at ease within the walls of the abbey than he had out in the open upon Moot Hill. With he and Boyd standing shoulder to shoulder, their hands resting on the pommels of their swords, an assassin would have to be completely mad to make an attempt on the Bruce's life at the moment.

As the night wore on, the laughter grew more boisterous while the tankards of ale and goblets of wine emptied and refilled.

Well after the tables had been moved for the dancing, Boyd again prodded James with his elbow. "Look who's dancing with Campbell. Isn't that the lass you were ogling at the crowning?"

"Bloody hell." James gulped as he watched Arthur Campbell place a hand on the waist of the loveliest lass in the hall—the girl with the sable hair, of course. "Campbell has always had a way of turning ladies' heads, the bastard."

"If that's the case, then why is he not yet wed?"

Clenching fist, James shrugged. "Lucky, I'd reckon."

"Luckier than either of us."

"Nay, the pair of us are standing behind Robert the Bruce," said James, even though his stomach was roiling, and not from hunger.

"Do you fancy her as well?" he asked, his eyes transfixed on the woman as her silken tresses swung about her hips, her movement as graceful as a doe lightly stepping through the forest. Everything about her was perfect—except she kept looking at Campbell and smiling. If only she knew the knight's sole purpose in his feigned kindness was to raise her skirts.

"Not likely," Boyd replied, pulling James from his thoughts.

"Oh?" James asked, annoyed. "Why the bloody hell not?"

"Och, she's bonny and all, but I've more important things to tend to than women."

"As do I. I'll be riding for Douglas lands as soon as the king has received the oaths of fealty on the morrow." *With a wee detour, but Boyd doesn't need to know about that.*

"Douglas? What? Are you planning to face Clifford on your own?"

"I aim to assemble my men first. Then Clifford will wish he'd never set foot in Scotland."

"You have a pair of cods, I'll give you that."

"Best compliment I've ever had from the likes of you."

"Do not grow accustomed to it."

"I'm nay planning to."

Boyd yammered on, but James tuned him out. He was too busy watching Campbell take the lass by the elbow and accompany her out the door. If only James could follow and whisper a warning in her ear.

Blast it all, why did he care?

I don't. Only after I regain my lands and rid Scotland of Edward's vermin will I ever allow myself to care for any woman.

3

After Ailish kneeled before the king and pledged to honor and obey his royal decrees on behalf of her brother and Clan Maxwell, she changed into her heavy woolen nun's habit and readied the mule for the long return journey to the priory.

She tied her satchel to the saddle and patted the gelding's hip. "I'll walk for a time. The old nag will make it farther that way."

Coira raised her skirts enough to reveal her booted foot. "I'm the one who ought to be walking."

"Och aye? And annoy your rheumatism?" Ailish tugged either side of her attendant's veil and gave a warm smile. "Ye ken you'd last but three-quarters of an hour afore your knees started swelling."

"I am not an invalid, m'lady," Coira replied as she turned in place. "I thought you said we were to be escorted by one of the king's men. If I may say so, we're all but being ignored."

"Before I took my oath the steward told me a knight would meet us right here under this oak tree when the bell rings the tenth hour." As Ailish spoke the words, the tower bell began to toll. "See? We're exactly on time."

Coira craned her neck, searching the clusters of people

milling about. It seemed everyone was busy readying for their journeys. "Now all we must do is to find our escort."

Ailish squinted, peering into the stable's dark corridor. "I was rather hoping he and his retinue would find us. I see no other nuns about."

"Does he ken we're disguised as nuns?"

"I told the king we'd traveled to Scone wearing habits."

Coira snorted as she pulled the bridle up over the mule's nose and slid the bit into his mouth. "I'll wager our man has no idea."

"Patience." A number of people came out leading their horses, but nary a one paid them a mind. Then Ailish's breath stopped when a knight clad in full armor from head to toe led an enormous black palfry out of the stable. And once she saw him in the light, she recognized yesterday's champion, James Douglas—the hero who had saved the king only moments after the Bruce had been crowned. Surely a man such as he would stride past without giving them a second glance. He might have offered her a wee grin at last eve's ceremony, but the man was obviously far too important to be assigned to the ordinary task of accompanying a mere woman home.

Pretending to be unaffected by the braw Highlander, she shifted her gaze beyond him.

Goodness, her fingers trembled. What was it about Douglas? Several knights had already walked past, why did this one make her so self-aware? Truth be told, traveling with a man like Sir James would be distracting. And Ailish could not afford to be distracted in any way. She had protected her younger brother and sister for six years and *they* were her only care. Her sworn duty was to guard Harris with her life, and she must continue to do so no matter what may come.

Besides, the king was as intelligent as he was shrewd. Surely, he'd appoint an old knight—a wizened man, weary from years of battle—to see her safely returned to her kin.

"I beg your pardon, Sister," said Sir James in a very deep-sounding brogue. He stopped beside her, though she didn't dare meet the hard stare she sensed was boring through her veil. "You wouldn't be the lass...*er*...the *nuns* in need of an escort to Lincluden Priory? I was told they'd be waiting here beneath this oak. Ah...an *important* woman?"

Coira thrust her fists onto her hips. "Och, so a pair of women dressed as nuns cannot possibly be important? Well, I'll have ye know—"

"Enough," Ailish said, chopping her hand through the air, glaring at the maid and willing her to hold her tongue. "We are indeed traveling to the priory," she explained before her knees buckled.

Please not this man!

Slowly, she raised her chin, allowing her gaze to meander up to his face. As sure as she was standing, James Douglas stared down at her with a pair of piercing black eyes—eyes so dark, they were almost the color of obsidian. And the severe slash of his eyebrows demanded she take heed. By the saints, she could not help but do so. The man was even more braw up close than he'd been standing guard upon Moot Hill last eve.

His presence alone was that of power, of unquestioned strength.

"You will be our escort?" she asked, her voice losing confidence with every word.

"A nun?" He stepped back and gaped as if she were vermin. Then he shook his head and looked to the heavens. "Forgive me, Sister. Were you expecting another?"

Ailish clapped her fingers to her cheeks, positive she'd turned as red as scarlet flax petals. Of all the men at the coronation, James Douglas was the absolute last she expected to be assigned to protect her on the journey home. "Nay. I had only assumed a knight such as you would have far better things to do than accompany me and my..." She stopped herself from uttering "lady's maid". He obviously believed her to be a nun. Perhaps it was best if he continued to do so. "...ah...me and Sister Coira."

Sir Douglas narrowed his eyes and stroked his fingers down his thick black beard. "Were you not at the coronation?"

Ailish stood a bit taller. "I was there, of course."

"Hmm, I do recall. And you were sitting with *Sister Coira* during the feast as well."

"Perhaps I was."

"Interesting. I did not realize that novices were permitted to dance or wear fine gowns or attend coronations without their heads covered."

Blast him. What hadn't he noticed last night? "I assure you, my attendance at the coronation and feast thereafter was of grave import."

He pursed his lips. "So says the king."

Ailish nodded as if she were the most important woman in Scone this day. "So says the king."

"Forgive me." He bowed. "I am Sir James Douglas at your service. His Grace, himself, asked me to escort you safely to Lincluden, and I intend to see you behind her walls with haste."

She searched behind the man for his retinue. "Only you?"

A wee storm brewed in Sir James' black eyes. "Perhaps the Bruce felt two nuns traveling with a knight would look less conspicuous than two nuns accompanied by an army," he replied with a sardonic air with no hint of a smile. "Pray tell, what do I call you aside from Sister?"

"Ailish."

"Very well." Sir James examined the mule. "This fella's fine for carrying your effects, but where might your horses be?"

She squared her shoulders. If she possessed nothing else, she most certainly had Maxwell dignity pulsing through her blood. If this man intended to spend the next few days traveling with them, she'd best start acting like she knew what she was about. "Sister Coira and I share the priory's mule."

"I beg your pardon, but that old neddy will not be able to keep pace."

Coira smoothed her fingers down the mule's neck. "He managed to carry us here. He mightn't be fast, but he's steady."

"Agreed, unless you have another horse you'd prefer us to ride," said Ailish, hoping he did have an alternative. It would be ever so nice to ride a real horse for a change. At one time, she'd been quite accomplished in a saddle.

Sir James frowned and, though Ailish couldn't be certain, he may have colored a bit. "I'm afraid I haven't at the moment."

She bent down to give Coira a leg-up. "Very well."

"What are you doing?" asked the knight.

"Helping my m—I mean *Sister Coira* mount."

"Not on my watch." Sir James handed her the reins of his enormous warhorse and laced his fingers together. "Come, we haven't all day."

Waggling her shoulders, Coira patted Ailish's cheek, then placed her boot in his makeshift step. "Thank you, sir."

James glanced to Ailish. "Now you."

Rather than blatantly obey, she returned his reins. "I thought I'd start the journey by walking."

"Walk? It'll take us a bloody week if you walk."

She gaped at his vulgar tongue. "But the mule's stamina will last longer."

He rolled his eyes. "You are riding, and I'll entertain no argument on the matter."

Before she had a chance to object, he grabbed her waist and hoisted her in front of Coira. Then he slapped her thigh, the rogue. "*You* will last far longer up there."

Sir James looked none too happy as he marched over and climbed aboard his enormous palfry—a horse far more capable of carrying two than the priory's mule. "We ride."

As Ailish slapped the reins, Coira whispered in her ear, "He's rather arrogant, is he not, you being the daughter of an earl and all?"

Letting the mule fall back a few paces, Ailish cupped her hand to her mouth and kept her voice low. "He thinks me a nun."

Coira shifted in the saddle. "And I'm a cabbage. Good heavens, he admitted to seeing you at the coronation. And you were quite a vision, I'll say."

"Would you leave it be? Clearly, he has no idea why I wasn't wearing a habit last eve. We are traveling as nuns for our own safety. The fewer people who ken our identities, the better."

"Och, have it your way, m'lady. But I reckon the only person you're fooling is yourself."

Sir James turned and beckoned with a wave of his gauntleted hand. "Keep pace, Sisters."

THE SUN HAD TRAVERSED BELOW THE WESTERN HORIZON WHEN James steered his mount toward a copse of trees. "We'll rest the horses and make camp ahead," he said, though he could hardly call the old mule a horse. First of all, it truly was no horse, and secondly, Sister Ailish had been right about walking. They might have made better time if the animal had been carrying only one of them.

Regardless, there was no chance in hell he'd ever allow a woman to bloody walk. If need be, he would be the one to take to his boots, but if James had his druthers, they'd all be riding at a fast trot, not ambling along like an old crofter taking a wagonload of hay to market.

"Do you ken where we are?" asked Sister Ailish.

"Three miles from Dunblane near enough." He glanced over his shoulder seeing they'd fallen back once again. Bloody hell, he could crawl to Lincluden faster than the mule. "Come. There's good cover ahead and we've enough daylight to set up a shelter and have a wee bite to eat."

"Oh, thank heavens, I'm half-starved," said Sister Coira, who was as round as a heifer's rear end. If anyone looked famished, it was the younger nun.

Nuns? I'll burn in hell afore I believe the sable-haired lass has taken her vows. First of all, she had to be a maid, else she would have had her head covered last eve—especially when attending the coronation of a king. Besides, if she were merely a nun, the king wouldn't have mentioned her importance. Neither would he have taken such an interest in personally seeing to her protection.

Whatever the reason for her disguise, James wished she'd be forthright with him. He'd been appointed by the King of Scotland to see to her care and either Robert the Bruce wanted James out of his craw, or that lass was no nun. And by the sizable amount of coin the steward had given him to raise an army this morn, he reckoned it was the latter. James' orders were to deliver the woman to the priory and then set to recruiting men and forming an army to operate out of Selkirk Forest—Wallace's old den. Aye, the legend hadn't set up camp in the caves for his health. It was a brilliantly secluded location from which to orchestrate raids on the English.

Only a handful of Scots knew how to negotiate the thick wood—men James needed to find and recruit to the Bruce's cause. Such a task would take coin for certain.

After he led the women to the clearing, they dismounted and Sister Ailish released the girth strap on the mule's saddle.

James stilled her hand. "What are you doing?"

"Removing his saddle, of course."

"Nay, this is a time of war. Loosen the girth a wee bit, but the nag's saddle stays in place. I'm certain I don't need to say the further south we go, the more likely we'll encounter English spies." He set to hobbling both animals. "I've a chicken from the abbey's kitchens. We'll need firewood but cannot risk smoke afore dark. Can one of you fashion a spit whilst I set up a tent?"

"Do we need a tent?" asked Ailish.

James looked to the sky. They'd been blessed with fine weather this day, but clouds were rolling in. If there was one thing about Scotland that was a surety, good weather never lasted. "Mark me, we'll see rain afore dawn."

Sister Coira picked up a sturdy branch. "I'll fashion the spit, m'lady."

Ailish shot the woman a heated glance. "I'll fetch the firewood, *Sister*."

James sniggered to himself. He kent the *novice* was a lady. And he highly suspected the other woman was her servant. Coira certainly was built for labor. But he wasn't about to concern himself overmuch. Once he left them at the priory's gates, he'd most likely never set eyes on the wee sable-haired lass again, no matter her station.

As he went about his task, stringing a rope taut between two trees, he watched Ailish out of the corner of his eye. She collected sticks and good-sized pieces of wood without a word of complaint. And by the stars, she was bonny. Even beneath the drab woolen habit, her form was lithe, just as he'd remembered from last eve.

If only her hair weren't covered with that hideously drab veil. It wasn't hewn of finely spun wool either. The weave was coarse and had to be scratchy even though she wore a white linen under veil.

Why was the lass staying behind the walls of a nunnery and where was she from? Was her father still alive or had he been a victim of Edward's tyranny as James' da had?

He grew more curious as he worked, draping his leather oilcloth over the rope, and securing the edges with stakes. Inside, he cleared out stones and spread some rushes on the ground to ensure Her Ladyship's comfort.

Once he'd finished, it was nearly dark. "I'll set to lighting the fire."

"The kindling is ready with a handful of flax tow beneath, and we're ready to start working Coi—*ah*—Sister Coira's spit."

James frowned. "I'll crank the spit."

"That's very kind of you," said Ailish, producing a flint and rod and efficiently lighting the fire, blowing at the base to encourage the flames. God's bones, the lass was independent for a noblewoman. Though in truth, he ought to respect her more for it.

By the time James had the chicken ready to roast, the blaze was crackling. He couldn't have built a better fire himself.

Coira rubbed her belly. "It will be the witching hour afore the meat is cooked."

Ailish started for the mule. "I'll fetch a few oatcakes from my satchel."

"Good heavens," said the older woman, barreling past the younger. "I'll fetch them and spread our bed rolls as well. You need your rest."

The wee novice impersonator harrumphed and crossed her arms, her hip jutting to the side. "Very well. If you insist."

James patted the grass beside him. "May as well sit. Sister Coira is right about resting. We'll have a long day on the morrow."

The lass eased down beside him and tucked her legs beneath the folds of her habit. "We all need a respite."

"Agreed." The breeze brought with it the scent of woman, sweet like honey and mulled wine. James leaned toward the lass and breathed in. Och aye, this was no commoner. She smelled too good. He plucked a yellow primrose, twirled it between his fingers and offered it to her.

"What's this?" she asked, accepting the gift.

"A wee bit of beauty in the midst of turmoil."

She drew it to her nose. "Thank you. I love primroses."

"They are my favorite." He plucked another. "My mother said they symbolize underappreciated merit."

"Mm hmm." James reckoned she would look ever so bonny with a crown of primroses, but he'd risk sounding like a lovesick bard if he owned to it. "Ah...how long have you been a resident of Lincluden Priory?"

"Six years," she said, her voice taking on a faraway tone. "When..."

"What happened...*ah*...to your kin?" he asked, his mind

reflecting back. Edward's raids into the borderlands had been particularly savage in the year of our Lord thirteen hundred.

"I do not wish to speak of it."

"I ken exactly how you're feeling, lass. 'Twas a bitter pill to swallow when Edward murdered my da and the English took my lands. I was just a lad at the time, else I'd either be dead or the blood of Clifford's army would have fertilized my crops."

Ailish smiled. Albeit sad, her wee grin made her face more radiant as the amber glow from the fire sparkled in those crystal eyes. "I've oft wished I were a lad so I could take up my father's mantle and ride with..." She wiped a hand across her mouth before she continued, "Scotland's army."

Pursing his lips, James put a piece of wood on the fire and resumed turning the makeshift crank. Obviously, she continually caught herself, hiding what she really wanted to say. Why didn't she trust him? Hadn't he proved himself worthy? Was not being knighted and appointed by the king enough?

"I beg your pardon, sir," said Coira coming into the fire's glow. "But your bed roll is in the tent."

He looked up, his hand continuing to spin the chicken. "Aye, and what of it?"

"I thought the shelter was for Sister Ailish and me."

"It is."

"Where do you plan to sleep?"

"Beneath the oilcloth." A raindrop splashed James' nose. "There's ample room for the three of us."

The woman planted her fists upon her hips. "Pardon me, but—"

"I'll entertain no argument. The Bruce told me to escort you safely to the priory, and that is exactly what I will do."

"Very well, then *I* shall be sleeping between the pair of you."

"As you wish." James turned the chicken faster. Wonderful. Coira most likely snored louder than a saw in a forest of hardwood.

4

Ailish startled awake with a gasp. She wasn't only freezing cold, several drops of water splattered her face in quick succession. But the rain wasn't what woke her. Through the cobwebs of latent sleep, she shivered, not caused by the chill, but with a clammy dread crawling across her skin.

Something's out there.

Sitting up, she gasped again as she realized she was staring at the immense form of Sir James crouched at the tent entrance. "What is—?"

"Sh!" He commanded in a pointed but very audible whisper.

As Ailish clamped a hand over her mouth, rain pattered upon the oilcloth above. Through the blue light of dawn, only the whites of Sir James' eyes pierced through the shadowy tent—and the glint of the sword in his hand.

Soggy footsteps squished the wet earth beyond.

Oh, no!

Ailish's heart hammered, thundering in her ears. She clutched her fists beneath her chin, willing herself not to move.

"This horse is a beauty," came a low rumble from a man with an English accent.

Beside her, Coira snored and blubbered, making every

muscle in Ailish's body tense all the more. James' gaze snapped back, his eyes now wider and far more menacing.

The air around Ailish grew charged as swelling silence beyond the safety of the oilcloth made Coira's breathing sound like the bellows in a smithy shack. Even the rain stopped pattering.

"Quickly, let's spirit away before they wake," whispered another Englishman.

With Ailish's next blink, James burst out of the tent, bellowing like a madman. "Back away from the horses or I'll cut you down, ye worthless curs!"

Coira jolted awake, with a shocking gasp. Ailish wrapped her arms around the woman. "Wheesht!" she squeaked, unable to stop the fear from warbling her voice. "We're under attack."

The metallic sound of a sword being stripped from his scabbard hissed. "I'll sever your cods and stuff them down your gullet," growled one of the English.

Another laughed. "And we'll take your women."

"No!" Ailish screamed in a hushed whisper as the clang of iron meeting iron screeched in her ears.

She darted for the opening, only to be pulled back by Coira's powerful grip. "What the blazes are ye up to?"

"He needs my help."

"Nay! We've seen that man fight. He can hold his own."

Grunts and clangs resounded outside, merely paces away. "But he's outnumbered by Lord kens how many men!"

The dawn sky grew a tad lighter as Ailish pulled her dagger from her sleeve.

Coira tugged her elbow. "Do *not* go out there!"

She wrenched her arm away as a man grunted followed by a thud. "I must do something!"

Gripping the knife with both hands, Ailish ignored the pleas of her maid and lunged outside, ready to strike. "Leave us be!" she shrieked so loudly, her throat burned.

Sir James whipped around, his eyes wild as he yanked his

sword from the chest of a brigand. Good Lord, another lay dead beyond. "Quickly," he snarled. "We ride."

She stood for a moment and clutched her dagger to her squelching stomach. So much blood spilled into the soil. Gripped by the onslaught of memories from the siege of her father's keep, the death cries of the Maxwell men rattled in her head. The fear, the fires, the night she'd run for her life with Harris in her arms.

"Sister Ailish!" the big knight boomed.

The sound jolted her from the terrors of her mind. With a new wave of courage, she returned her dagger to its hiding place and turned to Coira. "Roll up the bedding. I'll tend the oilcloth.

"There's no time." Hefting Ailish over his shoulder, Sir James carried her to the palfry and hoisted her onto the saddle. "You're riding with me."

"You mustn't treat Sister Ailish like a sack of grain!" Coira hastened toward them with her arms full of sodden woolens.

Sir James frowned yet gave her a leg up. "Your first concern is to keep pace. Ye ken? And the bedding stays."

"I can tie these in place as we go." Clenching her bundle tighter, the lady's maid bobbled in the saddle. "Aye, sir?"

James grumbled under his breath as he mounted behind Ailish and kicked his heels. "Those were English scouts, mark me. We've no choice but to ride hard." He steered the palfry beside the mule and pulled away Coira's reins. "That means this fella stays at my flank."

"But—"

"Do as he says!" shouted Ailish as James demanded a trot.

Westward.

Good Lord, they needed to travel south. But she knew better than to correct him. Instead, she closed her eyes prayed the big knight knew where in heaven's name they were headed.

THEY'D RIDDEN ALL MORNING THROUGH SLEET AND DRIVING rain before James' blood finally cooled. Killing men was never easy, even Englishmen. Though he refused to admit how much taking a life disturbed him. After what Edward and his bloodthirsty savages did to his father, he'd personally flay every last man in Longshanks' army. God's bones, he hated the English to his core.

James had been trained by the best swordsmen in Scotland. And now he was stronger than he'd ever been. Faster, smarter, and hungrier for vengeance. Moreover, in Scone, he'd proved himself to the king.

Though now he was on a mission that galled him to no end.

In front of him, the wee lass shivered. But despite the damp and cold, she sat erect and held on to the horse's mane for balance—mighty uncomfortable posture for a day-long ride.

He closed his arms tighter around her and tilted his lips toward her ear. "Rest against me. I have enough warmth for the both of us."

Ailish glanced back toward Sister Coira who was hunched over as if she were dozing. With a nod, she rubbed her hands and relaxed into his chest. "I'm so c-cold."

James closed his eyes and drew in a deep inhalation. Even soaking wet, she smelled like a field of wildflowers. "With a bit of luck, the sun will dry us soon. Either that or this ghastly wind."

"'Tis the wind that is cutting through to my bones."

"I'm sorry," he whispered.

"You have no power over the weather."

"Nay, but I should have insisted we ride farther last eve. I thought we'd be safe in the copse."

"Have not Edward's scouts infested all of Scotland?"

"All but the Highlands and the far north. Certainly, West Lothian, where I hail from, is crawling with miscreants and I've a duty to rid the vermin and reclaim what is mine."

"Me as well," she whispered.

"You're from a highborn family, are you not?"

To his question she provided no response.

"Och, lass," James pressed. "You do not need to hide your identity from me. I ken you're of noble blood. And Sister Coira is your lady's maid. 'Tis as clear as the nose on my face."

"Aye." Ailish groaned and looked up, her blue eyes meeting his, making his breath catch. They weren't only blue, they were shocking like the color of the sea just before the foam rolls onto a beach. God save him, he'd never forget such eyes.

"My father was Johann Maxwell, murdered and hung from the walls of Caerlaverock Castle by Edward and my imposter of an uncle."

Maxwell? James knew the name well. "Your da was an ally of the Douglas."

"I remember. I'm sure your father dined at our table when I was but a wee lassie—before..."

"Before?" James asked, looking to the trail, trying not to stare into those captivating eyes.

"Before my brother was born."

"Johann's heir survived?"

"Aye," she said, her voice haunted. "He's my only care. Harris and my sister, Florrie. I traveled to Scone to pledge fealty to the king on behalf of the lad and declare his rightful place as Earl of Caerlaverock."

James chuckled. "Well then, 'tis a good thing your uncle wasn't present."

"He wouldn't dare show his face to Robert Bruce. He's in bed with the English and enjoying my father's wealth as well as Edward's spoils."

"Not unlike Clifford, the thief who is growing fat in my father's keep."

"'Tis why we cannot travel west any longer."

James arched his eyebrows. The lass had been smart not to question him earlier. "I turned the horse south about an hour past but 'tis difficult to tell with the cloud cover. We needed to give Stirling a wide berth."

Coira stirred and gave a loud sigh.

"How are you faring, Sister?" James asked, raising his voice.

The maid wiped the spittle from her mouth. "Aside from an insatiable hunger and a pain in my backside, I'm well, thank you."

Ailish patted the palfry's neck. "Coira's not particularly fond of traveling."

James almost laughed until a pair of burly men stepped out from the trees, crossing their battleaxes and blocking the path.

As he tugged on the reins, he reached for the hilt of his sword, steeling himself for another fight.

"I wouldn't do that if I were you," said one, baring his teeth as a dozen brigands dropped from the trees and surrounded them.

Spotting a crossbow archer with an arrow trained on Her Ladyship's heart, James raised his palms in surrender. The leader motioned to one of his men. "Take his weapons. My da will be interested to have a word with these trespassers. That is, unless they'd rather die now."

5

"Stay close to me," James growled in Ailish's ear while the outlaws led them deeper into the forest and farther away from Lincluden Priory. "Say nothing."

She wanted to shake her fists. She and Coira had fared much better on their journey north. Though they'd been stopped by patrols, they had no trouble convincing the soldiers that they were on a pilgrimage to Dunfermline. Now, they were traveling the byways with a knight who was supposed to be protecting them. They'd been gone a day, had nearly lost their horse and mule before dawn, and now were being taken hostage by a mangy lot of tinkers...or whatever they were. Though the scoundrels were Highlanders in speech and dress, she doubted there was an honest man among them.

After riding about an hour higher into the Highlands, the trees opened to a glassy loch. As they continued along the shore, Ailish prayed Sir James would do something soon to enable their escape. Lord knew the tension emanating from his body felt as hot as a smithy's fire. Surely, he would not allow these brigands to run roughshod over them for long.

Though the odds were not looking good at the moment.

About a mile on, they were once again led into the thicket

until the grey walls of a stone tower peered through the skeletons of trees still leafless from winter.

"Dismount," grumbled a man with a craggy face—the one who'd been issuing orders.

But there were too many of them not to do as they were told.

The cur pointed to James. "You come with me."

James shouldered himself in front of Ailish. "Not without the nuns. They're in my charge."

With a dozen leering eyes raking down her body, she emphatically nodded, ever so glad to be in disguise.

Coira lumbered beside them and scowled. "Och, you lot best never think to defile a nun else ye'll be damned for eternity!"

A few of the men took a step back. But the leader jabbed James in the shoulder with the butt of his axe. "Move your laggard arse."

Inside, the walls were crude with exposed stone. Thresh crunched underfoot as they were led into the great hall. A man with grey in his beard sat paring an apple at the head of a table near the hearth.

"We caught these travelers trespassing through Duncryne Forest," said the craggy-faced varlet.

Slipping a slice of apple into his mouth, the man looked up. "Is that so?"

James' eyes shifted as if he were assessing everything in the chamber. "We were set upon by English scouts just before dawn. If you retrace our tracks, there are two dead men not far outside of Dunblane. We're heading south, but I took a wee detour to ensure we ran into no more trouble."

The man eyed James from helm to mail and tunic to the tips of his boots. "And why is a knight riding with a pair of nuns?"

"To provide safe passage to the borders."

"For mere nuns?" asked the man while Ailish bit her tongue, praying her escort would not reveal her identity.

James moved his fingers to his sleeve. "I've another task to perform. The journey was *convenient*."

"Keep your hands where I can see them," ordered craggy-face.

The man at the table stood and planted his palms on the table. "A task did you say?"

With a grim nod, James stepped forward and pointed to the wooden shield hanging above the mantel. "I see you display the seal of the lion rampant emblazoned on your targe."

"Aye, given to my da by Wallace himself."

"And you've heard they've crowned Robert Bruce as king?"

The man gave a curt nod. "I have."

James took in a deep breath and ran his fingers down his beard. "I attended the coronation and received my spurs that very night."

The man's gaze narrowed. "You side with the Bruce?"

"I've a letter in my possession commanding me to establish a borderland army bearing his seal."

Ailish squeezed her fists so tightly, her nails bit into her flesh. What was Sir James doing? These men could not be trusted.

"Aye, and where do you aim to hide these men with a multitude of English spies mulling about?"

"Ye ken Wallace." James smirked as if he were comfortable with the guards encircling them, ready to chop of their heads with their axes. "The Bruce aims to start where the great warrior left off."

"Selkirk," said the man. "And who might you be?"

"Sir James Douglas, Lord of Douglas."

The man's eyes widened. "Le Hardi's son?"

Ailish held her breath. Sir James' da had lost Berwick, and many Scots held him accountable for the carnage.

But the knight continued to act as if they were merely having a passing conversation rather than about to be run through. "Aye."

The elder's face split into an enormous grin. "Well why did ye not say so in the first place?"

"No one gave us the courtesy of asking." Sir James threw a

thumb over his shoulder. "This ragged lot behind me has forgotten their manners. They did not even grant me the civility of giving me your name."

"Erloch Cunningham, chieftain of these lands, and the guard holding a battleax at your throat is my eldest son, Torquil." He walked around the table and clapped James' shoulder. "Welcome to Duncryne, friend."

As Torquil's axe lowered, Ailish exchanged a relieved glance with Coira.

"My thanks," James mumbled rather unconvincingly as he rubbed his neck. "But seeing as we've been waylaid by your *hospitality*, I reckon we'll be needing lodgings for the night—and I'll be taking back my sword and dirk."

Ailish gave him a nudge. These men mightn't have robbed them on the trail, but she had no doubt if they were on the wrong side of the war, the blackguards would have skewered James and ravished her and Coira or worse. "Perhaps if we left now, we'd make it to Dunbarton before nightfall."

"Och, 'tis dusk already," said Torquil, pointing to the balcony above where absolutely no light shone through an archer's crosslet loop, blast it all.

"The sisters will require privacy, of course," James added as one of the men returned his weapons.

Erloch shrugged. "They can use Torquil's chamber for the night."

The young man eyed Ailish like he had been doing since they blocked their path in the forest. "Och, I'd rather have the bonny one in me bed for the eve."

James pulled her behind him. "I beg—"

"Stand down, Son. It will not hurt ye to sleep in the hall for a night." Erloch sliced his hand like he was chopping wood. "Can you not see she's a holy woman? These are our guests, and I expect you to treat them as such, else we'll have a reckoning."

"I'll have a bloody reckoning," James mumbled into Ailish's ear.

Coira, looped her arm through her lady's elbow. "If it would not trouble ye overmuch, might we be able to venture above stairs now to refresh ourselves afore the evening meal?"

"Aye, and Torquil will show you the way."

Ailish squeezed Coira's arm tightly and fingered the dagger inside her sleeve. His father may have offered hospitality, but she didn't trust the son in the slightest.

And to prove her point, he smiled like a lecherous cur. "This way, Sisters."

"Leave the axe," said James, stepping aside and giving Ailish a nod. "I'll see you anon."

She inclined her head toward the stairs. "Do you not want to ken where we'll be staying, sir?"

"Och, you can climb a few stairs without your guardian," Torquil growled over his shoulder.

"Come along," said Coira as if she were readying herself for battle.

ERLOCH GESTURED TO THE BENCHES AT THE LONG TABLE. "SIT and rest your weary bones." He clapped his hands. "Bring us some ale."

James climbed over a bench, ever so happy to see Torquil return directly. He'd been of two minds in letting the young man take the ladies above stairs, but he would have broken the laws of hospitality had he insisted on tagging along. Nonetheless, had the man dallied above stairs, James would not have hesitated to intervene.

"Torquil, go see to the horses," said Erloch.

"Och, the men will take care of them."

"Just do as I say."

An ewer of ale and two tankards were placed on the table as the lad pushed outside.

James poured. "His beard has come in, surely he's not as young as he behaves."

"The lad's ten and seven. He needs to be fostered by someone who can turn him into a man." Erloch picked up a tankard. "Sláinte."

James followed suit. "Sláinte."

"I'd like him to ride with you."

Blowing frothing ale out his nose, James looked at the man as if he'd grown two heads. "Not only am I tasked with ridding our borders of English vermin, I'm amassing an army. Moreover, how in God's name can I trust him to keep his hands off Sister Ailish?"

"Because you'll sever his cods if he tries anything untoward." The old man grinned behind the pewter cup. "I ken what I just witnessed, sir. You would protect the wee lassie with your life."

James kept his expression impassive and shrugged. "The women are in my care. I'll do what I must to protect them. To prove it, there are two dead Englishmen in a wee clearing near Dunblane."

"I kent I liked you as soon as you stepped into me hall." Erloch poured himself another ale. "If ye are forming an army like you said, Torquil would do well to serve under a man like you—James Douglas, son of le Hardi."

"Oh aye?"

"Aye. And I reckon you've a chip on your shoulder larger than my arse."

"What of it?" James regarded the shield over the hearth. Bloody oath, he had something to prove. But that was none of Erloch's concern. "I've been here for less than an hour. You've formed a great many opinions in the time it took to exchange *pleasantries*."

"I ken the look in your eye, Son. And you've the girth of a prized bull. Mark me, you're a fighter."

At least the Cunningham chief wasn't wrong about that. "If I agree to take your son with me, what others can you send as well? I need numbers. Good men, mind you."

"I'm growing old, else we'd all ride into hell with you." Erloch shook his head. "But I need my army to defend my keep."

"Mayhap you think you need them, but your king needs them more," James said before taking a long, slow drink.

"Och, with English patrols riding through Duncryne whenever they please? I'm lucky they haven't burned me out."

Saying nothing, James' eyebrow quirked as he swiped the froth from his beard—staring. Not smiling. Just leveling a hard stare directly at the man's face.

Erloch tilted back his head and groaned. "Very well, Caelan will ride with ye. He's my best archer. Not bad with a sword in his hand either."

"That's all you can spare?"

"Aye."

"Then I'll be needing two horses for the nuns."

"One."

"Two."

"Apologies, but I can only spare one." Erloch leaned in. "Are they nuns or is there something you're hiding?"

James fingered the handle of his tankard, unwilling to say more.

Fortunately, Torquil chose this moment to make another appearance. "The horses have been turned out for the night."

"And my palfry?" James asked.

"We've put him and the mule in the yard. They've plenty of hay and water."

"My thanks."

"I've news for you, Son," said Erloch, sitting back and gesturing to James. "Come morn, you and Caelan will be riding with Sir James. This is your chance to fight for king and country, lad. And this knight will see ye turned into a man."

Torquil cut James a leer. "*Him?*"

"Aye."

"God's bones, Da. He's barely older than me."

James pushed the bench back and stood, making the lad crane his neck. "I beg to differ. I'm four years your senior, and I've spent the past ten in the service of Bishop Lamberton, training with the finest knights in Scotland."

"Hear him, lad," said Erloch. "If you apply yourself, you'll attract the king's eye. I ken what I'm on about."

To the tune of the boy's snort, James planted his hand on Torquil's shoulder and squeezed. "Let us step outside. I reckon we need to talk afore I agree to your father's terms."

James led the way into a paddock, far from any prying ears. "Your da told me you could benefit from a turn in the wars. But I have my doubts."

"Is that so? I bloody disarmed you. Came upon you unawares—"

"Came upon a man and two nuns minding their own affairs and acted like a rogue. Heroic of you."

"You were trespassing."

"Hardly. We were passing through—on a well-used road. And mind you, I *let* you take my sword and lead us here. I could have dispatched you and your men at any time."

Torquil toed the dirt. "Then why did you not?"

"You're a Highlander for one. Moreover, I didn't want one of the women ending up harmed in the scuffle." In truth, had James been alone, he may have tried to outrun them, but fleeing was not an option with a mule in tow.

"Likely story. I can best you any day."

James snorted. "Mayhap with a crossbow."

"Ye are full of shite."

He drew his sword from its scabbard, the hiss echoing between the trees. "Let us have a go, shall we?"

"But I have no weapon."

"You do now," said James, presenting the hilt of his sword.

Torquil took it and smirked, swinging the blade in a figure eight. "You're mad."

Crouching with his hands level and ready, James gave the lad a nod. "Give it your best."

The lad turned his shoulder as if he were planning to walk away, then spun on his heel with a bellow, swinging the blade over his head.

James thrust up his hands, crossed his wrists, and stopped the attack while grabbing the back of Torquil's hand and twisting, making the boy drop to his knees. With his next breath, he grabbed the sword's hilt and continued to twist until the braggart lay on his back and James leveled the point of the blade at his neck. "Ye were worried I wouldn't be able to defend myself without a weapon?"

"You tricked me."

"Is that what you'll say on the battlefield when an Englishman has your cods in his fist?"

Torquil kicked his feet and squirmed. "Release me."

"Very well." James stepped back and presented the hilt of his father's sword once more. "Again."

This time, Torquil attacked with a thrust aimed to skewer James' heart, but with a simple counter move, the lad was again relieved of the weapon and on his back with the pointy end pressed against the wee pulse throbbing at the base of his throat.

James leaned over, looked him in the eyes, and lowered his voice to a growl. "If you ride with me, you will treat all women with honor and respect, starting with the nuns sleeping in your bed this eve. And if you ever attempt to backstab me, I promise it will be the last act of your maggot-infested life."

6

Ailish opened her eyes, certain something had rattled. "Did you hear that?"

Her question was answered with one of Coira's snores. The woman would sleep through a raid from marauding Norsemen.

Something shifted outside the chamber door. Clutching her hands over her heart, Ailish peered toward the sound, the coals from the fire casting a shadowy light through the chamber.

What should I do? Scream? Rouse Coira?

The maid snored.

Ailish patted her arm. "Are you awake?"

Another snore.

Well, she certainly was not about to lay abed and wait for some beast to burst inside and ravish them. Besides, her father always said the best attack is when the quarry is taken by surprise.

She slid her dagger from beneath her pillow and silently swung her feet over the mattress. The floorboards felt cold beneath her bare feet as she tiptoed to the door. Her hand perspired as she rested it on the latch, listening for another sound.

Closing her eyes, she steadied her breath and offered a silent prayer for strength.

In one swift motion, Ailish yanked open the door and lashed out with her blade. Before she could recoil, a hand grabbed her wrist and squeezed with the strength of a vise, making the dagger fall from her grasp as she spiraled downward, landing on top of the blackguard.

"Och, m'lady, I'd have a wee peek at who I'm attacking afore I blindly thrust a dagger about."

"Sir James?" she asked, pulling away and peering through the blue-black ingress, lit only by a moonbeam shining through an arrow slit in the stairwell.

"Aye, lass, and you'd best be glad 'tis me."

"But why would you be here, making noises outside my door?"

"I was sleeping afore you came barreling out here with this."

As he held up her dagger, she snatched it from his grasp. The movement caused her bottom to shift, his thighs flexing beneath. Only then did she remember she was sitting on his lap. A flood of awareness gushed deep and low in her belly, and she quickly tucked her legs. Heavens stars, only her shift and his plaid separated her skin from his. "Y-you were..." Her gaze dipped to his shirtless chest—a very nice, very braw chest. Even in the dim light, she could discern the outline of musculature obviously developed after years of wearing mail and wielding a gargantuan sword. "Um...you were sleeping in my doorway?"

"The king entrusted me with your safety, did he not? It wouldn't be forthright of me to make up a pallet below stairs in the great hall and leave two nuns alone in a keep full of Cunninghams, now would it?"

Ailish gulped. "For our protection?" she murmured absently, her gaze slipping to his mouth. Curiosity made her run her finger over his bottom lip, leaning nearer as her blood pulsed faster. "Do your lips always glisten in the dark?"

James' warm breath caressed her cheek as his hand tightened

on her waist and another slipped up the back of her neck, making tingles flutter down her arms.

As if pulled by a magical force, she inched closer until his lips brushed hers.

She gasped.

His fingers slipped into her hair while his mouth grew harder, more urgent. Unable to stop herself, Ailish followed his lead, closing her eyes. When his tongue lightly brushed her lips, she opened ever so subtly. She must have interpreted the cue correctly because with a feral moan, that devilish tongue swept into her mouth and danced in the most languid, erotic, entwining strathspey she'd ever imagined.

Impulse took over as she met him stroke for stroke, weaving her fingers through his thick mane of hair.

As they pulled away, he tapped his forehead to hers. "Forgive me."

She swallowed against the thickening of her throat. Aye, Ailish knew sitting on a man's lap and kissing him in the wee hours was enough to see her ruined. But no one and nothing had ever stirred her blood as James Douglas had done in this moment. "I must go."

He helped her to her feet. But as she pulled away, he kept hold of her hands between his much larger palms and touched his lips to her forehead. "Sleep well, m'lady."

Dazed, Ailish stumbled back to bed. Who knew her first kiss would leave her utterly breathless?

AFTER THE DEPRESSION IN THE MATTRESS POPPED UP WHEN Coira arose, Ailish rolled to her back and stretched. "Ahhh," she sighed in a singsong warble. "What a fabulous day."

Water trickled into the washbowl. "Aye, I slept sound which was a nice respite after suffering the rain and the mortifying English attack the night prior."

Ailish smiled, her heart lighter than goose down. "A good night's sleep is better than any tincture, for certain."

"That it is, m'lady." Coira blotted her face dry with a cloth. "You'd best wash. We've another long day of riding ahead of us."

Ailish tossed aside the bedclothes and skipped to the washstand. She'd be riding with James this day. "Fa la de da fa la," she sang.

"My heavens, I don't believe I've seen you this happy since afore we fled Caerlaverock."

"Oh?" Ailish hid her cringe by bending over the basin and splashing her face. Squeezing her eyes shut, she fumbled for the cloth. "I suppose I'm anxious to see Florrie and Harris."

"I am as well," Coira said, waving a hairbrush. "Though we've another night on the road afore we reach Lincluden."

Ailish feigned a groan as the maid began to work through the knots that always managed to knit through her tresses when she was sleeping. "Do not remind me. I'm not comfortable to have Torquil riding with us, either. I loathe the way he ogles me."

"Hmm, though he behaved better at the evening meal. Perhaps his da set him to rights."

Deciding not to tell Coira that Sir James had slept outside their door obviously to protect them from the rogue, she grabbed her habit from the back of the chair and pulled it over her head. "Perhaps, but how will he behave when his father isn't watching?"

Coira held up the veil. "You'd best stay close to me. No wandering off the trail when we stop to rest the horses, ye ken."

Ailish wouldn't mind wandering off the trail and stealing another kiss from Sir James, no matter how sinful the notion. Though in truth, she mustn't lose her head. She was duty bound to her kin and he to the king. Once they reached the priory, they would part and most likely their paths would never again cross.

Coira started for the door. "Come, we must break our fast. It may be the last good meal we'll have in days."

When Ailish stepped into the great hall, she immediately

spotted Sir James already seated at the table. "Good morn, everyone," she chirped.

He didn't look up but shoved a bite of sausage into his mouth. "You'd best eat your fill. We ride within the hour," he said, his voice gruff.

Suddenly not very hungry, Ailish's throat swelled. Had she done something wrong? Was he angry with her?

Torquil rose from the bench. "You can take my seat. I'll go see to the horses."

As she sat and served her plate, Ailish watched the big man through the fans of her eyelashes. He hadn't glanced her way, not even once. What the devil? And after they'd shared the most passionate kiss she'd ever imagined. Did he think her a harlot for letting him kiss her last eve?

How dare he? Sir James kissed me, not the other way around.

His aloofness needled her to no end. How could he have been so passionate and completely flip his manner within a few hours?

When Sir James stood, his gaze met hers for the briefest of moments before sweeping across the hall. "Eat your fill but do not dawdle. I'll see you ladies outside anon."

"But we've only just started," said Coira.

"Wheesht," Ailish snapped, her good spirits completely dissolved. "We won't be but a moment."

"He seems rather cantankerous this morn," the maid whispered as Sir James walked out the door.

"His pallet was most likely as hard as stone. I'll wager he didn't sleep a wink." The man had slept on a hard floor, and she had awakened him—unless he went about kissing women in his sleep. "I only hope I don't have to ride with the beastly curmudgeon," she added while the porridge churned in her belly. Oh, how she'd been looking forward to curling against Sir James' powerful chest and enjoying his warm breath upon her neck. But everything had changed as soon as she'd stepped into the hall.

But why?

After they'd finished their meal, paid their respects to Mr. Cunningham, and headed outdoors, Ailish looked twice at the horses the men had assembled. With Torquil and Caelan, there were five riders, but only four mounts with saddles and the mule was packed with stores.

James grasped her elbow. "Not to worry, Sister. Erloch has given us a garron pony for Coira to ride, and you'll be doubling with me as before."

"I could double with her."

He gave her a leg up onto the palfry. "You could, but mine's the larger mount. We'll travel faster if you ride with me."

She glared down at him. "I'll have you know I am an excellent horsewoman."

"Did I say you were not?"

Ailish pursed her lips. He hadn't said as much, but she reasoned if he had his druthers he'd prefer not to have her ride with him. He most likely was concerned with moving as fast as possible and rued the fact they'd be sharing the warhorse. After all, the sooner they reached Lincluden the sooner he'd be rid of her.

7

A tic at the back of James' jaw annoyed him like flies in a privy. And it had everything to do with how miserable he felt about grousing at Lady Ailish this morn. But it had to be done. Each of them had lost their sense of duty in the wee hours of the night. No matter how much he wanted to tilt that lovely chin his way and devour her with kisses, he must not.

After Ailish returned to her bed last eve, he'd felt like an unmitigated arse. He hadn't slept, either.

James had no business wooing a proper lady—aye, a tryst with a widow or an alehouse wench might suffice, but Her Ladyship was neither of those. She was the daughter of an earl, and the eldest to boot. Obviously, the Bruce wanted to ensure her safe passage to protect her virtue, not for James to take it. And to make matters worse, she was traveling in a nun's disguise. Riding off into the thicket and having a wee roll in the grass was out of the question, no matter how much his cock throbbed every time she moved her shapely backside.

Aye, sharing a mount was pure agony. Having Lady Ailish so close and being unable to embrace her had already twisted his heart into knots. Yet, in no way would he allow her to ride with anyone else. Especially Torquil. And though Coira might be a splendid lady's maid, she wasn't equipped to protect the lass.

At least he felt a bit more confident riding in a star formation with Torquil taking up the rear. Coira and Caelan rode at the flanks with the palfry in the lead. And being a good five and twenty miles west of Stirling, they were well and truly beyond the reaches of any English troops. This was Bishop Wishart's territory and, thus far, Edward's men had given the burgh a wide berth.

Thus far.

It was nearly midday and the lass riding in front of him hadn't uttered a word since they set out this morning. Even though Lady Ailish's posture reflected angry tension, every time James inhaled, he bathed in her scent. And the woman's alluring perfume drove him to the brink of madness. Never before had he wanted to take a lass into his arms as much as he wanted Lady Ailish now. If only he could dig in his spurs and make love to her in a fortress of peace—a place free from war, where the sun shone every day.

But such a place did not exist. At the moment, James did not even have a chamber to call his own let alone a humble shieling in the Highlands. And if it hadn't been for Bishop Lamberton's generous gift celebrating James' knighthood, he wouldn't even own the warhorse beneath them.

A wisp of her hair slipped from under her veil and swept across his face. He shifted his reins to one hand and wound the tress around his finger. Bringing it to his nose, he closed his eyes and inhaled. The winsome fragrance made his heart squeeze all the more. He glanced over his shoulder. The others were far enough back, if he kept his voice low, he could try to calm the waters without being overheard.

"Are you looking forward to rejoining your kin?" he asked.

Ailish immediately stiffened as if his question riled her. "There's no need to make idle chat."

James unwound the lock of hair and let it drop. "No, there isn't."

"Hmph."

If only she'd allow him to tighten his arms around her and urge her to recline against his chest as she'd done the day before. But showing her how much he cared would only cause hardship for them both in the long run.

"I'd like to meet Harris and Florrie," he whispered, trying again. She might be angry with him, but he didn't want a rift between them when he left her with her kin. At least there was no harm in attempting to rebuild the wee friendship they'd begun.

"They're both sweet dear ones," she replied. "Neither of them deserves to be orphaned, hiding behind the walls of a nunnery."

"Nor do you."

She turned her head and glared up at him with those bonny yet unnerving ice-blue eyes. "No, I do not."

The corner of his mouth ticked up. "I'm glad we have that settled."

"Aye."

He ground his molars as she faced forward again and laced her fingers through the palfry's mane. She fashioned the coarse hair into a plait, mussed it, and started again, her fingers working furiously.

"I'm sorry for being a mutton heid this morn."

"Och, so ye own to it, do you?" Ailish's fingers stilled as she leaned out and glanced back to the other riders. "You kissed *me*," she whispered. "Then come dawn, you acted like *I* was a harlot."

"Nay. It was not you at whom my ire was directed."

"It did not seem as such to me."

"Forgive me. I cursed myself for..."

She waited while an air of awkward expectation swelled between them. "Ugh," she groaned. "Are ye going to tell me why you transformed from Lancelot into Mordred in a matter of hours or nay?"

He chuckled at her metaphor. "We are both tasked with duty to king and clan. You pledged an oath to your father to protect your brother. And I have been assigned with the forming of an army to defend our border."

"No small task."

"You are right there."

"Where will you find men to support you? We've been at war for so long, Scotland's sons are either dead or bone weary."

"Och, that doesn't sound like the spirited lass who impersonated a nun and traveled to Scone to pledge fealty for a king who some consider an outlaw in his own realm."

She gave him a sardonic leer. "Was that your attempt to make amends? I woke this morn floating like a soap bubble but someone below stairs took his eating knife and made it vanish with a single barb."

"Ye do have a way with words."

"And you haven't answered my question. Where are you planning to find your army?"

"They'll come. Caelan and Torquil are just the beginning. Once I make it known I've taken up the sword in the name of Robert Bruce, my clansmen will stand behind me for certain."

"You sound confident."

"I *am* confident. Like you, I was orphaned at a young age. My kin sent me to Bishop Lamberton to shelter me from the English. They kent I'd receive a fine education and train to become a knight like my da. Though I left fighting, I now realize there was wisdom in their actions."

"Aye," she said on a sigh. "I've never seen a man wield a sword with as much ferocious passion as the likes of you."

"Is that a kind way of telling me I'm brutish?"

"Nay. The way you fight reminds me of the legends of William Wallace. The question is..."

"Hmm?"

"Whether or not you have his heart."

James gulped. Indeed, he believed he had such a heart. He'd pledged his life to Scotland and the king and he would rid the land of Edward's vermin or die. Now he just needed to prove it to her.

They rode in silence for a time as he reflected on the enormity of the task he was to undertake. For the past ten years, he'd been driven by the intense desire to take back his father's lands. He'd lived, breathed, and trained with an ever-growing hatred for the English king, knowing in his blood he would have vengeance. He needed to prove it to himself. Prove it to clan and kin. And when Robert the Bruce stepped forward to take the Scottish crown, James was further galvanized to prove he was worthy to his king. Now, for some reason he did not grasp, it meant the world to him to prove his worth to the wee sable-haired lass he'd only met less than a sennight ago.

Lady Ailish's shoulders relaxed with her next exhale. "We both have our crosses to bear, do we not?"

The woman had no idea exactly how right she was.

THE FOLLOWING DAY, AILISH DECIDED THE ONLY GOOD THING about this journey was having it come to an end. Riding with Sir James was difficult, painful, and frustrating. Yesterday, they'd chatted a bit and it seemed to ease the tension between them a little. But today, nothing had changed. Ailish didn't want to say goodbye with an awkward misunderstanding dangling between them but knew the inevitable would come within hours.

It was well after midday and they'd been riding since dawn.

Trying to think of something clever to say, Ailish bit her bottom lip. She couldn't tell him that after one silly kiss, she'd been smitten. Such a thing was not only daft, it was trifling.

She sighed, her head swimming. Oh, what a marvelous kiss it had been. If she ever experienced such rapture again, it would be nothing short of a miracle. In fact, Ailish had no illusions that her stolen kiss in the wee hours would be the one and only reckless indulgence of her lifetime. Hidden behind the walls of a nunnery, there was no chance for her to fall in love. Besides, highborn lassies never actually fell in love. As the king had alluded to in Scone, he might one day arrange for her to marry a nobleman. Then again, who knew how long this war would last? How long would it be before Harris regained their ancestral lands?

Too long.

Ailish's brother was only nine years of age. She'd be an old spinster by the time he no longer needed her.

Again, she sighed. At least she had the memory of Sir James' kiss and she would lock it away in her heart for the rest of her days.

As the horses crested one of Scotland's rolling hills, a tower caught her eye. "Look. 'Tis Closburn Castle."

"We'll be at the priory in time for the evening meal," said Coira, sounding immensely thrilled that their journey was coming to an end.

James slapped the reins. "Let us not delay."

As he urged the palfry to a fast trot, Ailish threaded her fingers though the horse's mane and held firm while her backside bounced against Sir James' thighs—very solid, comforting thighs that she ought to be loathing at the moment.

Except she didn't loathe anything about the man. Sitting between his thighs made her want to kiss him all the more. Made her desire him all the more.

If only he'd decided to slow down rather than make haste for Lincluden. If only he'd stop, take her into a thicket, hold her in his arms, and never let go.

But all too soon, the two stone towers of the priory loomed above the church walls with the stained glass sparkling over the bailey walls. Unfortunately, the warhorse bounded ahead of the others and they arrived at the nunnery's gates well before anyone else.

After James dismounted, he held the reins and offered a hand. "Allow me to help you."

"I can do it."

"Aye, you can." He patted her thigh, making gooseflesh skitter across her entire body. "But I'll not be here to assist you the next time you dismount, m'lady."

"Very well." Leaning forward, she placed her hands on his shoulders as his enormous hands clamped around her waist.

His face didn't register the slightest strain as he lifted her clear out of the saddle and brought her against his chest. Ailish couldn't breathe as she slid down the length of his body until her toes touched the ground.

"I...ah..." he said as breathlessly as she felt.

"You're back!" Harris yelled from behind the iron grille of the gates.

Ailish hopped away from Sir James' grasp. "Aye," she said, suddenly at a loss for words.

Florrie stepped into view. "Where's Coira?"

"Here I am," said the maid, reining her horse to a stop beside the palfry with Torquil and Caelan close behind. "Heavens, when that mammoth beast has a mind to run, there's no stopping him."

"I'm glad you made it home in one piece," said Sister Louisa as she used an enormous key to turn the lock. The young novice had become one of Ailish's dearest friends.

"Did you meet the king?" asked Harris, his brown curls flopping about his head as he bobbed up and down.

"I did, and told him everything," Ailish replied before she made the introductions. Then she squeezed Sister Louisa's hand. "Would we be able to invite Sir James and his men in for a meal? 'Tis the least we can do after he risked life and limb fighting the English to see us safely home."

"I'll ask," said the novice, stepping aside and ushering everyone into the courtyard.

"You battled the English?" Harris' eyes grew round as if instantly captivated. "Did you fight them with your great sword?"

James mussed his hair. "I did, m'lord."

"And that was afore we met up with Torquil and his da," said Coira, pointing to the Younger.

"What an adventure you had. Please excuse me while I ask the prioress permission to feed you," said Sister Louisa, gesturing to a bench. "You may wait here."

"I'll stay with you," said Ailish, giving Sir James a polite smile.

Harris took the knight by the hand and pulled him to the bench while the other two followed, though Torquil and Caelan opted to stand. "Ye must tell me everything about your adventure. 'Tis ever so dull living with nuns." The lad thumped his chest. "After all, I'm a man, ye ken."

Sir James sat and pulled Harris onto his lap. "Aye, you're an earl, and you have one brave sister who made certain your fealty was pledged to the new king."

"When can we move back to Caerlaverock?" asked Florrie.

"As soon as my army rids Scotland of the English vermin," said Sir James.

Ailish bit her lip. There was no use telling the children James first must raise an army, train them, then fight a great many battles, all which would undoubtedly take years.

Harris' jaw dropped to his chest as he gaped. "You have an army?"

"I will have now that I'm close to clan and kin."

"Did you hear that Ailish?" said the lad. "Sir James is from Galloway, too."

"He's actually from West Lothian, just north of here," she said. Sitting back, she watched her brother hang on the knight's every word. Of course, any lad would pine for an audience with a real knight. And the Maxwell Clan could certainly benefit from allies such as Douglas. Even the Cunninghams would make good allies after Torquil and Caelan had behaved with utmost respect during their journey south.

Sister Louisa returned with the gate's key in her hand. "The prioress will allow you to bed down for the night in the stable's loft. There's a well out the back where you can wash afore the evening meal."

Sir James stood and set Harris on his feet. "Thank you. We're grateful for your hospitality."

"I'll show them where to go," said Ailish, taking the key from the nun.

Harris was already rattling the gate. "I'll come, too."

Ailish's sprits fell. She desperately wanted a wee moment to speak to Sir James alone and now it seemed her chance had slipped away.

8

After Ailish kissed Florrie and Harris goodnight, she tiptoed down the rear steps of the abbey's dormer and slipped through the bars of the rear gate. Not many adults were able to fit through the gap, but she'd been doing it since her arrival six years past.

Though well after compline, there was still at least an hour of daylight remaining—plenty of time to bid goodnight to Sir James. She stopped behind the hedge for a moment and listened.

Water trickled near the well, but she heard no voices.

May as well make my presence known.

Stepping out, she clasped her hands over her heart and gasped. Merciful saints, the knight stood stripped to the waist with his back to her.

He wore only a plaid belted low about his hips, his muscles rippling with his every move. He splashed under his arms and over his head. Rivulets of sparkling water trickled down his flesh, accentuating dozens of puckered scars—a true sign of a swordsman.

Moving nearer, Ailish reached out as if to trace her finger over the longest mark, starting at his flank and running diagonally across his back. But as she stepped within touching distance, he spun around with a dirk in his fist and fire in his hawkish eyes.

She froze, completely speechless.

In a flash, his gaze changed from deadly to daring, drawing her in like a moth to a flame.

He broke the spell as he reached for a cloth while streams of water meandered their way through the black hair on his chest—a chest so powerfully sculpted it didn't appear to need to be covered by armor at all. "Forgive me, m'lady. I didn't expect to see you," he said, wiping his face.

Ailish blinked, staring at the silver cross he wore over his heart. "Nay, I shouldn't have come."

He tossed the cloth aside and stepped nearer—so close the heat from his body made her mouth go dry. "I'm glad you did."

"Truly?" she asked, glancing over his shoulder. "Where are the others?"

"Gone to the village for a pint of ale—at least one with a wee kick."

"Aye, the nuns water the wine and ask the brewer to make the ale weak." A high-pitched chuckle tittered from her throat. "When do you plan to leave?"

"At dawn."

She scraped her teeth over her bottom lip. "Oh."

When Sir James grasped her hand, Ailish's very breath caught in her chest with a wee gasp. And then she could have floated to the skies as he held her palm over his heart. "I wish we lived in a different time."

Her gaze shifted to his lips as she licked her own. "I do as well."

He dipped his chin. "But we must stay the course."

She inched up on the tips of her toes, needing to be a wee bit closer. "We both bear a heavy burden."

"Aye," he whispered, cupping her cheek with his hand—oddly warm since he'd just been bathing with cold water.

As those bold, masculine lips neared, every inch of Ailish's skin tingled. A deep growl rumbled from his chest, vibrating through her while his intoxicating mouth claimed hers. Slipping her arms around his waist, she deepened the pressure, craving more. Sir James drew her nearer until her breasts crushed into his scar-ridden, rock-hard chest, making her crave more, more kisses, more of him, more of something she did not begin to understand.

His lips wandered across her cheekbones, her ears, and down her neck. Sighing, she dropped her head back and gave in to pure pleasure.

"I wish..." he mumbled.

"What do you wish, sir?" she asked breathlessly.

Sir James inhaled deeply and leaned his forehead against hers. "Forgive me for taking liberties, m'lady."

"There is nothing to forgive." Looking into his fathomless eyes, eyes of a man who fought like the devil, yet he was more tender with her than she ever dreamed possible. "Our lives were not meant to be easy."

"Mine will never be. Ye ken I have sworn an oath to King Robert—one which may see my end."

"You will prevail. But first we wait. You will build your army."

"And wait for the king to grow stronger."

"Aye." Ailish took his hand and kissed his knuckles. "Day and night, I will pray for justice and liberty."

"And I pray when our paths again cross, the kingdom will be at peace."

With one last kiss, Ailish left him, as if she were floating. But she was not only dazed, uncertainty kept her from floating all the way to the clouds. Merciful saints, she might be old and bent before Scotland saw peace.

AMONG THE LETTERS JAMES CARRIED FROM THE KING WAS A missive of introduction to John Blair, an old monk who James found on his knees in the church at Fail Monastery. It had taken a bit of persuasion to be allowed an audience with the monk who had taken a vow of silence.

But James, if not gifted with a silver tongue, was nonetheless a persuasive man. He walked into the nave and sat in a pew beside Blair. His shaved head bent in prayer, a ring of silver locks revealing the monk's advanced years.

Rather than speak, James tapped Blair's arm with the missive.

The monk glanced back, crossed himself, took the letter, and slid into the pew.

James clenched his fists as he waited for Blair to read the contents, nearly holding his breath to keep from demanding Blair leave with him at once.

"The rumors are true," mumbled the monk, his voice barely audible.

"I thought you'd taken a vow of silence."

Blair glanced over with bloodshot eyes, the bags beneath sagging against his cheeks. "I did."

"But you choose to speak now?"

"I suppose no one bothered to ask me why I entered into holy silence."

"Why, then?"

"After they executed Wallace, I vowed to never again speak until someone with big enough cods stepped forward and put the Scottish crown on his head."

"You're a vassal of Robert the Bruce?"

"Och, I never thought much of the fellow when his father was alive."

"And now?"

Blair held up the missive. "If what he's written is true, then I have had a change of heart."

"He said you could lead me to Wallace's hideaway in Selkirk."

"How many men have you?"

"At the moment, two."

"Pardon?"

"Three, counting you. But not far from here are Douglas lands. I reckon I'll raise fifty, mayhap more."

"You'll not survive a fortnight with an army that small."

"Aye? Then let me ask you, how many men did Wallace have when he first ventured into Selkirk?"

"You think you have a point, but things are no longer the same as they once were. The people are tired. They've been beaten down and left with naught but a few sickly sheep, their crofts burned and left to the buzzards."

"Mayhap you're right. But soon the sons of the fallen will rise again. Men like me who saw their fathers murdered at the hands of the English tyrant."

The friar adjusted the ropes belted around his waist. "You are not wrong there. Lord kens we cannot endure much more of his oppression."

"Will you come with me?"

"Aye." Blair stood, and seemed taller, certainly robust for a monk. "But you'd best prove to me you are a worthy leader of men."

"I welcome you allowing me the chance to do so." James released a long, pent-up breath. "I'll return on the morrow. Be ready to ride."

"Have you a horse?"

"A palfry. What about yours? Did you not ride with Wallace?"

"Upon entering the monastery, all our worldly possessions are given to the abbot."

James pushed to his feet. "I'll secure you a mount by morn."

THE DAY WAS NEARLY AT AN END WHEN JAMES SAT ATOP HIS palfry and looked across the valley of his birth. Jutting above the walls stood the round tower built by his great-grandfather. Black smoke belched from the chimneys, settling above the castle, making it look as dark and ugly as it had become.

Bile burned his throat as he craved sweet revenge. It should be he sitting before the hearth in his great hall, his wife at his side with a babe in her arms. Had things been different, his da might have arranged his marriage to Lady Ailish.

James chuckled to himself. How sweet it would be to hold such a woman in his arms every night. Make love to her every night. Awake each morning to her bonny smile.

And where was he now? A landless knight, staring at his ancestral lands like an outsider. Damnation, the mere thought of what might have been stirred his ire—made him want to barrel through the gates and put the lot to fire and sword. Aye, soon James would face Clifford and rid his lands of the English vermin.

But not this day.

He rode into a copse and waited until darkness fell. Only then did he make his move and slip through the back door of his father's most trusted man's cottage—the very man who had delivered James into the care of Bishop Lamberton eleven years ago.

A woman saw him first, dropping a wooden trencher to the floor of packed earth.

"I'm James Douglas, son of William Douglas and it is time to take back what is mine."

Sliding his fingers onto the hilt of his dirk, Hew, now far older, his face worn like old leather, his hairline receded halfway up his skull, rose to his feet. "God on the cross, 'tis as if ye returned from the dead."

"'Twas you who took me to Saint Andrews."

"Aye."

"The bishop trained me well." James picked up his heel and pointed to his boot. "Earned my spurs from the king at his coronation."

"Sir James," Hew whispered, marching across the floor and offering his hand.

"I've been tasked by His Grace to establish an army nearby. We'll raid like Wallace, attacking the English when they least expect it."

"Dear Lord, no more," said the woman.

Hew held up his palms. "Wheesht, Sara."

"I ken Scotland's people are weak and hungry, but as long as we remain beaten, the English will continue to plunder our homes and our crops. They'll take our lads to fight their wars and rape our women until..." James thumped his chest. "*We* put an end to it."

Hew pointed to the houseboy sitting in the corner, cutting beans. "Seumas, go fetch Davy, and be quick about it."

Davy was Hew's son, as well as a lad James had played with when they were young. It wasn't long before they were sitting at the table together. Now in his prime, Davy had turned into a sturdy Scotsman.

"I ken of a dozen who we can trust," said the man.

"Only twelve?" asked James.

"If ye spread word wider, you'll risk having your plans exposed," said Hew. "Clifford has us all by our throats."

"Then we'll cast a wider net. Recruit trusted allies outside of the clan." James picked up an ewer from the center of the table and poured himself a pint of mead. "I ken some of the Maxwells to the south are not fond of the new earl."

"Aye, they have his protection, though." Davy plucked a hazelnut from a wooden bowl in the center of the table, slammed the shell with a hammer, and popped the meat into his mouth. "They might be afraid to take up arms."

"Mark me, they're being oppressed by the murderer who calls himself earl." James tossed a nut into the air and caught it. "Mayhap we test the waters—Davy go see what you can find out. Bring any willing souls to Selkirk. I'll have a sentry posted to lead you in."

"Very well. Shall I pay a visit to the Johnstone as well?"

"Anyone ye ken who's had a gutful of Longshanks' tyranny is welcome."

By the time they'd finished plotting, five trusted clans would be visited on the morrow and given news the King of Scotland needs an army. In the wee hours, James headed back to Fail, a tad deflated that he hadn't immediately recruited his fifty men. Nonetheless, his numbers had increased tenfold and that was a start.

If only he could ride to Lincluden and tell Lady Ailish of his plans—ask her which Maxwell men might support the king.

Hold her in my arms and kiss her under the stars.

Alas, the priory was the opposite direction to Selkirk Forest. And like it or not, the sooner he put the beguiling lass out of his mind, the better off he'd be.

9

Ailish tried to smile as Harris played at being a knight, galloping across the courtyard, using a stick as his horse.

"I'm Sir James and I'll smote ye where ye stand!" the lad yelled at the top of his lungs.

Cringing, Ailish wiped a hand across her mouth. The braw knight had been gone for a fortnight now and her heart still ached as if he'd taken it with him and left a gaping hole.

On the bench beside her, Sister Louisa gave Ailish's hand a pat. "You've been melancholy ever since you returned from Scone."

"I suppose."

"But why? You should be overjoyed that your brother's earldom has been recognized and preserved, thanks to your bravery."

"Perhaps, but who kens when Robert will march his army to Galloway and remove my uncle from Caerlaverock Castle."

"Would it not be nice if they could do so peaceably?"

"You're too kindhearted." Ailish gave the nun a friendly nudge. "I simply pray the king will rise up and use whatever means necessary to reclaim Maxwell lands."

Harris galloped past again. "Sir James, Sir, James! I'll save you!"

The lad's antics made Ailish's heart twist. Where was the knight now? Was he in harm's way? Had he raised the army he'd hoped?

Has he thought of me half as often as I've thought of him?

"Ye ken," said Sister Louisa, "Harris will need to be fostered soon."

"Oh, aye?" Ailish threw up her hands and looked to the skies. "And where might you suggest he go for such fostering whilst the kingdom is infested with Edward's men?"

"It is not for me to say, but the lad was obviously impressed with Sir James."

"Aye, and he will not stop talking about him."

The sister covered her giggle with slender fingers. "I reckon you cannot stop *thinking* about him."

"Sh. I have my duty to Harris and Florrie. There is still much I can teach them, which is all that matters."

"Mm hmm." Sister Louisa picked a daisy from beside the bench and handed it to Florrie who was sitting on the grass making daisy crowns. "But you'd best think on my suggestion. The lad needs to be trained as a knight. One day he will be the leader of men and if he cannot wield a sword, no one will respect him."

Ailish rolled her eyes. She was the daughter of an earl, not Louisa. "Do you think I do not ken? And my journey to Scone only opened my eyes wider."

"I understand, but I do believe you need to start thinking about his future training."

"Och, he's only nine years of age."

"And soon he'll be ten...then afore you know it, he'll be interested in the fairer sex."

Ailish snorted. "What would you ken about that?"

Sister Louisa picked another daisy. "I had older brothers.

And mind you, they all were practicing swordsmanship with wooden wasters by the time they were Harris' age."

Folding her arms, Ailish watched the lad take the stick horse and thrust it into the air, pretending it was Sir James' great sword. Though Sister Louisa had put it into words, she was well aware that when the boy showed the first signs of manhood, the prioress would insist on sending him away. If only Ailish could entrust the lad to Sir James. But the king's knight had no time for children or fostering of any sort. For the love of God, he was living in a forest, sleeping on a bed of rocks for all she knew.

"Mayhap I'll write to the king," she mumbled, thinking aloud.

Sister Louisa stood and brushed out her apron. "That would be a start."

A racket came from the main gate and three nuns hastened to open the iron viewing panel.

Ailish headed toward the noise, signaling for Sister Louisa to follow. The priory didn't often receive visitors and when they did, they usually came without so much banging. "I wonder who's there?"

She ushered the nun against the wall where they could hear but would not be seen.

"We require food and ale," said a man with an English accent.

"I am sorry, but we are only poor nuns," said one of the sisters. "We have very little to spare."

"Ye all are alike, hoarding. Bring us bread and cheese, else we'll break down this gate and burn ye out!"

"Arrragh!" Harris roared as he galloped toward the gate. "Stop, you fiend!"

"Harris, no!" Ailish cried, catching him before he reached the soldiers.

"Let me go!" the lad shrieked as she carried him toward the wall, catching the eye of one of the three men peeping through the panel.

Ice shot through her blood.

Flay it all, she knew him. He was a vassal of her uncle and

every bit as deceitful. Turning away, she sheltered Harris' face from the man's view and hastened into the dormer.

THROUGHOUT SCOTLAND, SUBTLE PRAISES OF ROBERT THE Bruce were whispered among the common folk, as well as the request for all able men to take up arms. Once word spread that James was recruiting with the intent to liberate the border, crofters and lads as young as eleven wandered into the camp, some armed with nothing more than a shovel.

Over the past month, they'd cleaned out the cave and established a command post exactly as the king had asked. And now it was up to James and a handful of trained warriors to turn this bedraggled lot into fighting men. Good God, feeding them was a chore in itself, not to mention the bows, arrows, clubs, and pikes to be made.

With his hands fast on his hips, James stood atop an enormous boulder and watched the men spar. "Better!" he hollered. "Never forget the best offensive attack is good defense. Let them come at you, protect your vitals and bide your time whilst they tire. Only then should you attack, and when you do, aim for the gullet. If his trunk is covered with mail, sever the inside of his leg. He'll bleed out afore he can raise his weapon."

"Again!" bellowed Torquil, who, despite his skirmish with James at Duncryne, had proved his prowess with a blade. To be honest, James was glad to have the lad in his ranks. He might be a bit course with his manners, but gallantry had no place on the battlefield.

"I've a missive for Sir James," bellowed a messenger, holding a letter aloft and riding into the clearing.

James hopped down from his rock. "'Tis nigh time," he said, taking the missive and examining the seal. At last, word had come from the king. He ran his finger under the wax, shook it open, and read.

"What does it say?" asked Torquil.

Davy stepped beside James and peered over his shoulder. "Where are we off to first?" He rubbed his hands together. "I'm ready for a fight."

Torquil patted his sword's hilt. "Past ready."

Though James wanted to leap back onto the boulder and dance a reel, he held his tongue and affected a scowl. Bless the saints and all the stars, he'd been given word to take Castle Douglas and rid her of the infesting vermin. "*...take no prisoners and ensure no Englishman ever again sets foot in her keep*."

"Torquil, ready fifty of our best soldiers to march," he said, shifting his gaze to Caelan. "And I need a dozen of your best archers."

"Not all of us?" asked Davy.

James started for the wood, motioning for Davy to follow. "'Tis too soon for most of them," he said as they approached the river.

"You're right." Even though the rushing water provided enough noise so they would not be overheard, James checked the area to ensure no one was lurking. "We're taking Castle Douglas."

"Praises be."

"I aim to burn it."

Davy gaped so widely his jaw nearly hit his chest. "I beg your bloody pardon? Have you lost your mind?"

James tolerated no disrespect, except from Davy. The two of them were as close as brothers. Rather than argue, he shook the missive. "The Bruce is on the run—heading west where Edward's forces cannot touch him. It will be a year or more afore he's ready to ride into battle. Meanwhile, he's asked us to conduct raids against English forces on our lands—small acts of rebellion to weaken them so when the time comes, they won't stand a chance."

"Does that wee letter tell ye to burn your own keep?"

"It demands that I ensure none of Edward's men ever again

set foot within her walls." James slid the missive into his jerkin. "Look, if I cannot live in my own home in peace, no one will. Besides, if I raze the castle, they'll ken I'll stop at nothing to see justice."

"They'll think you've bloody lost your mind."

"Then so be it." James shrugged. "I care not what they think of me. But, by God, I want the bastards to *fear* me."

HIDING IN HIS FATHER'S STABLES AFTER DARK, JAMES MET with Gilchrist, his da's old butler, one of the few servants whom Clifford hadn't murdered. "We attack at dawn. Ensure no one loyal to Douglas is trapped in the fray."

"Aye, sir."

James clapped the man on the shoulder. "'Tis good to see you."

Gilchrist rubbed his hands together. "I cannot tell you how much it warms my heart to see you've grown into a man. You are the image of your da."

"Truly?"

"He'd be brimming with pride if he could set eyes upon you now."

"I pray he's watching." James gestured toward the keep. "Now go, you mustn't be missed. I want nothing to alert Clifford of my presence."

"Aye, sir." Gilchrist started off, but before he reached the door, he stopped and turned. "Might I say 'tis a shame you do not plan to stay."

"Soon I will return and set things to rights with clan and kin. You have my word."

James watched as Gilchrist quietly returned to the keep, his back stooped and his strides stilted. The years had not been kind to the old man.

He remained in the loft for the night. Hiding just beyond the gate were Davy and the Douglas men. The plans had been carefully laid. Now all James needed was to wait.

He dared not close his eyes as he waited in the dark, the sounds of the animals below his only company.

Before dawn, he made his move. Inside the keep, it was inky black and though he'd been away for eleven years, he knew every passage, every hall, and each winding curve of the stairwell as if he'd never been gone.

When he arrived at the half-sized door to the wall-walk, he crouched in an archer's recess and listened. Beyond, a breeze whistled. And soon, footsteps sounded.

Gilchrist had confirmed two guards were posted—two of Clifford's men who'd been awake all night and undoubtedly were eager to head for their pallets in an hour's time when the guard changed.

It will all be over by then.

The mummer of their voices resonated through the timbers as James cracked open the door.

"Did ye hear that?" asked one.

"Aye."

James pushed the door a bit further with the point of his sword. *Come closer, ye maggots.*

Footsteps shuffled nearer as James' heart thundered in his ears. He could smell their fear as weapons hissed through scabbards. When they pulled the door wide, he burst through, thrusting his blade across the throat of the first, and plunging his dirk into the heart of the second.

He dashed to the brazier and lit a torch, waving it over his head, alerting Davy and the others. Almost immediately, the Douglas set the bunkhouse alight while the shouts of trapped Clifford men rose.

But James had no more time to waste. Caelan and his archers knew what they must do.

James sprinted down the stairs directly to the master's chamber—where his da had slept for years. As he burst through the door, Clifford still slumbered beneath a mound of bedclothes, barely discernable by the light of the coals in the hearth.

"Up with ye!" James seethed, moving forward, ready for the snake to pounce.

Clifford stirred, though barely. "Who are you?" he asked, his voice wary.

"I am James Douglas, come to take what's rightfully mine."

The bastard guffawed. "Your lands were forfeited over a decade ago. Your traitorous father saw to that."

Propelled by rage, James darted toward the bed with his sword raised. As the coverlet moved, a glint of iron caught the light from the fire. Just as Clifford sprang off the mattress with a thrust of his sword, James spun away, losing his balance.

He crashed to the floor and rolled to his knees, while the blackguard pounced. James ducked, caught the cur's wrist, and twisted him downward.

"I'll cut your throat and hang you by the neck from the walls of *my* keep," Clifford seethed as he fought to counter.

But James was stronger and thrust his blade into the man's gullet. "It is not I who will be on display for a buzzard feast," he growled, levering up his sword. "Know this: The son has returned. And Edward's men will have no rest until the Scots have their vengeance!"

10

During vespers, Ailish bowed her head in prayer as did Harris kneeling on her right and Florrie on her left. Of late, her prayers had been more focused on the welfare of Sir James rather than for the poor and oppressed. Certainly, she prayed for everyone. But given Scotland's misery, the knight needed as many prayers as he could get.

News from the outside had been spotty at best. The king was in hiding and she'd heard not a word of Sir James or anyone else, for that matter. It was as if the coronation happened and then nothing changed.

"God bless my sister, and please help her not to worry so much," whispered Harris.

How perceptive the lad had become. Did she worry unduly? Perhaps, but she had an enormous burden to bear. On top of it all, soon he'd be too old to live in a nunnery. What would she do then? It would destroy her for the family to be separated—at least until...

A clamor of heavy footsteps resounded beyond the nave. Ailish turned as knights with swords drawn burst through the oaken doors.

"Where is he?" bellowed a man wearing a helm, his surcoat emblazoned with the Maxwell coat of arms.

Recognition gripped her while the sound of his voice made Ailish's blood turn cold.

Uncle Herbert.

She wrapped her arms around Harris. "No!"

The usurper sauntered toward her, leveling his weapon with her eyes. "Release the lad or I'll run you through."

"Stop at once!" ordered the prioress, hastening from the choir. "This is hallowed ground. You are interrupting God's holy prayers."

Ignoring the nun, Uncle Herbert grappled for Harris.

"You will not take him!" Ailish screeched, scooting away.

Florrie stomped on his instep. "Go away, you fiend!"

The blackguard whacked the lass with a backhand, sending her to the stone floor. The nuns screamed while Ailish watched in horror. But Herbert had not come for Florrie.

Making a snap decision, she grabbed her brother's hand and broke into a run, heading for the rood screen and the sacristy beyond—a place to hide.

"After them!"

"Haste," she growled, as the child stumbled, his legs not long enough to keep pace. Before they passed through the screen, a beastly man grabbed her arm while another ensnared her brother by the scruff of the neck.

"No!" she screamed, fighting to keep hold of the lad and wrapping an arm around his waist. "Release me!"

The tyrants tried to pry them apart. Gnashing her teeth, Ailish held tight while Harris kicked his captor. "Let go!"

No matter how much she resisted, her efforts were in vain. It took three knights to peel the lad away. The boy fought like a hero, stretching his arms out to her. "Don't let them take me!"

She twisted and struggled to break free, but she was no match for the two brutes gripping her by the arms. "I will find you!" she shouted as they dragged her to a pillar and tied her wrists around it while Harris disappeared out the door.

Herbert looked her up and down with a nasty sneer before he turned.

"You cannot kill him," she spat. "Harris is the true Earl of Caerlaverock."

The imposter stopped and glared over his shoulder. "You are quite mistaken. *I* am earl. And if you cannot own to it, you will suffer the same fate as your father."

As she clenched her fists, every fiber of her body turned to fire with the force of her hatred. "You are a deceitful liar!"

Her uncle pointed his sword at her throat. "Your arrogance is exactly why you are unfit to care for the boy. You are just like my brother."

Ailish stopped fighting and glared at the cur while a flicker of hope flashed through her mind. If she was unfit to care for Harris, then what did her uncle intend to do with the lad? "Where are you taking him?" she demanded.

"Far away from here. The whelp must learn respect for the crown."

Her brother would live?

Refusing to allow a modicum of relief to show on her face, Ailish narrowed her eyes and curled her lips. "You mean *Edward*?" she said as if the King of England's name were a curse.

"I most certainly was not referring to the murdering, self-proclaimed King of Scots."

"Robert Bruce *is* the king—he's the only true heir."

"You and your misplaced sense of birthright." Herbert snorted, sheathing his sword. "Your cowardly king is not only in hiding, he sanctioned James Douglas to sack Clifford's keep. The lunatic murdered His Lordship and impaled his head on a spike above the main gate. And, by God, Douglas will meet his end in the Tower where he'll join his father in hell."

"Clifford?" Ailish jerked against the ropes. Sir James had

begun his raids with his own castle? And sacked it? "Lord Clifford was a tenant at best."

"And you will never be tamed." Herbert backed out the door. "But Edward might have a place for your father's devil. *If* he cooperates."

NO SOONER HAD THE DOORS OF THE CHURCH SLAMMED WHEN Coira dashed to the pillar and untied Ailish's bonds. "Are you hurt, m'lady?"

"Only my pride." Rubbing her wrists, she was far more concerned about her sister, now sobbing in Sister Louisa's arms. "More importantly, is Florrie well?"

The child wiped her eyes and sniffled. "T-that man hit me."

"There's a bruise coming up on her cheek," said Sister Louisa.

Ailish examined her sister's face. There was a red mark on the side of her cheek, but the strike hadn't broken the skin. She kissed the lass' forehead. "Are you sore anywhere else?"

Florrie shook her head.

Ailish bent down and looked her sister in the eyes. "I need you to be strong for Harris. Can you do that for me?"

"A-aye."

"You have the strength of the Maxwell Clan running through your blood. I want you to return to the dormer with Coira. She'll mind you whilst I have a word with the prioress."

"After vespers has concluded," said the mother, clapping her hands and urging the nuns back into their pews.

No matter how much Ailish wanted to argue, she took to her knees. But now she prayed for God to protect Harris, remaining in place until the service concluded and the nuns filed out of the nave.

"Come," said the prioress, leading Ailish to her chamber. "We cannot abide soldiers forcing their way into the priory and taking children."

"No, Mother."

"Your uncle must have discovered Harris was here when you went to Scone."

"Nay." Ailish clearly remembered seeing her uncle's man's face in the gate's viewing panel. "'Twas when the soldiers demanded food a few weeks past. I recognized one of them."

Mother sat at her writing table. "Well, whatever the reason, your brother is gone. I must write to Bishop Wishart at once."

"Agreed, the bishop must be informed." After all, Ailish and her family had received sanctuary with his blessing. Turning, Ailish casually clasped her hands behind her back and examined the map of Southern Scotland on the prioress' wall. It marked all the holy abbeys and priories. Interestingly, just near Jedburgh Abby was Selkirk Forest, and in two blinks, she had the journey memorized. "I also must take word to Sir James."

"Hmm." The prioress picked up her quill and smoothed her hand over a piece of vellum. "Perhaps we ought to send him a missive as well."

Ailish took a step toward the table. "What if I carried the letter to him?"

The woman glanced up with a dour frown. "The ordeal in the nave must have addled your mind, child." She dipped the quill into her ink pot. "Oh, no. It has become far too dangerous for you to step outside these walls."

"With all due respect, the priory's walls have already been breached. Moreover, if my uncle wanted to do me harm, he'd have taken me with him."

"Nay, the kingdom is again in turmoil. Surely you heard the man. He said Sir James Douglas burned his own keep. I cannot allow you to leave the priory again. Not only is it too dangerous, your reputation would be ruined if you sought him out. Think of how your actions might reflect on your siblings."

"You are concerned with my *reputation*? What of Harris? He's merely a child and has just been abducted from the only home he's ever known."

"God will prevail." The prioress dipped her quill. "But hear me now, if you leave our walls, you will not be welcomed back."

Ailish's face grew hot while the nun scribed a salutation. Yes, she had been a burden to the nuns for the past six years but, prior to that, her father had been a benefactor to the priory. He'd paid them ten times over the cost of her maintenance. "After my father's generosity, I do not understand why—"

The mother pointed the feather of the quill between Ailish's eyes. "I agreed to let you dress as a nun and travel to Scone to claim your brother's rights as earl, but now things have changed for the worse. Soldiers broke into our house of prayer."

"And took my brother."

"And you believe a man who would raze his own keep is your answer to rescuing Harris from your uncle's army? Your ideas are substantially flawed. 'Tis nothing short of madness, and if you leave these walls, you will put the order in further peril."

Ailish pursed her lips. She'd known the prioress long enough not to pursue the argument. Doing so could see her locked in her cell for a sennight. "Very well. We shall send a missive...with haste."

PLAGUE TAKE IT, AILISH DIDN'T GIVE A HOOT ABOUT HER reputation. Her brother had been abducted by the vilest man to whom she had the displeasure of being related. Harris must be terrified out of his wits, the poor lad.

Aside from Robert the Bruce who, as far as she knew, was in hiding somewhere in the Highlands, the only person who might help was Sir James. True, she could send the knight a missive, but who knew how long the letter would take to reach him...if it did at all?

Well, if she'd learned anything from her father's demise, it was to take charge, not to idly sit by and pray for something good to happen. Despite the prioress' intentions, good things *never* happened on their own no matter how much one prayed.

By the saints, leaving and not being allowed to return hurt deeply. Had she posed such a burden over the years to warrant the woman's ire? How could she remain behind the priory's walls while Harris suffered?

I cannot.

After Florrie fell asleep, Ailish slid a dagger up her sleeve and one in her boot. As she pulled the nun's habit over her gown, she looked fondly at her sister, sleeping on her side with her mouth open. She hated to leave the lass alone, but she'd be far safer with the nuns and Coira would see to her care. Ailish set a note on her bed and donned her cloak. Barely making a sound, she slipped out of the dormer and through the postern gates. She tiptoed to the stables where the mule and the horse from the Cunninghams were silent in their stalls.

By the moon's light, Ailish found a bridle and saddle, then clucked to the gelding. "Hey, laddie. Are ye up for a wee ride?"

The horse nickered and pawed the ground as she opened the stall and slipped inside. He seemed to be eager for a bit of freedom because he took the bit like a hungry hound. Mayhap he didn't care much for the abbey as compared to the Cunningham keep.

She led him to a mounting block, but when he blew out a snort, she walked him in a circle to calm him. The last thing she needed was a wily horse to take off like he was being chased by the devil. "'Tis dark out there. We'll both break our necks if you set out at a gallop."

With a nod of his head, the gelding sidled to the block. "Very well, then. We ride. But we must not make a sound. We shall pick our way like fairy folk in the forest," she cooed, keeping her voice soothing.

After she mounted, she used the bit to keep the gelding's head low, demanding they slowly walk to the road. By the time they reached the milepost, the horse had settled into a gentle gait, easily carrying his head, his hoofbeats silenced by the grass at the side of the road.

Ailish may have managed a stealthy escape, but she knew exactly how perilous her circumstances were now. One wrong turn could very well mean her death. Worse, there was no option to turn back.

II

James held out his arm while Seumas buckled his gauntlets. "Are the men ready to ride?" he asked Davy, his friend leading his horse out of the pen.

"Aye, sir."

"Torquil," James bellowed. "I expect to see marked improvement in your men by the time I return. In swordsmanship as well as archery."

The Cunningham lad looked up from where he was making arrows with Caelan. "You will, sir."

"And do not allow idleness. If we worked without stopping for a year, we would not have all we need. Repair the fences, dig deeper privies, sweep the spiders and vermin from the cave."

"Sir James," called a guard, leading a horse and rider into the camp. "You have a visitor."

James pulled his arm away. New men were arriving at the camp every day, but they were never announced as visitors. As he craned his neck, a burst of fluttering wings erupted in his stomach—not exactly the reaction suited to a warrior about to ride to defend his king.

His gaze homed in on the rider wearing a black nun's habit. And though her eyes were covered by a blindfold, he knew in his bones it was none other than Lady Ailish Maxwell. Every fiber in his body yearned to race across the camp and wrap her in his arms, but the worry tightening the corners of her mouth stopped him—that and the dozens of men looking on.

The guard tugged her horse along and as she tottered in the saddle, James realized the man had not only made Her Ladyship wear a blindfold, he'd also bound her hands.

James marched across the sparring paddock. "What the blazes is this? Untie this woman at once!"

The guard glanced back. "Thought she was a spy."

"I am no spy and I've told this man the same a hundred times, yet he has refused to pay heed to a word I say."

"A spy she is definitely not." If he had any doubts, her sauciness in the face of doom made James smile. He grabbed the lead line, unsheathed his dagger, and cut the bindings himself. "Good day, Lady Ailish."

She pulled down her blindfold and gave the guard a heated glare. "I told him you accompanied me from the coronation, but he chose to call me a liar."

"Beg your pardon, sir. But my orders are—"

"I ken your orders. I'm the one who gave them." James helped Her Ladyship dismount. "Did he harm you?"

"Nay." She held out her palm to the guard. "But I'll have my dagger back, thank you."

The man first looked to James and, receiving a nod, he returned the weapon. "Women have no place here."

"Agreed. However, Her Ladyship is here now, and I'll have it known she is under my protection." James ushered Ailish down the path to the river where they could talk. When they were out of sight, he stopped, took her hand, bowed respectfully, and kissed it. "Forgive me. I did not greet you as I should have done."

"Not to worry," she said, blushing and giving him a grateful smile. Och, he'd missed the bonny lass ever so much. "I imagine my arrival comes as quite a surprise."

"Aye, you were the last person I expected to see." He placed his palm in the small of her back and headed for the shore. "Why did you not send a messenger? You could have been killed by coming here. Not to mention traveling alone. Where is Coira?"

"She is with Florrie, but I have grave news." Her eyes grew haunted as she clutched James' hand and squeezed. "My uncle stormed into the nave whilst we were at prayer and took Harris."

James groaned, his head dropping back. Was no one safe? What of the sanctuary of the church? "How did Herbert discover you were harboring your brother in Lincluden?"

"I cannot be positively certain, but I believe one of my uncle's men was riding with some soldiers who stopped to demand food. I tried to hide Harris from him, but he must have seen us—and I ken for certain he recognized me."

"Blast." James paced. "Where have they taken him?"

She fell in step beside him. "My uncle said to a place the lad will learn respect for the English crown."

"South of the border, most likely."

"Please, we must ride after him at once."

James stopped. "Nay."

"I beg your pardon?" Ailish shook her fists. "Harris is the *Earl* of Caerlaverock, a peer of Scotland, mind you, and he has been kidnapped by a tyrant!"

"'Tis an outrage, and I know you must be beside yourself with worry, but if we ride blindly after him now, we'll never find the lad."

"You cannot mean what you say!" A tear slipped onto her cheek. "Bless it, the longer we wait, the deeper into England he may go."

James didn't doubt her reasoning, though it still didn't make the lad's whereabouts any clearer. "Or he could be held at your father's castle."

"I doubt that. I feared my uncle would kill the boy until he said Harris would be taken to become a vassal of Edward." Ailish knit her brows, giving him a wary once-over. "He also told me you razed your own keep—said you'd gone mad."

"Hmm, I'm glad they took notice. I also wonder if Herbert kens of our alliance." James scratched his beard as he paced. "We must take every care to ensure whatever measures we take to rescue Harris will not be thwarted. I shall send out scouts first, else we risk riding into a trap."

"Scouts? I cannot possibly sit idle whilst my brother is in fear of his life."

"Aye, we're all in fear of our lives." James grasped her shoulders and looked into those captivating eyes. Och, he'd missed them so. "Let me ask you this; if I am killed acting like a raging bull, what good will I be to Harris then?"

Ailish turned and buried her face in her hands. "I just want him back."

His heart twisted as he smoothed his hand across her shoulder. No matter how much he wanted to ride to Caerlaverock and put the castle to fire and sword, it was a mighty fortress—one only conquerable with thousands of men and siege engines. Six years past, Edward had taken the castle with three thousand men and four catapults, hurling trebuchet balls day and night. And if James had learned anything from his years of training, it was always to ride into peril with a solid plan, preferably when one has the highest ground.

"We both want the same thing, lass," he whispered as gently as possible. "But when I go after the lad, I must do so with a clear head and a solid plan."

"What if your scouts do not discover where he is?"

"If nary a soul sees a Maxwell retinue ride south or mayhap east, then we'll ken your brother is at Caerlaverock."

"Oh, Lord in heaven, my insides feel as if they're being torn to shreds."

James slid his hands around her waist and pulled her into his arms. He knew her pain. He knew all too well the rage clawing at her insides. If only he could tell her how happy he was to see her again, but now was not the time. He closed his eyes and savored her scent. "M'lady, you have my oath I will find him. Now, I need to arrange for an escort to take you back to the priory where you'll be safe."

"Nay." She pulled away from his grasp, a new bout of worry filling her eyes. "The prioress said if I left to find you, I could never return."

"What? Why?"

"She thought it was too dangerous for me to come."

"Well, she was right there."

"Please, Sir James. I have nowhere to turn."

He gestured back toward the camp. "I'm living in a cave with hundreds of men. 'Tis crude to say the least. This is no place for a woman, let alone the daughter of an earl."

Her lovely lips parted as if she had much to say but could not bring herself to form the words. "It seems there is no place for me, then."

"Nay, once you are in my care, there you will remain." James groaned. "I was about to ride to the Highlands to gain an audience with the king—tell him of our progress here."

"May I go with you?" Ailish's eyes lit up as if she were already plotting. "Perhaps His Grace can help us find Harris. He might also suggest a place for me—and then I can send for Florrie."

James could only imagine the king's solution, and it included holy matrimony with some overstuffed, elderly lord. Moreover, since he'd dispatched Clifford and burned the Douglas keep, reports were the English had stepped up their patrols as well as their raids. "I'll send a missive—advise the Bruce as to what's happened to Lord Harris and why I've decided to remain here. I'll figure a way for you to stay here until I receive word of your brother's whereabouts."

The furrow in Ailish's brow eased as she wrapped her arms around James' midriff. "I kent you would help. Thank you. From the bottom of my heart, I thank you."

His throat thickened as he cradled her in an embrace. Every

night since he'd left the priory, he'd dreamed of having her in his arms but, deep down, he knew she mustn't remain in Selkirk Forest for long. He prayed the king would see reason. After all, Harris was a Scottish earl, too important for the future of Scotland.

SEUMAS, A SELF-PROCLAIMED SQUIRE TO SIR JAMES, SAT BESIDE Ailish as he helped her trim a stack of beans they were preparing for the evening meal. "Are ye a real nun?"

Ailish snipped a bit of stem with her eating knife. Though she continued to wear the habit, Sir James had already introduced her as a lady and had given the men a stern warning that she was under his protection. "Nay, but I've lived with nuns for the past six years."

The lad tossed a bean into the pot. "That's how long I've been with Hew and his wife."

"Are you an orphan?" she asked, covering her yawn with her hand. After riding all night, she was ever so tired.

"Aye, lost my parents when Lord Clifford stormed the Douglas keep when I was a wee bairn."

"I'm so sorry. It seems war has made too many orphans."

"You're not wrong there, but I aim to be a knight just like Sir James."

"You sound like my brother."

"Is he a lord?"

"Mm hmm. He's an earl."

"Holy merciful fairies. A real earl," said the lad, his eyes round and his voice filled with awe.

Ailish chuckled. "He's a couple of years younger than you, but I reckon you'd make fast allies."

"And then we could both train to be knights together."

"Indeed." Ailish mussed the lad's brown hair. "Tell me about Hew. He's a Douglas man, no?"

"Aye, and he was ever so glad to see Sir James return. He's the one who took him to Bishop Lamberton, ye ken."

"Was he?" No wonder James seemed fond of the man. "And what do you know of the other men here?"

"Well, Davy is Hew's son, but he's as old as Sir James—has a wife and everything." The lad went on to rattle off a list of names as if he were reading from a scroll. "...and I mustn't forget Friar John. He led us to this camp—rode with William Wallace he did."

"I am duly impressed." Ailish had met the monk. He was in charge of the cooking and had set them to preparing the beans to go with tonight's stew. "How many rabbits do you think it takes to feed all these men?"

The lad shrugged. "The friar uses whatever the hunters bring in. Sometimes it is not very filling, though."

"Mayhap we can assist by gathering roots and berries."

After she sent Seumas to the cooking tent with the beans, Ailish stretched and looked out over the camp, spotted with dozens of tents. Every man seemed to be going about his task, reminding her of a shipping port busy with the affairs of the day. If they weren't chopping and carting wood, or putting up tents, they were making arrows, sharpening blades, or fashioning spears. A number were in the sparring ring with Torquil and at least a dozen practiced archery with Caelan, shooting arrows at straw targets. Some of the men showed promise, but none of them were near as skilled as Sir James.

Just as his name crossed her mind, the braw knight stepped into the sparring ring and eyed a pair of fledglings with his fists on his hips. "Halt!"

They stopped, their chests heaving.

James shook his head at one of the men who stood with his hands on his knees, sweat streaming from his brow. "If ye're planning to wield your blade like a lass, I may as well run a blade across your throat now and be done with it."

The fellow straightened. "I ken how to fight as well as the next man."

"Och aye?" James drew his great sword and stood *en guard* with both hands securely gripping the hilt. "Then come at me."

The man looked to his sparring partner who gave a nod, then with a feral roar, he attacked. With the first strike, James countered with an upward swing, ripping the sword from the man's grasp.

"How did ye do that?" asked the bystander.

James shook his weapon and held it aloft. "This is how you hold a Highlander's blade. Both hands, else you'll tire more quickly."

"But what if you're holding a targe?" asked Torquil.

"Then you ought to be fighting with a lighter sword—shorter, too. The English carry shorter weapons and that gives us the advantage. When wielding a great sword, there's no need for Highlanders to move in so close. We can defend a strike without their blades running us through."

James circled his hand over his head. "Go again."

Ailish moved her fingers to her lips to cover her smile. Sir James was certainly a sight to behold. Every time he stood before his men, there was no question as to who was in command. The Bruce was right to appoint him to general of the borders, for a fiercer Highlander did not exist.

He caught her eye and gave a nod while he walked toward her. "Seumas said you're helping in the kitchens."

"Aye," she said, thinking of the crude conditions in the cooking tent—a spit fashioned from tree limbs, a fire pit, a few iron pots—not exactly *kitchens*. "I want to help wherever I can."

"I'm glad of it. No one here is idle, even if they are nobility."

"Are there other nobles present?"

"Nay, but if there were, they'd be working alongside the others."

"As it should be." Ailish yawned and patted her chest. "Apologies."

"You're weary are you not?"

"A bit. I haven't slept since the night afore last."

"I should have thought to tell you I've fashioned a pallet in an alcove of the cave. You'll have a guard and privacy there."

Ailish almost swooned. The mention of sleeping sounded heavenly. "That is very kind of you. I'm certain I will fall asleep as soon as my head touches a pillow."

"Would you like to rest now?"

"Nay. Though I might be bred of nobility, I'd be looked upon as a laggard, would I not?"

The corner of his mouth turned up while his eyes grew even darker. "I reckon we ought to give you quarter this once."

"No matter how much I'd like to slip into the alcove and close my eyes, I'd best wait. I truly do not wish to draw attention to myself."

"I'm afraid with you being the only woman within a good five and twenty miles, every time you take in a breath the men notice you."

"You exaggerate."

"Nay. *I* notice you, for certain."

Before she could stop herself, she tittered, her face suddenly hot.

He tucked a lock of hair under her veil. "I came over here to tell you the missive to His Grace has been dispatched and two scouts are heading south to see what they can uncover as to Lord Harris' whereabouts."

"Bless you." She pressed praying hands together and looked to the heavens. "I kent in my heart you were the one man who could help us."

"Do not go making me out to be a saint. We need to find where Herbert has hidden the lad, then taking him back will be the true challenge."

"But we will. I feel it in my bones."

12

Smoke from the torches and fire pit hung above, making the cave seem surreal. Ailish, the old monk John Blair, and Seumas sat off by themselves, eating the evening meal of tasteless rabbit stew with beans. It was thickened with barley and served on rough wooden trenchers.

Ailish had thought she'd become accustomed to hardship at the priory, but living among a group of poor nuns was nothing like this. The cave was rocky, dank, cold, dark, and full of spiderwebs. There wasn't a single chair, let alone a table. And the stench of men was only tempered by overtones from the wood burning in the firepit.

Many wore their beards thick and long, sweeping chests. Some even had matted hair—possibly where a few of the spiders had taken up residence.

Ailish shuddered. Of course, the nuns at Lincluden Priory were fastidious about cleanliness. Though the priory was small, there was a bath house. And Ailish and her siblings always washed at the bowl morning and night.

She turned to Seumas. "Do you have many opportunities to bathe?"

The lad made a sour face. "Only when Hew makes me."

"Do you wash in the river?"

He scooped a bite of stew with his eating knife. "Aye."

"Well, at least you do not smell like a heathen, nor does Friar John."

"I suppose some of the men are a bit rank," said the monk. "I'll mention bathing to James. It wouldn't be good if the English found our camp on account of the stench."

She chuckled. "After being blindfolded and having it take ages for the guard to lead me here, I doubt we're likely to be raided any time soon."

"Aye, that's why Selkirk makes an ideal hideaway. We're close to our enemies, yet if the blackguards attempt to set foot in the forest, they'd never leave."

Seumas used his teeth to scrape a morsel of rabbit from his eating knife. "We have spies in the trees as well as around the perimeter."

"Well then, I will sleep soundly this night." Honestly, Ailish most likely would sleep through an all-out siege as soon as she found the alcove James had promised.

At the moment, he was across the cave, deep in conversation with his inner circle of men.

One of the others who had been standing guard when she was preparing beans stopped by and tossed his trencher in front of her. "I thought with a woman here, the fare might have a bit of flavor, but I was wrong."

"Haud yer wheesht." Blair lumbered to his feet. "*I* prepared the pottage, and you ken we've naught but what God sees to provide around us and any kind donations the men may bring."

"Well, if she cannot cook better than the likes of you, what good is she?"

Heat spread across her face as Ailish lowered her gaze. She had never cooked a meal in her life, though she'd helped a great deal in the kitchens at the priory. "I'm sure Friar John's cooking is far better than mine."

"Is that so?"

"Is there a problem here?" James asked, coming up behind the ungrateful fellow.

No one said a word, including the grumbler who'd just insulted the friar's cooking abilities. Ailish gave him a hard glare before she smiled at Sir James. "This gentleman was just telling us how much he enjoyed the beans."

"Pshaw," Seumas blurted with a snort.

James looked to Blair. "Is that so?"

The friar gave her a wink. "Aye, one of the new recruits brought a bushel along. I reckon they added some flavor."

Seumas licked his lips and rubbed his belly. "It was delicious. I could eat rabbit stew every meal."

"So, Graham," James said to the man. "Why is it I sense these three are feeding me a line of drivel?"

The man shrugged, looking about as innocent as a dog who'd stolen a leg of mutton from the kitchens. "Not certain, sir."

"Let me make it clear. You are not to speak to Her Ladyship unless spoken to—"

"But I wasn't just speaking to her."

James grabbed the man by the collar. "Did you understand what I said?"

Growing red in the face, Graham sputtered. "A-aye, sir."

"Good. Then we've no quarrel." James pushed the man away and offered his hand to Ailish. "Would you like me to show you to your quarters, m'lady?"

Seumas laughed. "Aye, as if there's a castle within fifty miles."

"Keep the smart-arsed comments to yourself, ye wee pup," said Friar John.

Ailish said nothing and took James' hand. But after they were several paces away, she turned her lips toward the knight and whispered. "I wasn't certain how much longer I'd be able to hold my head up." Her insides might be roiling with worry, but if she didn't sleep soon, she'd risk falling on her face.

"I noticed. Even from across the fire, you looked as if you were fighting to keep your eyes open."

"Was it that obvious?"

"Aye," he said, stopping outside an opening covered by deer hide. He pulled the shroud aside. "When we arrived, not even Seumas could stand straight in this wee nook."

Ailish stepped inside. "No?"

"I took a pickaxe to the ceiling and now at least you can stand. It isn't much but ought to give you a modicum of privacy." He pulled a flint from his sporran. "Would you mind holding the curtain aside whilst I light the fat-burning lamp?"

She grasped the pelt, noticing a large clam shell in a wee hollow with a wick buried in tallow. "Not at all."

In two strikes of his flint and knife, James lit the lamp, turning the alcove into a private little sanctuary. It was no larger than the silver closet at Caerlaverock but was perfect for sleeping. A pallet had been made up and covered with fur pelts—no bed linens, but what ought she expect in a cave?

"This is lovely, thank you."

"'Tis rough at best. I pray you sleep well."

Ailish removed her veil, dropped it to the pallet, and shook out her hair. "I am grateful."

James plucked a wavy curl and wound it once around his finger. "Though you're a maid, I reckon 'tis best for you to wear a veil whenever in the presence of the men."

"Of course. I'm wearing a gown beneath my habit. Do you wish me to remain dressed as a nun?"

"'Tis for the best." He cupped her cheek and dipped his chin. Ailish's very breath caught in her throat as he softly brushed his lips across hers. "Forgive me, but I've wanted to do that ever since you arrived."

A delightful shiver spread across her shoulders. All day, she'd waited for him to kiss her, but with an army of men about, kissing ought to be the very last thing upon her mind. She placed her palm in the center of his chest. "If I am going to continue to be pious, perhaps kissing should be off limits?"

"Hmm." He kissed her again. This time, he lingered while his tongue lazily swept across hers.

"What would Friar John say?" she asked, breathless.

"I reckon the old monk would turn a blind eye." James glanced back. "But you are right. In Scone, the king entrusted me with your virtue and I cannot deny that kissing you makes me want ever so much more."

James left Hew to guard Ailish and set out on his morning rounds, ensuring everyone was set to task. When he returned to the alcove, Hew was still there, sitting against the cave wall, cleaning his fingernails with a dagger.

"Where is Her Ladyship?" James asked.

"Hasn't come out as of yet."

Though she had been exhausted, it didn't seem likely for her to still be asleep. Had she fallen ill? "Lady Ailish?" Hearing no reply, he pulled the fur aside and peeked in, but it was darker than charcoal. "Are you well, m'lady?"

His query was met with a gasp and some rustling. "Is it morning?"

"Aye, has been for some time."

"My heavens, I must have been exhausted. I never sleep past sunup."

James' eyes adjusted a bit—at least enough to see the lass sit up with a fur clutched beneath her chin. "There's the conundrum. The sun never shines in here."

"Mayhap that's why."

"I'll have Seumas fetch you a bit of porridge."

"Thank you."

James dropped the shroud and looked to his man. "I'm trusting you to keep an eye on her. Lord kens having a woman in camp can bring out the beast in men."

"Will do. I'll put Davy on alert, as well."

"Good man."

Her Ladyship may have slept like the dead last eve, but James had barely closed his eyes. What the devil was he to do with her? Aye, he could think of dozens of things he'd *like* to do with her, but nary a one was possible.

"She should have sent a damned missive," he growled under his breath as he stepped outside.

The recruits were only beginning to come into their own and there was much to be done. James also should have left for the Highlands yesterday. The king had sent word that he needed every sword. The MacDougalls had refused to declare fealty to Robert Bruce and because the English were chasing him like hounds, he had been forced to send the queen and his daughter north to Kildrummy Castle.

Given the MacDougall threat in the west, the king's position was all the more precarious.

And I should be at his side.

If they found Lord Harris' whereabouts quickly, James might only be detained a fortnight or two. And then he'd have to walk away from Ailish once more. If only he could give her a proper home, he might consider wooing the lass. Well, he'd already started down that path—even though his amorous leanings needed to stop. The problem was every time he was alone with the woman, he couldn't help but kiss her.

In the command tent, James met with Torquil, Davy, and Caelan. It was time they identified the strongest fighters and allocated them to different schiltrons. A cohort of the best would be assigned to James, but there were enough strong soldiers to name a sergeant to lead each group.

After the meeting ended, the first thing that drew his gaze was Ailish heading down the path to the river with a bucket in her hand.

"M'lady," he called, hastening after her.

She stopped and looked at him expectantly. "Good day, sir knight."

He looked to the skies. How could she be so guileless? "You weren't about to head for the river *alone*, were you?"

The lass held up the bucket. "Friar John needs water."

"Well, he should not be sending you to fetch it."

"He didn't. I volunteered."

"Nay." James took the bucket from her fingers. "I do not want you leaving the camp without an escort. Where the blazes is Hew?"

She shrugged. "Not certain."

"Come," he groused, heading down the trail. "I'll catch up with him later."

"Do not lose your temper with Hew. He left me in Friar John's care."

"Then I'll have a word with Blair and tell him you're not to leave his bloody sight."

Ailish's footsteps pattered the ground, as if she were struggling to keep up with James' strides. "Are you angry with me?"

He stopped and thrust his fists onto his hips. "Nay." In truth, he was angry, but being angry with Her Ladyship seemed absurd.

She eyed him. "I sense you are troubled."

When was he not? "Word arrived that the king has sent Her Grace and his daughter to Kildrummy Castle."

"But that's in the far north." Ailish clasped a hand over her chest. "Do you believe they will be safe there?"

"I do, else the Bruce would have sent them elsewhere."

Nodding, she glanced down the path. "Oh, I found something of yours." Her smile radiated warmth as she pulled a silver chain over her head and held out his cross. "This was between the furs in my pallet."

He stood for a moment watching the silver flicker in the sunlight. "'Twas my mother's," he whispered, as he took the cross and put it on, his stomach clenching. The piece was the sole possession he had of his mother's memory. He never took it off—had it slipped over his head in the fits of a night terror? Most likely.

Gulping, he swallowed his deep-seated emotions and tucked the keepsake under his shirt where he always kept it close to his heart. "How did you ken it was mine?"

"You were wearing it the evening you spent at Lincluden." Ailish turned the color of a blood rose, her gaze meandering to his chest. The shift of her eyes, the slight parting of her lips made her all the more irresistible, more entrancing. "Remember? You were at the washstand behind the stables."

James had only relived that moment every night since. At the time, it had taken all his self-restraint not to whisk the woman into his arms, carry her to the loft, and have his way with her. Just as he felt like doing now. They were alone aside from the muffled sounds coming from the camp. But, alas, this was not the time and most likely would never be.

Ailish turned and continued toward the river. "You gave me your pallet in the alcove, did you not?"

Of course he did. It was the gentlemanly thing to do. "I put you in the only place in the entire camp where there was no chance you would be harmed."

"I suppose you slept outside the alcove as well."

He grunted, taking the pail from her hand. "His Grace asked me to protect you."

"On the journey to Lincluden."

"Aye, but I'm certain his orders would have been perpetuated had he known you would venture to Selkirk Forest...*alone*."

"I apologize if I have caused you inconvenience, but I had nowhere else to turn."

"And that is why I have not sent you away."

"You would have cast me out otherwise?"

No, his heart wouldn't allow it, but he'd best not admit it to her. "Let us say I would have done and will do what is necessary to find Harris."

Her smile was even brighter this time, setting alight a flicker in his heart. But she said nothing. Instead, she continued along the path, letting her fingers brush the shoots of leaves, turning green with the promise of spring.

After a moment or two, she turned and asked, "You said the cross was your mother's. What happened to her?"

James brushed his fingers over the heirloom. "She was taken by fever when I was but two years of age."

"I'm sorry," she said, the smile fading.

He almost asked her to smile again but doing so would make him sound like a careless rogue. "And your mother?"

"She drowned in the Firth of Solway when I was an infant. My father remarried, but my stepmother died giving birth to Harris."

"Forgive me. You have endured so many sorrows."

"'Tis the way of things. And 'tis why we must live for the now."

He stopped at the river's edge. "I like that. For the now."

"Which is also the reason I've decided I must accompany you once we learn where my uncle has taken Harris," she said as he stooped to fill the pail with water.

James' blood boiled as he stood. What the devil? Had she been scheming to hit him upside the head with her unthinkable notion all along? Did she believe she was some sort of warrior princess? He set the bucket on the shore, straightened, and hovered over her. "I disagree."

She scoffed, thrusting her fists onto those saucy hips. "I beg your pardon? You fob me off without at least asking for my reasoning?"

"I do not need to ask. Not only are you female, you are pint-sized at that." He thrust his finger toward the camp. "Any man in my army could flay you."

Seemingly unaffected by his pointed remark, Lady Ailish defiantly turned up her chin. "Och aye? Then where would you like me to go once you leave? Ride north to Kildrummy?"

"Good God, no. I'd rather have you stay in Douglas with Hew's wife."

"And you believe such an arrangement is safe for the daughter of Johann Maxwell?"

"No one would suspect—"

"I *disagree*," she said, spitting the word. Fuming, she pulled a dagger from her sleeve and held it aloft. "Besides, I am not completely unable to defend myself."

James snorted and rolled his eyes to the tops of the trees. "What the blazes do you intend to do with that wee knife?"

She drew an X through the air. "You'd be surprised."

"Show me." He beckoned with his fingers. "Come, have a go."

"You? That's hardly fair. You're the king's champion."

James almost grinned. She thought of him as a champion? If she weren't being so contentious at the moment, he might climb to the highest hill in Selkirk and beat his chest. "You said you were skilled with a dagger. As the Bruce's general on the borders, I'd like to see what you can do."

"Very well, but I'll not be held accountable if I hurt you."

"Agreed."

Sliding a foot back, Her Ladyship addressed him as if preparing for a swordfight. Then she proceeded to dance around him as if either deciding upon his weakest point or waiting for him to move.

James clenched and unclenched his fists. "I haven't all day."

The lass' crystal eyes flashed wide as she lunged straight for his heart. Before she had the blade completely extended, he stepped off the line, grabbed her wrist, and bent her hand inward, putting stress on her fine sinews and relieving the weapon from her grasp.

"Ow," she said, rubbing her arm. "I hardly see what you just proved by manhandling me. You have the ability to disarm any soldier in your army."

He returned her dagger, picked up the bucket, and headed toward the camp. "Aye, if they come at me directly."

"Wait a moment." She snatched the pail and dropped it on

the ground, making half the water slosh over the side. "You cannot just say something like that and be done with it."

"Nay?"

The saucy woman stamped her foot, jutting her face into his. "Nay."

He offered a mocking bow. "What would you have me do, m'lady?"

"I would have you explain and demonstrate what I should have done."

"Very well." James held out his palm into which she deposited the knife. "First of all, if you plan to attack someone with a blade this small, it must be a surprise."

"But you already knew I was going to thrust at you."

With the speed of an asp, he grabbed her wrist, twisted her into his body, and held the knife against her neck, ensuring his thumb kept the blade away from her skin. "Did ye ken I was going to do that?" he growled, making his tone menacing.

"Or this?" Kicking his foot, he swept the woman's legs out from under her, using one hand to break her fall as he followed the momentum, carefully placing his knee on her chest so as not to crush the lass while leveling the dagger at her throat.

"See my point?" she asked, wide-eyed and unruffled as if she almost enjoyed being wrestled to the ground by a brute of a man. "You are a well-trained knight, sir. Not a common crofter."

"That allays nothing. You are not powerful enough to overcome me or anyone else in this camp."

She smirked. "Aside from Seumas."

James stood and offered his hand. "I wouldn't underestimate that lad. He's a Douglas scrapper."

After allowing him to pull her to her feet, she brushed the dirt off her skirts. "Then what would you have me do when I'm threatened?"

"Do you know a man's weak points?"

Suddenly coy, Her Ladyship scraped her teeth over her bottom lip, her gaze dropping to his loins. "Mm hmm."

Lord have mercy, he wasn't expecting that. But she was right. "Aye, a good kick or knee to a man's unmentionables is a start. But what if you're thwarted? Men have an ingrained ability to protect their loins. Where would you strike next?"

"The throat?"

"Where on the throat?"

She traced a line across the base of her neck.

"A good option." He raised his chin and pointed to the vein throbbing along his throat. "If you plunge your blade into either side where the pulse is strongest, he'll bleed out afore he hits the dirt."

"Oh, that is amazing," she said, drumming her fingers against her chin. "Wonderfully gruesome, however."

"War is ugly. Barbaric."

"It is," she whispered. Her haunting tenor reminded James that she had witnessed battle on her own castle when she'd lost her father.

But he wasn't finished with the lesson. He drew an imaginary line where his leg met his trunk. "Cut your attacker here and he'll bleed out as well."

"Truly?"

"Yes. And if you sever the backs of his ankles and he will not be able to walk." James tapped his chest with the pommel of the knife. "Tell me, why should you not try to go for the heart?"

"Not the heart? Is that not where most mortal wounds are sustained?"

"Nay. Unless you are very strong and very skilled, your blade could be stopped by the ribs." He slapped his flank. "Go for the spleen or the liver or the kidneys."

"Good heavens."

"Let's say someone grabs you from behind. What would you do?"

"Well, I usually keep my dagger up my left sleeve. So, if I had my back to him, I'd reach in, grasp the hilt, and stab him in his..."

"Loins?"

"Nay. Where you showed me, so he would bleed out."

James returned her blade, offering her the hilt. "Good. How would you hold the knife when you make such a deadly attack?"

She replaced it in her sleeve, pulled it out, and awkwardly twisted her arm. "Och, that doesn't work terribly well."

"Because you're holding it like a fire poker when you ought to be wielding it like an iron spike." He changed the position of the knife in her grasp and tightened his fist over hers. "You'll have far more power if you wield it like this." He thrust downward with her hand.

"Barbaric," she whispered.

"Is that not what we just agreed was warfare? Is that not what it takes to fight for your life? Remember, if you decide to use a weapon, you'll have but one chance, and if you fail, odds are your life will be forfeit."

"Understood," she looked at the blade in her hand, thrust it downward then across and diagonally.

James gave a wee whistle, the fire in his blood thrumming with her unfettered inspection. "You look more dangerous already."

13

After her knife-wielding lesson with Sir James, Ailish decided to pay more attention to the training sessions happening around her. And for the past two days, she'd queued up with the archers. Moreover, to her surprise, no one questioned her joining in.

Caelan moved behind her as she pulled the bowstring taut. "Focus on your target. Block out every thought except one."

Easy for him to say. His brother hadn't been captured by a tyrant who thought nothing of breaking into a holy church and taking a lad from his kin. And Caelan most certainly wasn't being distracted by a powerful knight who managed to consume her every other thought. "Focus," she repeated.

"You must hit your target or all will be lost."

Those words struck a chord. There was no possible way she would lose Harris to the English. Drawing in a deep breath and holding it, Ailish homed in on the center of the target. Slowly, she let the string slip from her fingers until, with a whoosh, the arrow flew, hitting two fingers to the left of center.

"Well done. You're improving," said Caelan.

She beamed, glancing over her shoulder to see if James might have been watching, but he was nowhere in sight. As a lass in her father's keep, she had been quite a skilled archer, but she'd used a smaller bow. "Still not good enough," she said, loading another arrow and vowing to herself that when Sir James did watch, she would hit the bullseye.

Ailish focused harder as she practiced, shooting her cache of arrows, walking to the target, and pulling them out. She hardly noticed when the others stopped for the day. By the time her fingers had rubbed raw on the bowstring, she was hitting the center of the target nine times out of ten.

There wasn't much daylight remaining when she marched up to pull out her last round of arrows.

"Are ye aiming to join the archers when we march into battle?" asked Seumas, walking past with an armload of firewood.

Ailish gave the lad a look as she yanked on a shaft and examined the tip. "I'll do whatever it takes to have my brother home again."

"Do you aim to bring him to Selkirk Forest as well? Hew says the kingdom won't be at peace until every last English soldier has scurried back across the border."

"I'll have to think about where we'll go after I find him," she said, tucking the arrows under her arm. "Come, I'm hungry. What are we having for the evening meal?"

"The Friar's surprise."

"Which is?"

"You do not want to know." The lad twisted his face into a grimace. "But it helps if you're hungry."

Ailish followed Seumas into the cave, not worried about Friar John's awful cooking, but wondering what she would indeed do once they rescued Harris. Only weeks before her brother was abducted, Sister Louisa had mentioned he would not be able to remain at the priory much longer. And now that the prioress had forbidden Ailish's return, she had naught but to find another safe haven.

Sir James caught her eye, talking to someone she didn't recognize.

What about Bishop Lamberton? He wasn't only one of the most powerful holy men in Scotland, he had sheltered James Douglas for ten years—fostered him, too. She stowed her arrows, then marched across the cave floor and stood patiently with her hands folded until the knight averted his attention her way.

"I've news."

Completely forgetting her purpose, her heart leapt. "Of Harris?"

He placed a hand on her back. "Come. We must talk."

Ailish nearly bubbled over with excitement, and trepidation, and everything in between. Did he know where Uncle Herbert was holding her brother?

As soon as they were outside and away from the tents, she stopped and grasped his hand. "Please tell me you ken where to find my brother."

"I have a token lead is all."

"What is it?"

"A cohort of men wearing the Maxwell coat of arms on their tunics was seen riding south on the road to Carlisle."

"Oh, my heavens. That's just over a day's ride."

"Aye, but we've no confirmation of a child traveling in their midst."

"It makes sense, though. Carlisle boasts the greatest fortress in England's north."

"Which poses yet another obstacle."

Ailish paced. "The only way we'll know how much of an obstacle we face is if we find out for ourselves. Do we leave on the morrow?"

"We?" He cleared his throat and planted his hands on her shoulders. "Both of us will ride on the morrow, but you are going to stay in Douglas with Hew's wife, and I will be taking a handful of men south—in disguise, mind you. No matter how much I'd like to show our enemies the might of Scotland, I haven't yet built the forces to ride across the border and attack the most fortified fortress in the north. Moreover, if they ken we are coming, they'll move the lad afore we arrive.

Ailish scarcely heard a word after he mentioned Hew's wife. For the love of God, she had already refused to hide. She straightened while fiery ire shot up the back of her neck. "Do you not recall I said I would be going with you?"

"'Tis far too dangerous."

"Do you think I care?"

"Lady Ailish—"

She shrugged out from under his grasp. "You just said you need to travel in disguise. What better way than with a woman in your midst? I could pose as your wife, or a servant, or a nun for that matter. Being Sister Ailish worked quite well for me when I traveled to the king's coronation."

"I do not think—"

She silenced him with a chop of her hand. "No! You have obviously *not* thought. As a woman, I can slip into places unnoticed far more easily than a man. And I'm smaller to boot."

"What if you are hurt...or captured, or, or...?"

"Live for the now, remember?" Ailish shook her finger. "I *am* going with you. You ken I cannot stay here and if you leave me with Hew's wife, I'll find a horse and follow."

"But—"

She stood her ground. "I'm going. That's my final word on it."

"Oh, aye?" he asked, his eyes growing dark. "And who made you general of the border army?"

"Do not be ridiculous."

"Am I? In my opinion, my question is no more ridiculous than m'lady's misplaced sense of her own invincibility."

Fit to be tied, Ailish snapped her hand back and swung. Before her slap connected with his face, he caught her wrist. Fighting, she jerked her arm toward his thumb and wrenched away while his fingers brutally dug into her flesh. As she stepped out, he captured her left hand, pulled, and in the blink of an eye, she was on her back with the brute straddling her.

"Leave me be!" she shouted, trying to sit up and slap the living daylights out of him.

"Stop struggling," He growled, pinning her wrists to the ground.

"Stop trying to make me out to be nothing more than a prized virgin, waiting for a gallant knight to sweep me away and take me to an ivory tower where he'll lock me within and keep me sheltered from all the wickedness in Christendom!"

James opened his mouth. Then closed it, his eyes growing narrower and darker.

Ailish gasped as his gaze meandered to her lips. Suddenly, she had not an ounce of fight remaining in her bones. Her insides turned molten as her breathing sped.

He neared, lowering himself over her.

Unable to wait, she arched up and kissed him. In a heartbeat, his tongue plunged into her mouth, as if ravenous. He moved atop her, his body wild with raw passion, the intensity of his ambush ramping up the desire coursing through her blood. As he released her hands, she wrapped them around his neck, holding on for dear life, meeting the demands of his tongue, stroke for stroke, brutal suck for brutal suck. His hips rocked against her and she thrust in turn, while frissons of fire and ice swirled deep and low between her legs.

Panting, she clamped her hands on either side of his face. "I've never felt like this before. You-you have beguiled me."

The corner of his mouth ticked up and his belly shook atop hers. "Quite the contrary, m'lady. It is you who has ensnared me in your spell."

"Then I can go?" she asked, holding his gaze. Perhaps she had more power over James than she realized.

"I see no other way to keep you from harming yourself—though the going will not be easy."

"I did not ask for easy."

He kissed her again, slower this time, as if savoring a drop of fine wine. And when she rocked her hips against him, his deep, guttural moan vibrated through her. "We'd best return to the camp afore I do something we'll both regret."

Ailish scraped her teeth over her bottom lip. Aside from her time at the priory, she hadn't grown up oblivious to the desires of men and women. And she wasn't certain she'd regret it if he did *that*. At least she was not afraid for her virtue. What good was one's maidenhead when one pledged to protect her brother for the rest of her days?

He stood and pulled her up. "By God, woman, whenever you meet an adversary, I'll wager you'd best argue your way out of peril. No man can stand up against your wicked tongue."

Ailish chuckled to herself. If any man other than James Douglas tried to kiss her in the midst of a disagreement, she'd sooner stab him before she allowed some cur to plunder her mouth.

But the rules changed entirely when it came to kissing her black-haired knight. And doing so wasn't only dangerous, it was akin to toying with the devil himself. The man completely disarmed her when his lips met hers.

14

"Where is Lady Ailish?" James demanded as Torquil tossed the rope over the pelts piled on the wagon. Catching it, James looped the end through an iron ring and pulled taut, then secured the rope with a bowline knot.

The Cunningham heir moved to the next tiedown. "Why are you taking her? She will see us all killed if you ask me."

"'Tis why I haven't asked your opinion." James secured the second rope. "But she kens the lad and she'll make our ruse all the more convincing."

The problem was James still wasn't sure he was doing the right thing by letting Her Ladyship come along. Too many things could go wrong, and he'd never forgive himself if anything happened to Ailish.

"She's not bad with a bow," said Caelan, tightening the girth strap on his saddle. "I'd recruit her into my archers if she weren't a woman."

"Wheesht both of ye," James said, straightening his rough-hewn hood and heading for the cave and batting a hand at the naysayers.

Once his eyes adjusted to the dim light inside, he found Blair fussing over Lady Ailish's veil like a mother hen. The friar's portly form blocked Her Ladyship's face from sight. "What is taking so long?" James asked. "First I go against my better judgment and agree to let you accompany us. And now we have not even begun our journey and you're already holding us up."

"Forgive me," she said, patting her hands over the linen cloth and stepping out from behind the holy man. "But if I am posing as your wife, I mustn't look like nun."

James' mouth went dry as he gaped at the bonniest creature who ever shifted a saucy gaze his way.

"And her lady's maid is still at the priory," said Blair, his words barely sinking in. "I think we have her looking quite nice, do you not agree, sir?"

Gulping, James allowed his gaze to meander from her head to the hem of her gown. She wore only the white linen under veil, held in place by a braided circlet—perhaps hewn of horsehair. The headpiece framed her face, drawing his attention to the beauty of her eyes, fanned by long, alluring lashes.

She pursed those bow-shaped, moist lips. Lips he'd be kissing right now if there weren't a friar standing but a foot away. "Are you unhappy?" she asked.

"Nay," he managed as his gaze shifted lower to a blue gown, the neckline scooped from one shoulder to the other, plunging over a pair of succulent breasts. Aye, he'd noticed her breasts before.

Many times.

But he'd only seen Lady Ailish without a nun's habit at the coronation. Aye, she'd bewitched him then, but here in the cave where they were standing only a few feet apart, he was utterly entranced. "W-where did you find the dress?"

"You do not remember?" She smiled, her shoulders waggling. Had she any idea such movement drew even more attention to the perfection of her breasts? "I've been wearing it under my habit all along."

"Well," he grumbled, swiping a hand across his eyes. "It is a good thing you kept it covered until now."

"Why, because it might end up soiled?"

He grasped her hand. "Because the men would never be able to take their eyes off you."

"Your cloak, m'lady," said Blair, holding up the garment and handing her a black, woolen bundle. "And your habit in case you have need of it."

Ailish turned and allowed the friar to slip her woolen cloak over her shoulders. "It would have been very miserable without this," she said, tying the mantle closed at the neck.

James stood back, his gaze shooting straight to her breasts. Thank goodness the cloak covered most of the distraction. "That's better. Now come, else we'll not make it to the border afore nightfall."

"Is that where you plan to make camp."

"Just north of there. I ken of a crofter who will shelter us for the night." He helped Ailish onto the wagon's bench and then addressed the retinue of soldiers he'd hand-picked to travel with them. "Listen to me, men. We are hunters traveling to Carlisle to sell our pelts. If we are stopped, I will do the talking, do you understand?"

Everyone voiced their consent aside from Her Ladyship. James gave her a pointed look. "That means you as well, m'lady."

"Of course. I wouldn't dream of speaking out of turn."

"Very good," he said, climbing beside her and taking up the reins. The timbers of the old wagon creaked as he cued the horse to walk on.

Lady Ailish glanced to the rear where her mount was tethered and following behind. "Why are you not taking the palfry?"

"Because poor hunters do not own expensive warhorses."

She groaned. "I should have thought of that." She gave his arm a pat. "The men look very convincing in their hunters' hoods."

They traveled along the winding maze of narrow pathways that kept their camp well hidden from the enemy while a team of men worked to erase their tracks. Ailish examined the bow and quiver of arrows James had placed at their feet. "Why are the men not carrying their swords?"

Everyone but James had stowed their weapons beneath the pelts where they were easily accessible if one knew where to look. "Again, most hunters cannot afford swords."

"Except everyone seems to have their bows," she mused.

"Tools of the trade." James patted the dirk guarding his loins. "Not to worry. Every man is amply armed."

"If we're ambushed, will we be equipped to fight?"

"Aye, lass." He slapped the reins. "And the arrows are at our feet for a reason. Caelan tells me you've become one of his better archers."

"Did he?" She pulled an arrow out of the quiver and ran her finger along the shaft. "Surprising."

"Why?"

"Because he never said as much to me."

"Mayhap he wants to make you better."

"By not telling me I'm one of his best?"

"Possibly. If the student continues to practice day and night as you have, the student may one day become better than the teacher."

"Hmm." She replaced the arrow. "Where did you learn all this—the hiding of weapons, the training of men, the way you fight like a demon is chasing you?"

"Aside from growing up with a sword in my hand, 'tis what comes from eleven years of being a squire to Bishop Lamberton."

"But that's what I don't understand. He's a holy man."

"He's a warrior, and the knights who follow him are some of the best-trained fighters in Christendom. Some spent their youths on the Continent following the tournaments. Others paid their dues in the Crusades."

"Have you been to the Continent?"

"Nay. Lamberton had already been by the time I came under

his wing. But there were plenty of skirmishes for an apprentice knight to learn his trade."

"Tell me about the bishop."

"He's a great man. He was instrumental in seeing John Balliol sent to France and, afterward, he supported William Wallace. Lamberton's men led many of the schiltrons in the first war against Edward. He's rebuilding Saint Andrews Cathedral after the English razed it in retaliation for his actions against them."

"And he presided over the king's coronation."

"That he did."

"And I imagine he had a hand in your knighthood."

"If it weren't for Lamberton, I'd be making hay in Douglas, too poor to own a cow, I reckon."

"I admire him."

"As do I, m'lady."

"What was it like to be his squire?"

"There were no easy days, for certain. We woke every morning afore dawn for lauds. When we weren't fighting the English, there were never-ending chores amongst all the praying and training."

"What chores did you like best?"

James thought for a moment, easily swaying with the cart's movement. "I never minded spending hours in the stables grooming horses, cleaning stalls, learning a bit about the smith's duties."

"I like the solace of the animals as well. 'Tis always peaceful in a barn."

"That it is."

"Then what did you like least of all?"

"Cleaning the middens for certain."

"Eew. That must have been disgusting."

"Very."

"But I'll reckon it made you strong."

His gaze slid to her face. "Know what made me stronger?"

She shook her head while the cart pitched with a rut in the trail, making her press against him. "What?"

"I carried fresh water from the burn with a yoke across my back."

"A bucket on either end?"

"Two. Four in all."

"Oh, my heavens. I can hardly manage one from the river to the camp."

"And I had twice as far to go, straight up an incline."

"Astounding," she said, her voice filled with awe and making James feel like a king. "No wonder you grew to be as sturdy as an ox."

After they reached the North Road, neither of them spoke for a time until Lady Ailish grasped his arm, her fingers making a welcome shiver course up his arm. "What will happen if the king's response comes whilst you're away?"

"I left Davy behind with instructions to bring us word straight away."

"You must have thought of everything."

"Och, one never kens what they've forgotten until they need it."

"True." Ailish smoothed her hands along her skirts. "*Ahhh*... there's something I've been wanting to ask you."

He regarded her out of the corner of his eye. The melody of her "ah" made a certain appendage between his legs rouse to attention. "What is on your mind, lass?"

A lovely shade of rose colored her cheeks. "We are posing as husband and wife, yes?"

"We are," he said, his voice husky.

"Um..." She traced a finger along his forearm, the friction making him all but shiver. "What about when we sleep?" she whispered, checking to ensure the others didn't hear.

There was one thing he hadn't planned for—sleeping arrangements. But holy Moses, the lass had a knack for disarming a man. Of course, the first response that came to mind was to ask if she wanted to bed him. Lord knew he'd wanted to bed her so badly that he'd been hard ever since she set foot in the camp in Selkirk Forest. Hell, he'd been hard since he'd first set eyes upon her at the coronation. But his unsated lust aside, the lady did have a point. James slowly swiped his mouth, trying to come up with an appropriate reply until he recalled the night they'd spent in the tent when traveling from Scone.

"Err...ah...you've slept beside me afore."

"Not exactly. As I recall, Coira slept between us."

"Well..." A wry grin played on his lips. "Since you've left your lady's maid at the priory, you'll simply have to control your urges, m'lady."

As a look of complete shock crossed her face, she thwacked him on the arm.

Unable to keep a straight face, James threw back his head and laughed.

"Sir James!" she chided.

"Och, lass. Surely you must realize if you cannot trust me, then there's no hope whatsoever."

Then he looked away and cringed. More importantly, could he trust himself?

BY THE TIME THEY TURNED ONTO THE OLD CROFTER'S LANDS, the sun had become an enormous orange globe on the western horizon. Ailish shaded her eyes, but it was so bright she could barely discern the outline of the cottage.

As the wagon veered, she spotted an elderly gentleman leaning on a pitchfork.

"Finlay of Galloway?" asked James.

"Depends on who wants to know."

James reined the horse to a stop and hopped out. "I'm Sir James Douglas, son of—"

"Ye mean to tell me the Black Douglas is here in the flesh?"

"I beg your pardon, sir?"

"That's what they're calling ye." The crofter grinned, showing more missing teeth than otherwise. "From Glasgow all the way to Carlisle, I reckon."

"Truly?"

"Are ye the savage lord who razed his ancestral keep?"

James scratched his black beard, his gaze darting to Ailish. She gave him a reassuring nod. This fellow was obviously awed. "I am. And your son is one of my best men."

Finlay pounded his pitchfork onto the ground. "Bloody oath he is."

"The good man is a leader in my camp." After shaking Finlay's hand, James signaled for the others to dismount. "We need a place to bed down for the night—for my men and my wife."

Stopping herself from gasping, Ailish folded her hands and tried to look wifely. She hadn't expected their ruse to start quite this soon. But then that's what they had agreed.

The man gave her a quizzical onceover. "If you're out to raid an English garrison, why have you brought your wife along?"

"Just gathering information at the moment," said James, helping her down. "We're taking these pelts to market in Carlisle to raise some coin. And ye ken women at the mention of a market."

Ailish gaped. "I beg your pardon?"

Finlay rolled his eyes as if all women were afflicted by some market-day ague. "I reckon it is a good thing you're not going to Carlisle to put the castle to fire and sword, because that old fortress is impenetrable."

"So I've heard," said James. "We'd be obliged if you allowed us to bed down in your stable's loft."

"Och, there's no chance I'll allow the wife of the Lord of Douglas to sleep in a musty old loft. The pair of ye can take the bed in my wee cottage. I'm certain 'tisn't anything as grand as what Her Ladyship is accustomed to, but it provided comfort for my wife and me over the years." Finlay crossed himself. "God rest her soul."

A sudden swarm of butterflies swarmed about Ailish's stomach. "Nay, nay, we couldn't possibly—"

"'Tis very hospitable of you," said James with a bow of his head.

"Excellent." Finlay picked up his pitchfork. "I've a lamb pottage warming. Stable your horses and we'll have a wee bite to eat."

15

After the evening meal, Ailish had insisted on cleaning the wooden bowls, though in truth the pottage had been so good there wasn't much left to clean. She considered asking Finlay to go to Selkirk Forest to help Friar John with the cooking.

"There was more meat in my bowl of pottage than I've had in a month," said James, rubbing his belly.

"I'll say," Torquil agreed, watching Ailish hang the drying cloth over a rafter.

Most of the men had supped in the stables, though as James' men-at-arms, Torquil and Caelan had been invited to dine at the table. Ever since they came inside, the lad had made her a wee bit uneasy—but it seemed his nature was to be a bit too opinionated and abrasive. To be honest, everything had made her uneasy, especially the bed across the floor. The cottage consisted of one chamber.

One.

With one bed.

And as sure as he was sitting at the table like a presumptuous cat, Torquil was on the verge of taunting her. If Sir James weren't present, she was certain the blackguard would say something vile. Aye, he might be a good ally on the battlefield, but Ailish always felt ill at ease whenever the lad was near.

She wrung her hands, looking for something else to occupy them.

"You look a bit nervous, m'lady," Torquil said with a bit of mischief in his tone.

James patted the bench beside him. "Come and have a rest, dearest."

Dearest?

The endearment made her stomach flip. Dropping her hands to her sides, she did as asked hoping she wasn't blushing at the mere thought of being James' dearest.

"What would you have to be nervous about?" asked the crofter.

"Nothing at all," James said, patting her thigh.

Of course, such intimacy made Torquil snigger behind his tankard.

The rhythm of rainfall on thatch came from above. Ailish rubbed her arms, glancing to the bed. When would the others head for their pallets? What then? What would it feel like to be in a bed alone with Sir James?

She felt the color rise in her face as her mind wandered back to every kiss—in the wee hours at Duncryne Castle, behind the stables at the priory, and in the wood only a few days past.

All she could think about was kissing him again. Wrapping her arms around James and holding him as if he were her... her...*husband*.

'Tis scandalous!

But Ailish was already twenty years of age. Elizabeth de Burgh had only been ten and four when she married Robert the Bruce—the same age Ailish was when she fled Caerlaverock with Harris and Florrie.

With war a certainty, who knew if she'd ever wed. More than likely she would not, and most certainly not before the Maxwell lands had been reverted to the true earl, which could be years if not eons.

James poured her a tankard of ale. "Be careful not to swill it, Finlay's ale is as thick as his pottage."

"It helps a man sleep at night," said the crofter, his toothless grin appearing over the top of his mug.

"So tell me," said James. "What news?"

Finlay wiped the froth from his moustache with the back of his hand. "Last I heard, Edward's men have stepped up their raids along the borders."

"Because of the coronation?" asked Torquil.

"Aye." Finlay's gaze cut to James. "But from here to Glasgow, they're pounding on every door seeking information as to where the Black Douglas is hiding."

"They'll never find him," said Caelan. "Selkirk Forest is as impenetrable as any fortress I've ever seen."

Ailish smiled to herself. She rather liked the new moniker they'd given the king's most gallant knight. On a sigh, she took a long draw of the potent ale. She could use a good night's sleep as long as the brew didn't leave her with a sore head come morn.

"What about you?" asked Sir James. "Have they been here demanding to ken my whereabouts?"

"Aye. But they'll never get a sane word out of me. I always act as if I've lost my wits whenever those bastards come calling." Finlay raised his tankard toward Ailish. "Pardon my vulgar tongue, m'lady."

"Carry on," she said, saluting him in kind.

"That's bloody clever," said Caelan.

"This old fool still has a trick or two up his sleeve." He pointed a gnarled finger at James. "And ye'd best not tell them you've been hunting in Selkirk Forest."

"Och, did I not tell you? We're hunters from the Highlands."

As the conversation went on, moving from crops to the weather to boasting about how much better things would be once the English were banished from Scotland, Ailish's eyelids grew increasingly heavy until she tottered into James' shoulder.

He wrapped his arm around her and squeezed. "Och, if we have any hopes of sleeping afore the sun rises, we'd best head for our beds."

Everyone except Ailish stood. James walked Finlay to the door and shook his hand, thanking him for his hospitality.

Torquil sauntered around the table and whispered in Ailish's ear, "Next time, mayhap you can share a bed with me, *m'lady*."

Gasping, her back went ramrod straight. "How dare you," she hissed, her face fiery hot.

"Come, Torquil," said James who had obviously been too wrapped up in conversation with Finlay to have noticed the Cunningham lad's advances. "Her Ladyship needs her rest."

The cur bowed as if he thought himself a gentleman. "Good night, m'lady."

She pursed her lips and leered before she looked to the others. "Sleep well."

AFTER THE MEN HAD RETIRED TO THE STABLES, JAMES sauntered toward the table where Ailish sat, suddenly looking like a hen ready to fight off an annoying cock. Albeit an incredibly bonny hen.

"What did he say to you?"

"Nothing of any importance."

"Tell me."

"You ken Torquil. He likes to stir the pot."

"And he's about to have his tongue severed from his mouth. Now tell me what he said."

"Please, I cannot repeat it."

"Then I will ensure he keeps his comments to himself."

"Do not make a fuss on my account." She peered into her

tankard, then pushed it aside. "He's vulgar. And I pray I never have to endure a moment alone in that man's company."

"I shall ensure you do not."

"My thanks."

James gestured toward the bed. "Go on, you'd best take your rest."

She hesitated for a moment, those crystalline eyes searching his. Then, with a subtle nod, she pushed to her feet and strode to the bed. With her back to him, she removed her circlet and veil. "I—"

He suddenly found himself standing behind her, his hands reaching forward. How had he moved so quickly? "Hmm?" he asked, clenching his fists. Damnation, he needed to stop acting on his urges.

She turned with her eyes lowered. With a heave of her chest, she placed her palms on his midriff and slowly slid her fingers upward in tandem with her gaze.

God on the bloody cross. The expression on her face was enough to bring James to his knees. Her breath grew more labored, the warmth seeping through his tunic. A pink tongue slowly slid across her bottom lip as she glanced over her shoulder. "I... we...are...?"

He quirked an eyebrow. She was flustered, making her allure all the more irresistible. "I will sleep on the floor," he whispered, hating the words but knowing he must.

A furrow of disappointment creased her brow. "Oh."

"Unless..." James trailed off, stopping himself before he tried to encourage her. Damnation, she was too precious to bed like a common alehouse wench.

Her fingers tickled the base of his neck. "Unless?"

"You want..." He clenched his teeth.

"To kiss you?"

You have no idea.

He wanted to do so much more than kiss. But as she inched upward on her toes, his restraint vanished. Unable to utter another word, he captured her mouth, plunging his fingers into her silken hair, proving how deeply he desired this woman. His cock strained against his braies as his lips wandered across her cheekbones to her tiny earlobes. Ailish shivered and sighed as he kissed her neck, then trailed lower, finding a treasure between the glorious breasts swelling above the neckline he hadn't been able to block from his mind since he'd set eyes on her this morn.

Sighing, Ailish tilted back her head and rocked into him, her fingers clinging to his hips. She brushed her mons from side to side, rubbing his cock, ratcheting up his need.

Loosening the laces of her gown and the shift beneath, he captured a rosy nipple between his lips.

"Ahhh," she sighed, the ardent moan begging him for more.

It took but a moment to lay her down, and stealthily tug up her skirts. He nudge between her knees and ran his tongue along the silkiest, most shapely thigh he'd ever seen in all his days.

As he slowly inched up, she arched for him, the intoxicating fragrance of woman sending his mind into a fervor. When he pushed her skirts higher, his seed pulsed to the tip of his cock.

"Magnificence," he growled, admiring the slender legs, flair of hip, a mahogany nest of curls.

Ailish pushed the cloth just enough to hide her treasure. "Are you sure?"

Him?

Sure?

"Och, lass, all that matters is what you desire."

She eased back and let her knees drop, opening herself to him. "I want you."

"Then allow me to bring you pleasure."

Certain she'd gone completely mad, Ailish swirled her fingers through James' hair while he kissed the most sacred, secretive place on her body. She ought to be utterly mortified and embarrassed to her soul.

But she wasn't. She spread her knees, delighting in being prone to him—in giving herself to his wicked mouth. Heaven help her, his tongue turned her wanton as he swirled it so close to the place that ached for him.

"Och, ye smell like heaven," he growled.

She whimpered wanting, craving more, but not knowing what. Gripping the bedclothes in her fists, she rocked her hips while James watched her with those black eyes, his tongue working magic. With a devilish chuckle, he licked the most secret part of her body, making her sizzle with need while her thighs shuddered.

"Mercy!" she cried, arching her back.

Rather than ease away, the black knight grew ruthless in his attack. His fingers swirled in tandem with his wicked tongue. Ailish gasped again when he slid his finger inside her. Good heavens, her core was incredibly moist and slick as if her body knew what to expect.

Him. His manhood.

The fiend worked his finger back and forth as he continued his merciless kissing.

His delightful, ravenous kissing.

Her eyes rolled back, and her hips rocked erratically, unashamedly in tandem with the escalation of desire—a craving low in her belly demanded more, threatening to send her to the brink of insanity if he dared to stop. His finger worked faster. Stars darted through her vision. Her breath came in short gasps.

"More," she said, her voice far and distant as if it weren't even hers. But as the word escaped her throat, the rumble of his deep chuckle reverberated against her thighs. He swirled his tongue faster, matching the rhythm of his insistent finger. Ailish gasped, tossing her head from side to side as if she were a demon possessed, craving more, unable to focus on anything but the ripples of need pooling inside "Don't stop! Please!"

At once, her eyes flew open, a cry caught her throat as her body shattered. Her breath came in short gasps as if she'd just run for miles. What had he done to render her helpless?

When Ailish's vision cleared and her breathing eased, she shifted her gaze to James. "Have I gone completely mad?"

"Nay, lass." He grinned, his gaze filled with the same desire she'd just experienced. "I just made love to you with my mouth."

"Oh." She glanced to his loins, knowing full well what lay beneath his jerkin. "You still have not been pleasured?"

"My pleasure comes from seeing your desire fulfilled."

"But—"

He tapped a finger to her lips. "Wheesht. I'll not take your innocence, lass."

16

"Bloody hell," James mumbled under his breath as the wagon inched along, stuck behind a herd of cattle crossing the border.

"The bridge over the river is awfully narrow," said Ailish, holding an old blanket closed at her nape, doing her best to appear matronly.

"And we'll be here half the day waiting for those laggard drovers to move the herd across." James tilted his head to better see out from under his hood. Aside from the three sentries at the crossing, he counted only two archers standing guard atop the wooden ramparts just beyond the river. But no matter what he saw, there were more.

Ailish tapped her toes against the footrail. "This is making me nervous."

The whole debacle not only made him nervous, it made him want to be reckless and ride ahead to tell the drovers to move their beasts aside and let him pass. But doing so would only make the soldiers suspicious. "Act as if you haven't a care." James glanced back to Her Ladyship's horse tied to the back of the wagon. The beast was sturdy enough, but he wasn't a warhorse. He gave his men a subtle nod as well. All four had moved in closer for the crossing. "As long as everyone remains calm, we'll pass through without trouble."

The blanket slipped back on her crown as she craned her neck. "It's just so unnerving."

James tugged it back up and pulled his hood lower over his brow as well. "All you need to worry about is keeping your face concealed. The less they see of you the more difficult it will be for them to remember what you look like."

She smiled and batted her lashes. "Aye, sir."

When she looked at him like that, he thought of nothing but taking the lass into the wood and ravishing her. "Just do not bat those saucy eyes at the sentries."

"I would not dream of doing so."

At long last, James drove the wagon across the bridge. He was stopped on the far side by a snarly sentry dressed in mail and wearing a pointed helm with an iron nose-guard. The man stood in the middle of the road and held up his palm. "Halt."

James pulled on the reins while a tic twitched at the corner of his eye. It would be ever so easy to crack the whip and trample the cur.

"What is your purpose?" demanded the man.

To smite your kind from Scotland forever. One day soon, he'd speak the words on the tip of this tongue. Just not this day. James even managed a semblance of a smile. "We're hunters taking these pelts to market—they'll make fine vellum, they will."

A pair of sentries armed with pikes moved behind to the wagon for their inspection.

"Is that so?" asked the guard. "That's quite an impressive heap. Where did you fell these deer? The king will be very interested to know."

Not my king. "They're Highland roe deer—hunted far from the king's forests for certain." The admission made bile burn James' throat.

"Highlanders, eh?" The man tapped the pommel of the

sword sheathed on his belt. "You've traveled a long way to sell your wares."

"They'll fetch more coin in Carlisle."

"Perhaps." The guard rested his hand on the cart horse's rump. "Tell me, what news have you of the outlaw Robert the Bruce?"

James' ire ratcheted higher, his fingers itching to pull the sword hidden in the pelts behind his hip and plunge it through the miserable fiend's heart. "I heard there was a coronation at the end of March. It seems Scotland has a new king, though I've not seen hide nor hair of him."

"Hardly. The bastard is on the run. He'll be dead along with that demon zealot the Black Douglas."

James snorted. "I've heard Douglas is not of sound mind."

"Ah, so you're aware he razed his father's *former* keep and hung Sir Clifford's head from the bailey, have ye?"

Dear God in heaven, if only I could slit this miserable fiend's throat and be done with it. James shrugged as if he had all day to flap his mouth. "Most everyone's talking about him. First mention I heard of it was when we passed through Glasgow."

"Well, when we find him, I'm going to flay him and turn his hide into a belt."

"What's this?" asked one of the sentries, pulling a sword out from the middle of the pelts.

James feigned nonchalance. "Och, when ye have a wife as bonny as mine, a man needs to defend himself."

"All blades are to be confiscated by the king."

"A moment," shouted the other pikeman, his arm buried in the stack of furs. "Here's another!"

"Bless it, I kent you'd cause trouble the moment I set eyes on ye." James glanced back as he pulled his sword out from its hiding place. "Ye want the Black Douglas' hide? Well I dare ye to take it!"

The guard's eyes flashed wide as the hood dropped from James' head. Stumbling backward, the cur grappled for his sword, but James was faster. Leaping from the wagon, he drove the point of his blade into the guard's throat.

As he whipped around, a pikeman hurled his lance through the air. James ducked. Ailish's bow twanged, her arrow hitting the man in the chest and, as he gaped in shock, another arrow shot from behind the wagon lodged in his thigh.

James spun to the third pikeman, ready for a fight. But the man was already down with an arrow buried in his back.

"Haste!" Ailish said, standing in the wagon, her bow loaded and ready for another shot.

"Take out the archers in the ramparts!" James bellowed as he slapped the reins, cuing the carthorse to run. "Keep your head down, m'lady."

"I have a shot!" she hollered, letting her arrow fly, followed by a shrill cry from a falling man.

But as soon as one fell, he was replaced by another.

Charging around the wagon, Caelan led the way, riding toward the fort with his reins in his teeth. At breakneck speed, the warrior took two shots, each hitting its mark.

After James had driven the cart out of firing distance, he hopped down and offered his hand. "I'll help you mount."

"I can manage." Ailish slung the bow and quiver of arrows over her shoulder. "You tend to your horse."

James unhitched the carthorse as Torquil and the men swiftly grabbed the remaining weapons from their hiding places. "Is anyone hurt?"

"Not yet," said Caelan, kicking his heels. "But they're after us for certain."

James mounted while Ailish rode beside him. "Damn," he growled as they headed south. The last thing he wanted was a skirmish at the border. Now they either must outrun the patrol or set an ambush. Both options were fraught with danger. Worse, as they rounded the bend, the miserable mob of cows blocked the road.

"What are we to do now?" asked Ailish?

"May as well use these beasts to our advantage." With a wave of his hand, James rallied the men. "Walk your mounts through the mob and keep your heads down."

"Are ye daft?" asked Torquil. "We ought to be riding up the ridge and setting an ambush."

Ailish glanced upward. There was a ridge beside them, but there was no way to climb it unless they backtracked. Across was a forest of brambles, too thick for anyone to pass through.

James started into the herd. "Do as I say."

Torquil shook his head. "You're signing our death warrants."

"Just meander through these beasts as if it were a holiday. And pray we reach the front of the herd afore the bastards catch up with us," said the fearless knight.

Ailish glanced over her shoulder as she followed James. The hide of a beast brushed her leg, but they were walking slowly enough that the friction did nothing to annoy the animal.

"What are you doing?" yelled a drover from the side.

"Don't mind us," James hollered back. "We'll be through in no time."

As they slowly surged forward, James' eyes never stopped scanning the road behind.

The reins slipped in Ailish's hand as she forced herself not to dig in her heels and demand a gallop.

"Archers!" yelled Caelan.

"Turn the beasts around—make them stampede!" James bellowed, slapping his crop on the nose of a steer.

Ailish did the same, shouting at the top of her lungs. As the cattle spooked, so did her horse, rearing and making her feet slip out of the stirrups. She held on with her knees, leaning as far over the horse's neck as she could. When his hooves hit the dirt, the gelding charged straight for the open road ahead.

"Whoa," she commanded, tugging on the reins and forcing

herself to ease the pressure of her knees. No matter how much she wanted to squeeze, the only way to calm a frightened horse was to relax her seat.

She curled forward, pulling and releasing, pulling and releasing. "Easy now," she cooed. "Easy."

By the time she had the gelding slowed to a fast trot, James was beside her. "Are you all right, m'lady?"

She tugged again. "I am now."

He reached for the bridle and, together, they slowed to a walk.

"That was brilliant," said Torquil, reining his mount beside them. "But why didn't you tell us that was the plan afore we walked into the mob?"

"I wasn't certain we'd reach the front of the herd by the time the soldiers arrived." James glanced back. "Did you get a look at how many were following?"

"A half-dozen at most," said Caelan. "Every last one trampled."

Ailish cringed and crossed herself. "Merciful Father."

"Better them than us," said Torquil.

"Do you think more will follow?" she asked.

James leveled a hard stare her way, his black eyes intense. "There are always more—but none who can identify us, God willing."

Ailish craned her neck, searching for a milepost. "We'd best find a less traveled route to Carlisle."

James pointed as a detour came into view. "What say you men? We ride for Carlisle at a fast trot?"

"How much farther?" asked Caelan.

"Eight miles, give or take."

It didn't take long to ride the distance along the detour. The curtain walls of the city came into view as did the River Caldew skirting along the east side. In the foreground, an enormous cathedral dominated the sky, every bit as large as the cathedral at Scone Abbey. Walls at least as tall as three stories surrounded the city with a blanket of smoke hanging above. A tower presided over the gate's archway, but though the entry was grand, the gatehouse was dwarfed by the towers beyond.

Ailish's heart pounded. "To think, I might be embracing Harris afore the compline bell rings!"

"We must find him first," replied James as he held up his hand. "Slow to a walk, men. We do not want to draw any more attention to ourselves than necessary."

With market day on the morrow, laborers and craftsmen approached the gates, leading carts filled with wares. "I wish we still had the wagon of pelts."

"There's no replacing it now," said James before he turned to the others. "I'll do the talking."

Ailish ran her fingers over the bow she wore across her shoulder, praying there would be no bloodshed this time. When the sentry stopped them at the gate, she peered beyond the line of pikemen guarding the city's entrance. The clang from the smithy shack rang as commoners ambled about, some pushing barrows of hay or less pleasant-smelling goods. Others carried bundles of wood on their backs. Flagged on by a guard, a group of washerwomen walked right past them and through the archway, heading toward the inner castle gate carrying their baskets of laundered linens.

"State your purpose," demanded the guard as if he intended to order the pikemen to attack on the spot.

"Come for market day," said James. "Do you know of an inn suitable for my lady wife?" He leaned down and cupped a hand to the side of his mouth. "She's awfully particular."

The sentry's gaze shifted to Ailish. "'Tis not advisable to bring a woman into the city, especially."

"I'm in sore need of fine cloth and silk for the babe," she said, rubbing her belly. "And I'll trust no one else to purchase it on my behalf."

James gave her a dour frown and cleared his throat. "Ye see my predicament, sir?"

"Aye, I have a similar problem at home. And there's no changing a woman's mind when she's in the family way." The man thrust a thumb over his shoulder. "The Boar's Head down the close lets rooms to travelers, but you'd best be quick."

"My thanks." James picked up his reins. "How many ale houses are within the city gates?"

"Three, but nary a one is suitable for a woman in the family way." He waved them on. "Ye'll find The Boar's Head is the smallest and least likely to entertain a brawl."

17

The innkeeper opened the door to the chamber on the top floor. "Apologies, but this is all I can offer."

A narrow bed sat in a corner and beside it was an old wooden stool. There was no hearth. An open gap posed as a window, skirted by a ratty fur tied back. Above, a pigeon cooed, roosting in the crumbling masonry. A white trail of bird droppings stained the wall beneath the bird.

"This will do," said James, dropping a coin in the man's palm, no matter how much he wanted to tell the innkeeper what he could do with the bed and the pigeon.

The man removed his cap and swatted the nest, sending the pigeon on its way. "Many guests have stayed in this chamber. Just pull the fur across the window when you're ready to sleep."

"Do you have a candle?" asked Ailish.

"I'll have the lad bring one up."

Her Ladyship turned in a circle, looking at the exposed rafters as the innkeeper took his leave. "At least it is better than sleeping in a tent."

James chuckled. The only time they'd slept in a tent, they'd been attacked by a couple of English spies. "Safer, if we're lucky."

As the door clicked, she grasped his hands. "Do you think we'll find Harris?"

"If he's here, we'll find him. I sent Torquil and Caelan to the tollbooth to inquire."

"After Harris?"

He raised her fingers to his lips. "Nay, to ask how many children are imprisoned."

"But *we* should have gone."

"Are you certain about that?" He arched an eyebrow. "If the Cunningham lads go now, no one will suspect me if I show up later."

"Ah." She slid her hands away and gripped her fists beneath her chin. "How are you planning to spirit him out?"

"One thing at a time." James pulled her into his arms and kissed her forehead. "So, you're in the family way, are ye?"

She turned up her chin with a saucy grin. "My wee fib worked, did it not?"

"Aye, but what happened to letting me do the talking?"

"I did."

"Perhaps afore you told the man you were expecting a wee bairn."

She pulled away. "Are you angry?"

"I'd put it no higher than annoyed."

"But why?"

"Because this is war and in war there can be only one general and his orders must be followed implicitly no matter how much you may think he's wrong."

"I did not think you were wrong."

"But you spoke out nonetheless."

"Nay! Well, I suppose I did, but the notion popped into my head and I blurted it out afore I remembered your orders." She dipped into a clipped curtsey. "Forgive me for my disobedience, oh master."

"Do not patronize me. Against my better judgment I've allowed you to come on this venture. We've already been chased by the border patrol. Lord only kens what we'll face next, especially if we attempt to spirit out of the most heavily armed fortress in Northern England with your brother."

She strode to the window and looked out, crossing her arms. "He and Florrie are my only care. My father told me to protect the lad with my life. And now..." Burying her face in her hands, she released an anguished sob. "I've lost him."

"Och, lass. We will find him." James moved behind her, placing his hands on her shoulders. "He is of noble blood, important to King Robert and the foundation of the Kingdom of Scotland."

Whipping around, Ailish faced him. "He *is* and nothing can happen to him."

"I ken, lass." He pulled her into his embrace and kissed her. "If you'll wait for me here, I'll go below stairs and find some food."

"May I go with you?"

He held her at arm's length. "Not if you're expecting a bairn. 'Tis too dangerous."

"You ken I'm not."

"You began the ruse, now you must play your part."

"But what if Torquil and Caelan discover Harris is in the tollbooth?"

"Then we'll have a rescue to plan, will we not?"

With a wee gasp, she covered her mouth with her fingers as if she were too afraid to hope. "Dear Lord, please make it so."

James took her hands between his much larger palms, turned them over and kissed each trembling finger. "I may be an overbearing brute and as rugged as the Highlands, but I promise you we will find your brother and then we will not rest until he is back on Scottish soil with you."

"What if they have him locked in an impenetrable tower? What if he's already in the Tower of London?"

"Then our king must negotiate."

"Will he?"

The lass was too perceptive. But James intended to do everything in his power to see Robert assert his kingship and take as many prisoners as the English crown had taken from Scotland. "In time. When he gains leverage."

"But that could take years."

"Wheesht, lass. Do not allow yourself to fret over that which we do not yet know." He headed for the door. "Lock the bolt after I leave."

BELOW STAIRS, THE NOISE IN THE ALEHOUSE WAS LOUD ENOUGH to shake the timbers. Men dirty from a day's work either stood three-deep at the bar or sat at one of the tables strewn haphazardly about the tavern. The odor of stale beer and tallow hung on the air in a hazy smoke.

When James spotted Torquil and a group of Douglas men huddled together at a table near the rear, he strode toward them. "What news?" he asked, annoyed they hadn't sought him out as soon as they returned from the tollbooth.

Caelan scooted aside, thumping the bench. "The clerk was gone for the day and will not return until the morrow."

James slid into the seat. "Did you ask a guard?"

"I tried." Torquil raised his tankard to his lips. "He threatened to run me through."

"Bastard."

James flagged a wench and ordered another ewer of ale as well as food and drink to take to Ailish.

"Are you certain the lad is in Carlisle?" asked Caelan.

"Nay, but it is likely."

"What will we do if he's not?"

James sat back as the wench brought the drink. "Find him."

"Search all of England?" asked Torquil.

Such a quest might take years—time James did not have. He was supposed to be building an army and preparing to wreak havoc along the borders, not chasing after a child. But then again, his own father had been abducted by Edward's forces and taken in chains to the Tower of London where they tortured Da to death.

Who kens what they will do to a lad of nine?

"We'll do what we can," he said as the heavy door at the front creaked open. His spirits lifted a bit as he beckoned the Douglas man. "Davy!"

But as his friend strode toward the table, his face appeared drawn as if he'd aged a decade in the two days since they'd left Selkirk Forest.

Standing, James grasped the man's forearm in a handshake reserved for kin. "What is it?"

"Grave news, but first I must tell you the messenger from the Bruce returned with an arrow in his shoulder."

"Good God."

"Bloody fighter, that one. Blair is tending him." Davy pulled James aside and whispered in his ear, "The king has taken refuge on the Isle of Arran—was pursued mercilessly by those loyal to Comyn. He sent word to do what you can to find Lord Harris as long as your army will be ready to attack without mercy by midsummer."

James nodded. "I thought no less."

"But there's more." Davy's face grew ashen. "It cuts me to the quick to utter it."

"Make room," said James, urging his friend to the bench. "Tell me all."

The man slid beside Torquil. "Sir Henry Percy and his band of English fiends raided five Douglas crofts. Burned them. Took no prisoners."

"God, no."

"Me ma's dead."

"Jesu," James mumbled while bile churned in his stomach. Rage pulsed through his blood. "I haven't words."

"Nor I." Davy had been clenching his fists so tightly, his

knuckles were white. "My wife and children were unharmed." He blinked away tears as he looked to the rafters. "Thank God my cottage is a mile outside the village."

They sat in silence for a time while James fumed, ready to ride like a madman and set the entire border alight. "What of Hew? I can only imagine how bereft your da must be."

"He's gone to bury the dead. Left Blair in charge until he returns."

The food came but James hardly noticed. What if he'd refused to allow Lady Ailish to come on the hunt for Lord Harris?

My God, she'd be dead as well.

"One more thing," Davy said, biting off a chunk of bread.

James glanced up.

"There's a price on your head."

"I glad of it." He smirked. "Because I want them to ken I'm coming. I want them to fear the Black Douglas because after I'm finished, they'll all know what it's like to live in hell."

18

Now that she had a tallow candle burning in the wall sconce, Ailish closed the fur over the window and tied it down to keep the chilly wind at bay. Over the years, she'd grown accustomed to the musky odor of tallow. After all, it was used in the priory. Beeswax candles were only brought out in the church and that was for holy days and special occasions when the bishop paid a visit.

A thud sounded at the door as if someone knocked with their boot. "Who is it?" she asked.

"Sir James."

"Thank goodness. I'm famished." She slid aside the bolt and opened the door. But as soon as she saw his face, she forgot her hunger. "What is it?"

He strode inside carrying a trencher with bread, cheese, an ewer, and two tankards, turned in a circle and ended up setting them on the bed. "The lads will not be able to speak to the clerk at the tollbooth until the morrow."

"Oh, that is disappointing." She reached for a piece of cheese and clipped it with her teeth while James strode to the window, peeked through the edge of the fur and dropped it with a grunt.

Had he told her everything? "Why do I sense there is something else on your mind?" she asked.

"First of all, the king needs my army ready to march by midsummer. And..." He raked his fingers through his black hair, making it fan about his face.

"Tell me."

"Edward's savages attacked a number of Douglas crofts. They spared no one."

"No."

Reeling, James stumbled to the bed and buried his face in his hands. "I should have been there."

Hot prickles fired beneath her skin. What should she say? There were no words powerful enough to ease his pain. "Hew's wife?" she whispered.

"Murdered."

"I'm so sorry," she whispered.

He looked up, the rims of his eyes red. "It feels as if I've been thrown back eleven years. When will the madness ever stop? The senseless raids, the killing, the pillaging, the pointlessness of it all."

They'd both lost so much. And James was right, there seemed to be no end in sight, mayhap not in their lifetimes.

Ailish slowly slid her hand onto his thigh.

He clutched his fists over his heart. "Whenever we retaliate, they come back with more vengeance than before. No one is safe. Not our wives, our mothers, our children. They are unfeeling, wretched, hateful barbarians and the only way to break free from Edward's tyranny is to fight harder, and meaner, and more savagely than they."

A tear streamed down her cheek as she slid her palm across his shoulders. "Let the pain drive you toward greatness."

With an animalistic wail, he threw his arms around her, pressing his head against her breast. "I miss my da. I miss my ma. I missed growing up on my family's lands, breathing the air of freedom. Our people have been oppressed since the death of King Alexander—twenty bloody, miserable years."

"Since the year I was born," she whispered, suddenly realizing he was right.

"I've pledged my life and my sword to Robert the Bruce. I ken in my heart he is the man with the mettle to lead us to freedom. But as sure as you are my witness, I will not rest another day until we have our vengeance."

"I ken the king was right to knight you. With a man of your ilk by his side, he will succeed. You will preside over Douglas lands and Harris will take his place at Caerlaverock." She clutched her arms around him and pressed her lips to his head. "I, too, pledge an oath that we will live to see our children in a world without oppression."

The candle flickered and burned lower while she held him, rocking back and forth. The attack on Douglas was devasting news, for certain, though such mindlessness happed all too often. Raids were common, especially along the borders. The priory had been spared mostly because it was holy ground—same with the abbeys like Kelso, Melrose, and Jedburgh. But nowhere else in the kingdom could they expect sanctuary.

And how much longer would the church be able to provide protection? After all, once Uncle Herbert learned that Ailish was harboring Harris in Lincluden, he'd had no qualms about invading in the midst of vespers and taking the lad. What would have happened if James had been present? There would have been bloodshed for certain.

Perish the thought had he tried to face Herbert's army alone. This brave and compassionate knight mightn't be in her arms at this moment.

James rubbed his hand up and down her spine. "Forgive my hour of weakness."

"There is nothing to forgive." She kissed him again. "I do not see it as weak to express the depth of your passion. Not when we've been through so much."

"I should leave you to eat."

"Stay." She ran her fingers through his thick hair. "James..."

"Hmm?"

"Kiss me."

He sat up and cupped her face in his strong hands. "It was wrong of me to take liberties at Finlay's croft."

Her gaze slipped to the pulse throbbing at the base of his neck. She wanted this man and none other. No matter what happened on the morrow, he was hers to hold this night. "I do not recall pushing you away."

He moistened his lips, his eyes hungry and more intense than she'd ever seen them. He gazed upon her as if he could read her thoughts, then slowly dipped his chin and kissed her.

James' low growl vibrated through her as he plied her mouth like a man possessed, a man who knew exactly what he wanted and took it.

And Ailish reveled in his every touch, his every breath whispering across her searing flesh. "I want you to lie with me."

His lips stilled on her neck. "I must not."

Her heart squeezed. "Do you not desire me?"

"Och, *mo leannan*," he said, his voice deep and soft as he uttered the Gaelic endearment. "'Tis not what I want that matters. You are a highborn woman, and I must preserve your innocence."

"But we are children of war, you and me. We have naught but to take our pleasure when we can, where we can. And I choose you, James Douglas, Lord of Douglas."

"Jesu, Ailish, you make my blood thrum with fire."

Emboldened by his words, she kissed him, imparting every ounce of passion in her soul. And as he kissed her neck, she shivered and sighed. Oh, for the love of all that was holy, James trailed his lips to breasts. His fingers drew away her dress and shift from her shoulders and Ailish felt no shame, only the searing pull of desire as he suckled her nipples and kneaded her, his deft fingers making her want for him coil deep and low in her nether parts even more powerfully than it had done the night before.

"I want to see you bare," she whispered, both shocked and bolstered by her brazenness.

James chuckled, and stood, removing his belt, jerkin, aketon, shoes, stockings, and chausses, until all that was left was his linen braies, secured at the waist with a length of string.

Ailish gripped her hands over her heart and gasped, unable to shift her eyes away from the dark triangle of hair beneath the linen cloth that strained against the outline of his sex. Large. Hard. Aroused.

"Now you," he growled, pulling her to her feet.

The motion was enough to make her already loosened garments swoosh to the floor.

He opened his mouth, then closed, his Adam's apple bobbing. "You are the most beautiful creature I have ever beheld."

Heat rose in her face as Ailish crossed her arms over her breasts.

"Nay." James grasped her fingers and pulled them away. "You must never cover yourself in front of me."

She liked having his eyes on her, adored the admiration in his tone, however, his own beauty is what gave her pause. "You are bonnier than I," she said, her gaze trailing to his chest, to the rippling sinew beneath the flesh on his belly, the line of back hair leading below his braies.

"I am but an ogre compared to you."

"Never say that," she said, untying the cord holding up his braies. And as she revealed him, he rendered her utterly speechless.

They stared at each other while the air around them grew charged as if their passion were on the precipice of erupting into a rolling boil.

She eased to the mattress, her hair sprawling every which way. "Show me."

James slid beside her, his wicked hands caressing everywhere. "Are you certain?"

She nodded, her gaze drifting to his manhood. "More certain than I've been about anything in ages."

"I've wanted you ever since I saw you standing beside Coira at the coronation." He traced his finger around her erect nipple. "It can be painful the first time. I do not want to hurt you."

"A wee bit of pain will be worthwhile if it binds me to you." She kissed him, her lithe fingers reaching down and brushing the tip of his cock.

James sucked in a ragged breath.

Pulling her hand away, her eyes grew wide. "Did I hurt you?"

"Nay," he croaked, coaxing her hand back down. "Feel me. Feel my length. Know how much I desire you."

"Do you like it when I touch you...ah...*there*."

Rather than answer, he slid his finger inside her, letting Ailish know exactly how much he liked to have her hands on him. "Aye, it drives me to the brink of madness."

"Madness?" she asked all the same, gripping him, milking him.

"An insatiable madness." With a feral growl, he moved atop her, and knelt between her legs. "Let me show you pleasure."

"Please."

Parting her curls, he brushed the pad of his thumb over her.

Gasping, Ailish arched her back. "My stars, how can you make me so wanton with a mere touch?"

He grinned, swirling his thumb in a languid rhythm. "Close your eyes and feel."

She did as he asked and as her hips worked in concert with his thumb, he slid his finger inside her again. "Think of my cock entering you."

"Mm," she moaned. *Cock. What a deliciously naughty word.*

He added another finger. "But I am bigger. I will stretch you further than you think possible."

The rocking of her hips sped. "Yes, I want your cock. I want all of you."

James balanced over her and slid his member up her parting. Back and forth he tempted her, making Ailish's thighs shudder while her moisture spilled over him.

Needing more, she forced herself to open her eyes. Watching him, she arched up and caught the tip of his cock at her entrance. "Take me," she whispered.

"Jesu," he growled. "You are so tempting, I will not last long."

Ailish nodded, her hips swirling until gradually, he pushed inside. She sucked in a gasp as he filled her, stretched her, shocked her. But most of all, he ignited a ravening she never knew she possessed.

James froze. "Am I hurting you?" He pulled out. "If you want to stop..."

"Nay! She clamped her fingers on his buttocks. "I want more." With a firm tug, she urged him deeper while she bore the pain and focused on the deep love growing in her heart.

When at last he was fully inside, James released a long sigh. "This is the nearest I've ever been to heaven," he whispered.

"Heaven," she repeated, rocking her hips now that the pain had ebbed.

He worked slowly at first, building the tempo as if he felt the mounting passion inside her. And when she could take no more, her eyes flew open, a cry catching in her throat. In an explosion of pure passion, frenzy claimed her mind. And as she shattered around him, he thrust deep, bellowing as he withdrew.

His head dropped forward as he panted as if fighting to catch his breath. "Lord have mercy," he growled. "You have bewitched me mind, body, and soul."

And after they shared a bonding kiss, she moved aside. "You spilled into the bedclothes."

"Regardless of what you told the guard, I will not have you with child. Not until you take your wedding vows."

With you? She wanted to ask but knew neither one of them was at liberty to make such promises.

His lips moved to her neck. "Was it as good as you expected, *mo leannan*?"

"Better." She arched into him as his mouth claimed her breast. "Never in all my days did I imagine such pleasure."

"You are precious to me, m'lady." His eyes grew moist as he ran a finger over her lips. "I do adore you."

"And I you."

19

Come morning, James allowed Ailish to break her fast below stairs. Thank heavens. No matter how much she wanted to remain in his arms for the rest of her days, she must never lose sight of her quest to find her brother and the oath she'd sworn to protect him.

She took a bite of porridge and watched James across the table, not feeling a whit of remorse for what she'd done. He'd been rather quiet since she'd come awake when he'd tapped on her door. No, he hadn't slept beside her as she'd wished. She guessed he'd slept in the corridor to keep up appearances. Either that or he harbored regrets, which was possible since he hadn't kissed her this morn.

And now he shoveled porridge in his mouth as if she weren't there. But there was no time to fret about what he was thinking.

Beside him, Davy pushed his bowl away. "The sooner we leave this place, the better."

"Why is that?" James asked, his voice low. "Too many Englishmen?"

"Too many scoundrels if you ask me. Every city is the same on market day. Plenty of swindlers out to rob you of your coin and Lord kens what else."

Torquil and Caelan pushed through the alehouse doors. James stood as Ailish clasped her hands over her heart, praying they had news of Harris.

Torquil took the lead, sauntering toward them in his cock-sure manner.

"What news?" asked James. "Tell me they have him."

"The only child incarcerated in the tollbooth is a lass of six, caught for stealing bread."

"How awful." Ailish imagined a poor gel only wanting to help feed her family. "Did you pay her fine?"

Torquil snorted. "Are ye daft, woman?"

James grabbed the man's arm. "She's a lady, mind you, and your better. I'll not tolerate a coarse word toward her."

"Forgive me. I spoke out of turn." Yanking his arm away, Torquil looked anything but sorry. "The clerk did offer up a tidbit of information."

Ailish leaned in. "About Harris?"

"Not exactly about the lad, but he said a retinue rode in two days past. Looked as if they may have had prisoners of the crown —nobles and the like."

"Was there a child among them?" asked Davy.

"He wasn't certain. But he did say any prisoners of noble blood were kept in the castle—the tollbooth didn't have proper accommodations for the aristocracy."

Ailish nodded. It was common practice to imprison those of noble blood in chambers with latrines and the like. Though from what she knew, there were few comforts. High-ranking prisoners in the Tower of London were treated the same. Rather than being thrown in an overcrowded pit or worse, they enjoyed a locked chamber with a cot, plenty of rats, and perhaps a barred window looking out over the Thames.

"Not much to go on," said James.

"But at least it is something." Ailish pushed to her feet. "I saw some washerwomen heading for the castle when we arrived.

I'll wager if I venture down to the river, one of them may know more."

"Washerwomen?" asked Torquil. "They might be able to tell ye what the Lord Warden ate for breakfast."

"Aye," Caelan agreed. "Because they're the ones who clean *his* linens."

James held up his palms. "Wheesht." Then he turned to Ailish. "'Tis too dangerous for you to venture to the river alone."

"But—"

"I'll go."

"Where? To speak to the washerwomen?"

"The smithy shack. There's no better place to have a wee conversation with a soldier than when he's waiting for a repair." James shook his finger under her nose. "Wait above stairs and bolt the door. I have no intention of chasing after two Maxwells."

Ailish would have argued but decided not to waste her breath. She'd come to read James better than he realized and, right now, he thought he knew better than anyone. Just as he had said the day prior, he was the general and everyone else must mindlessly follow even if he made the most egregious decision imaginable.

Some things he said made no sense whatsoever. If only he would recognize her worth, her ability to think on her own. But no, he expected her to hide in a chamber while they were no closer to finding her brother.

Poor Harris must be beside himself with worry, terrified he might never see his sisters again. She clapped a hand over her mouth while images plagued her mind of how he might be suffering or even tortured.

Well, I will not sit idle and do nothing!

Wearing the nun's habit and an apron borrowed from the innkeeper's wife so she looked less like a nun and more like a servant, Ailish slipped out of the alehouse and hastened toward the river. She wore the simple linen veil, definitely common looking enough to play the part of a washerwoman. Under one arm she carried her only shift and in another hand a bit of lye soap. It felt awkward walking over the cobbled streets without her undergarments, but it couldn't be helped.

Besides, no one had any idea she was indecently clad.

Just as she suspected, a group of women were kneeling among the rocks at the shore of the river, bent over, scrubbing linens. First, Ailish walked down the line, picking out tidbits of conversation—some complaints, some chatter about a male servant or two, and nothing about any prisoners.

At the end of a line, an older woman worked, separated from the others by a good yard. She batted a shirt with a mallet.

"Stubborn stain, is it?" Ailish asked as she kneeled beside the woman.

"One would think His Lordship wiped his mouth with his sleeve."

Smiling to herself, Ailish dipped her shift in the water. How fortuitous to happen upon a wench who tends the Lord Warden's laundry. "Do not most men?"

The woman scoured the cloth with a bar of soap "Hmph."

"Have you been in service long?"

"A dozen years, I'd reckon."

"My, that is a long time." Ailish took her time lathering her shift. "I'll wager you have many stories to tell."

"You'd be astounded by the trickeries that abound beyond the castle walls." The woman rocked back and held up the shirt. "And that's below stairs."

"Look there, the stain is gone." Ailish pointed. "You must have a magical knack."

"There's nothing magical about hard work." The woman tossed the shirt into the half-barrel and smiled, albeit a sad smile. "'Tis why I'm head laundress. His Lordship allows only me to wash his shirts."

"Is he a kind man?"

"I would not venture that far, but I'm paid a fair wage."

"I suppose that's all you can ask for." Ailish rocked back and sniffled, wiping her eye.

The woman leaned in. "Are you bereft, lass?"

"Alas, I am."

"Whatever is the matter?"

"I've lost my brother."

"Your brother? Oh, my heavens, that is horrible news. Have you any idea where he may have gone?"

"Honestly..." Lowering her voice, Ailish looked to ensure none of the others were eavesdropping, and then pulled her mother's ruby pendant from beneath her robe. "I am *Lady* Ailish Maxwell. My wee brother was abducted not but a fortnight ago and I have reason to believe he may be imprisoned in the castle."

"Maxwell?" the woman asked as if trying to place the name.

"My family holds lands in England as well as in Scotland. I mean you no harm. I simply wish to find the lad and take him home."

"Well, I cannot help you. I'm not privy to the comings and goings of His Lordship's guests."

"I understand, but surely you must have some inkling of where they might be holding him—if he is indeed here. Please. I am sick with worry. And he's such a good boy—only nine years of age, he is."

The woman grabbed a shirt and doused it in the river.

"Have you children?" Ailish asked.

She glanced out of the corner of her eye and worked as if she were possessed by a demon.

"He is my only care. Our parents are gone and, because he is the heir, there are many evil men who would like to see him dead. Please. If you care anything for a lost child, you'll tell me."

"Generally, captured Scottish noblemen being transported

to London are held in the postern tower, from which no one has *ever* escaped. If your bother is here, then the king must have ordered his capture, and I cannot possibly be of service to you, my lady. Now if you will excuse me, I have washing to tend."

Ailish stood and wrung out her shift. "Forgive me. In no way did I intend to make you feel uncomfortable."

The woman didn't reply, nor did she look up. But whether she knew it or not, she had revealed where highborn prisoners were held. Now armed with a solid bit of information to share with James, Ailish started back to the inn.

When she reached the road, she glanced over her shoulder. Odd, there was no sign of the washerwoman with whom she'd been speaking, though the others still lined the shore.

Ailish hastened her pace, heading up the path to the city gates.

A guard stepped into her path. "Where are you off to in such a hurry?"

"I—ah..." She glanced down at the laundered shift in her hands. "My lady needs this straight away."

"But it is wet." Curling his lips, the man looked her from head to toe and leaned in as if he were interested in more than her purpose. "Surely she will not need the shift until after it has been hung out to dry."

"But you don't understand. My lady is expecting me to return forthwith."

"Not before you pay the toll."

"Toll? There was no toll when we arrived yesterday."

He pursed his lips, his breath sour like distilled spirit that had gone off. "Come, wench, just give us a kiss and I'll let you pass."

Ailish shrank. The man was vile.

"I haven't all day."

"Do you promise to let me pass?"

"After you pay the toll, aye."

Wrinkling her nose, she darted in and gave him the briefest of pecks. "There, now I'll be on my way."

He grabbed her shoulders and snarled. "Am I not fair enough for the likes of you?"

"Forgive me, but I am not accustomed to being accosted by guards." Ailish tried to twist away, but he only gripped her tighter. "And a man who is supposed to be protecting the people, not mistreating them."

"Ye disrespectful shrew, I ought to—"

Not listening to another word, with all her might, Ailish thrust her knee into his loins. Grunting, the guard released his grip and doubled over.

Ailish ran.

"Stop that woman!" bellowed a woman from behind. "She's a spy for the outlaw Bruce!"

A rush pulsed through her blood as she quickened her pace, racing for the inn. Where was James? Where were the other men?

Approaching a turn, she glanced over her shoulder.

No!

At least a half-dozen soldiers were chasing her.

She wasn't going to make it.

Hide!

As she turned, she smashed into a wall of a knight, hitting him with such force, her head spun. Staggering, she mumbled an apology and skirted around. But he grabbed her arm.

"No so fast, spy."

"I am not a spy. I'm searching for my brother."

The guards surrounded them, flanked by the traitorous washerwoman. "That's her. Lady Ailish Maxwell. She's the one asking questions, Lord Warden."

At the use of his title, she glared up at the man who was responsible for countless Scottish deaths. Aye, Andrew Harclay earned his position in Carlisle for his ruthless plundering of poor border clans and kin.

"Maxwell, aye? Any relation to the earl?"

"That *imposter* is my uncle," Ailish spat. "The true earl is my brother, Harris, son of Johann."

"Ah, the traitor King Edward hung from the walls of Caerlaverock if my memory serves."

Ailish bit the inside of her cheek as the guards tied her wrists behind her back. If she said another word against her uncle or spewed a slight about Edward, she'd be hung without trial or worse, burned. And there was only one thing she truly needed to know. "I demand you tell me what you have done with my brother!"

"Well, well." The man's eyebrows arched mockingly. "You, *my lady*, are in no position to make any demands whatsoever. Tell me, surely you did not travel all the way to Carlisle alone."

"You boorish brute. Do you not believe me able to walk across the border on my own two feet?" Ailish fought against her bindings but they only cut into her flesh. "My brother is my only care. He was taken from the priory during mass, of all things. Please, he's only a wee lad of nine. He would hurt no one."

"Interesting thing about displaced Scottish nobles. They grow up to be rebels and traitors. Right thorns in the king's backside." The knight beckoned the guards. "Take her to the postern tower."

"Straight away, my lord."

Led away by an escort of a half-dozen guards, Ailish frantically searched for any sign of James or his men. If only she could shout his name, but doing so would betray him to her merciless captors.

20

James walked into the chamber, and then his throat constricted and his heart with it. Leaving the door ajar, he dashed inside and turned full circle. "Where the devil is she?"

Davy leaned against the jamb. "I thought she was to wait for you here."

"So did I." Every muscle in James' body tensed as he marched to the window and pulled the fur aside. "The lass may be bonnier than a spring rose, but she will never make much of a soldier."

"Why is that? From what I saw, she's quite skilled with a bow."

"Talent does not make a lick of difference when she cannot follow orders for the life of her."

"Sounds like every woman I've ever met. My wife's the same." Davy moved beside him and craned his head out the window. "Want to know what I think?"

"I reckon you'll say it whether I want to ken or not."

"You're in love with her."

Love? James had never been in love with anyone in his bloody life. "And you're touched in the head."

"Admit it. Why else would you have allowed her to come?"

James slammed his fist into his palm. "Good God, man, we're at war. The woman of whom you are speaking has not only disappeared, I cannot afford to fall in love. Especially with a noblewoman who refuses to stay put after I've given her an implicit order to do so."

Rather than argue, Davy pursed his lips, which was a damned good thing, else he'd have a mouth full of knuckles to contend with.

Grumbling beneath his breath, James took as step toward the door. "We need to find her. Mayhap she's in the kitchens."

Before he crossed the floor, Torquil and Caelan arrived, ruddy faced and eyes wide.

The Cunningham man's gaze swept across the room, searching just as James had done only moments prior. "Plague take it, the bastard was right!"

"Who was right?" James demanded. "And about what?"

Caelan sidled around his friend. "There's a crier in the square announcing a reward to anyone who can lead the Lord Warden to Lady Ailish Maxwell's accomplices."

Torquil threw out his hands. "'Tis only a matter of time until they track us here."

James jammed his fists onto his hips. "I thought I told you to keep an eye on her."

"Me, sir?" asked Caelan. "The lass never ventured below stairs."

"Och, aye?" James asked. "Lady Ailish just floated out the window and landed in the arms of the Lord Warden, did she?"

"Mayhap she slipped down the rear stairs," said Davy, still at the window. "Did she not mention something about having a word with the washerwomen?"

"That's it," said Torquil, snapping his fingers.

James cut the arse a deadly glare. "She may have done, but the pair of you still have some explaining to do. Why the blazes were you in the square if you were supposed to be watching out for Her Ladyship?"

"There's no time to discuss it now." Davy dropped the fur across the window. "There's a half-dozen soldiers marching this way."

Could things grow worse? "You all should be aware my visit to the smithy shack wasn't in vain. I learned that Harris is not in Carlisle. Hasn't been here, either." James grasped Torquil's shoulder. "Slip out the back. Ride to Caerlaverock and do whatever you must to find out where the earl took the child. Someone in that godforsaken castle must ken where he is. Meet me at Fail Monastery a fortnight hence."

"Shall I accompany him?" asked Caelan.

"Nay—gather the other men. Camp outside the walls—near the cathedral. I saw a copse of trees that ought to give you a modicum of shelter. Wait there until I send word."

Loud voices rumbled below stairs as Torquil hastened away.

Caelan popped his head out into the corridor. "What are you planning to do whilst I'm biding my time with the men?"

James grabbed the satchels and beckoned Davy to follow. "I aim to spirit Lady Ailish out of this godforsaken hell."

As footsteps thundered on the stairs from the alehouse, James and the men slipped out the rear. Caelan strode for the stables while James led Davy through the shadows until they reached an awning that housed the smithy's wood pile.

"Tell me you have a plan," said his friend, glancing out from the stacks of wood. "We cannot hide here for long."

James grabbed his satchel and pulled out his hunter's hood and leather jerkin. "This is why I left no witnesses when I razed my own castle," he said, shrugging into the coat. "Even if they discover Lady Ailish is under my protection, they will not recognize me. They may have *heard* of the Black Douglas, but no one truly kens what he looks like."

"Aside from a man the size of Goliath with black hair and a black beard."

James pulled his razor out of his satchel. "I mightn't be able to shrink, but no one will ken the color of my hair if we shave it all off."

Davy slid down on his haunches. "Then what? There's only a handful of us. And no matter if ye are a brute of a man, we've no chance of standing up against the Lord Warden's army."

"Did I say anything about staging a siege?" James fished around for his cake of soap. "Now go find me a wee pail of water."

AILISH SPENT A SLEEPLESS NIGHT ATOP A PALLET MADE UP WITH musty straw and a rough-hewn woolen blanket. She'd been tossed inside a dank chamber like a sack of grain and left to rot without so much as a morsel. And this is where they imprisoned the nobly born? She might be alone in her cell, sealed with a thick wooden door with naught but three bars across a viewing pane, but the accommodations were akin to a cellar.

No one had said a word about Harris, and though she'd shouted his name half the night, the only response she'd received was from the guard telling her to shut her gob or he'd cut out her tongue.

This morning, a guard had cracked the door wide enough to push in a slice of stale bread and a cup of water. And either the oaf was mute, or he had been instructed not to reply to any of her questions.

She paced the floor, nibbling on her thumbnail, a habit she'd overcome years ago. But she didn't care. She desperately needed something to occupy her mind—to overcome the sickly feeling that something dreadful had happened to her brother.

And where was Sir James? Did he know she'd been captured? And how in God's name would he manage to rescue her without an army of a thousand men? From the ground floor, they'd climbed two flights of stairs before they'd led her through a dark passageway and shoved her inside, slamming the door behind.

Footsteps resounded in the corridor. As they stopped outside her door, Ailish turned, crossing her arms tightly. The Lord Warden's beak-nosed visage appeared in the viewing panel. "Ah, my lady. I see you've survived the night."

"No thanks to your *in*hospitality," she said, her voice hoarse and grating.

"If you do not care for your accommodations, I can arrange for you to be taken to the tollbooth. I'm certain there are a number of interesting souls who would find you quite appealing."

She pursed her lips. Good heavens, not even a man as vile as Andrew Harclay, the Lord Warden, would stoop to such a vulgarity.

A rueful chuckle rumbled through his nose. "I thought not."

"The only reason I have traveled to Carlisle is to find my brother."

"Yesterday you told me you had come all this way alone," he said, skirting the subject.

"Indeed." She dropped her arms and straightened. His Lordship might be inclined to believe her if she came across as unflappable. "I spirited away from Lincluden Priory after my uncle captured Lord Harris in the midst of—"

"Vespers. I know the story. You've repeated it often enough. But I fail to believe that a wisp of a woman like you managed to slip past my border patrol."

"Oh, but that part was easy," she said with a toss of her head. "Surely you are aware of the shallows not far east of the bridge?"

Thank goodness she'd paid attention when they crossed into England. The river had meandered around a bend, but she'd seen the sandy bank of a wee island that parted the waters. Though Lord only knew how deep the water was on either side.

"Well, if your accomplices are here, we shall find out soon enough. In the meantime, I've written to your uncle to see if he corroborates your story, and I've also sent a missive to the king to advise him of your presence." The Lord Warden's gaze shifted to her breasts. "I'm certain the king will be very interested to discover a nobly born waif is in my gaol. Especially one as fair as you. If, of course, you can manage to hold your tongue."

"You fiend. I am not to be trifled with."

"Is that what you think? My word, you are naive." His Lordship pointed a long, slender finger through the bars. "You would do well to heed me. Edward can be quite generous to those subjects in whom he finds favor, but he is ruthless with those who cross him. That is why your man Bruce will face the same fate as William Wallace."

Ailish gulped back her desire to scream. To tell him exactly what King Robert planned for Carlisle—once he organized his army. But boasting about battles to come did nothing to help her find her brother. "Are you harboring Lord Harris?" she asked without blinking. "Do you ken where he is at this very moment?"

"Goodbye, my lady. Enjoy your stay in my tower."

With a smirk, he slammed the viewing panel.

"You cannot leave without answering my question," she shouted, though she was so hoarse it came out sounding like a fledgling hawk.

Blast, blast, and double blast! She raced to the door and pounded until her fist ached.

The dagger in her hose came loose and she stooped to retie it in place. Her weapons hadn't been accessible once her hands had been bound, and the first thing the guards had taken from her was the dagger in her sleeve. Thank goodness they hadn't found this one.

Thus far, she'd been presented with no chance to use her weapon. Though she would have liked to plunge it into the Lord Warden's eye when he was smirking at her through the bars.

Sooner or later, a chance would present itself and she'd escape this miserable cell regardless if the tower was reputed to be inescapable.

Ailish's attention was drawn away by a bout of shouting and cheering resounded from the courtyard. Curious, Ailish moved to the tiny window, in the shape of a clover, yet impossible for even a child to slip through. The clang of iron on iron rose above the din. Down below, two men sparred, their swords flickering in the sunlight.

One was quite large like James, but his bald pate shone nearly as brightly as his weapon. His opponent, a guard wearing the Carlisle coat of arms emblazoned on his surcoat, was clearly outmatched.

The big man fought as if he were possessed by the devil. But he was toying with the guard. Ailish counted five times he could have delivered a mortal wound or demand his opponent beg for quarter, but he kept on as if he had something to prove. With a brutish upward strike, the big man ripped the sword from the guard's hands and sent it clattering to the cobblestones—a move she had seen James perform at the camp in Selkirk Forest.

Oh. My. Heavens!

Ailish's heart started racing. If only she could call out. But if she did, surely the Lord Warden would know her accomplice was he. With haste, she shoved an arm out through one of the clover circles and waved—not like she was trying to draw attention, but as if she were enjoying the cool breeze on such a fine day.

She watched as another challenger stepped forward. James made a show of taking a flourishing bow, clearly issuing an insult. Before he straightened, he looked up.

Ailish waved once more, then drew her hand inside.

What on earth was he on about, sparring in the courtyard with His Lordship's guards? Did he intend to be arrested? Good heavens, if they put him in irons, he'd be no use to her whatsoever. And why had he shaved his head?

Ailish gnawed her thumbnail, forcing herself to watch, yet flinching with every clanging strike. After James had faced three men, he was swarmed by the crowd and marched toward the keep. She craned her neck and pressed her cheek against the stone wall, trying to figure out where they were taking him, but with her next blink, his shiny head had passed out of sight.

She gripped her hands atop her churning stomach. Aye,

hunger pained her but, moreover, she knew how angry he must be. He'd warned her not to disobey his orders and she'd thought herself smarter. And where had she landed? Locked away in this ungodly tower.

If the Lord Warden had his way, this nightmare had only begun. If she didn't find Harris and escape soon, she might very well find herself in London, forced to marry some vulgar lord of Longshanks' choosing.

I would rather die than submit to that barbarous viper's whims.

21

"I cannot understand why you volunteered for the night watchman's post," Davy complained as they made their way around the west side, patrolling the curtain walls. "We've been on duty for seven miserable nights and we're no closer to our purpose than we were when you nearly had your arm cut off by that idiot in the sparring match."

At the mention of his arm, the gash in James' shoulder throbbed. But at least his efforts had served their purpose. They'd been hired on as guardsmen for the Lord Warden which was their best chance to rescue Ailish. "'Tis but a scratch."

"You're lucky it was your left, ye cavalier fool."

James grumbled under his breath. There were a handful of people in all of Christendom he'd allow to call him fool—the man walking beside him because he was right, Lamberton, the Bruce, and Hew.

In the wee hours, a blanket of silence fell over the city. The wind was louder, the river rushed more clearly, even the sparks from the braziers crackled with crisp clarity. James had spent this time atop Carlisle's wall-walk learning and listening. After the vigils bell, the only other guards posted were five at the postern and a dozen at the main gates, not to mention all the sentry patrolling the grounds.

Rounding the corner, he waved to the postern gate guards as he had done on every turn.

A few paces on, Davy inclined his head toward Ailish's tower. "We're but a stone's throw from her, and yet we may as well be marching around Edinburgh Castle's wall-walk."

"Wheesht," James thwacked the man's shoulder. "Enough of your naysaying. We've naught but to bide our time and when the opportunity presents itself, we'll act swiftly."

"Just remember, you told Torquil to meet you at the monastery in a fortnight—seven days hence, mind you."

"I do not need your reminder. Be patient, my man."

"Patient?" Davy raised his voice, then hissed and glanced over his shoulder. Resuming a heated whisper, he leaned nearer. "I've held my tongue long enough. When have you ever shown a lick of patience? You returned to Douglas, pulled together a ragged army, unleashed your ire as if you were possessed by Satan, and now me ma is dead along with half the villagers."

Sickly bile churned in James' gut. He should have waited before he retaliated against Clifford. And afterward, he should have posted fifty men around the perimeter of Douglas. He also should have taken Ailish back to Lincluden Priory and demanded that the prioress give the lass sanctuary.

Damnation, the litany of "should-haves" was growing longer by the day.

"Mark me, I will face Sir Henry Percy sooner than later. As long as I am breathing, no man will plunder my lands or murder those under my protection and live." Stopping, James grabbed his friend's shoulders. "Not a day goes by when I do not lament over your mother's death—all our kin's deaths. Know that she will be avenged. Know my purpose is not for myself but for the kingdom we must fight to set free from tyranny."

Davy swept his arms in an arc, making James release his grip. "I ken why it happened. I just cannot understand why we do not just storm into the tower, seize Her Ladyship and ride like hell-fire. We'd be in Selkirk by nightfall."

"Because when we do, I wish for no one to be hurt—or worse captured and tortured to death. Not you, not Lady Ailish, and not Caelan and the others. Mind you, I haven't been marching around these walls for a sennight with my mind in a muddle. Did ye ken tower guard changes twice per day with the lauds and the compline bells? And our best chance to escape this shite-infested hole is in the wee hours via the postern gate."

"I'll alert Caelan come morn—tell him of your plan. We ought to act on the morrow."

"Nay."

"I beg your pardon? We are solving nothing here and the longer we remain, the more precarious our situation. Sooner or later, some bastard will peg you as the Black Doug—"

"Enough! I will decide when the time is right."

"By the bloody saints, there's no talking sense into you."

James ground his back molars. Why could Davy not realize he *was* acting responsibly, mayhap for the first time in his life.

"It might pay you to know I've struck up a wee friendship with the postern tower's night guardsman."

Davy gave him a shove. "Why the hell didn't ye say as much in the first place?"

"I hadn't come around to it yet. Dammit all, you gave me a bout of melancholy with the mention of Percy's raid on Douglas." James stopped again. "Ye may bleat as bitter as you like, but we will have our vengeance. On that, I promise upon the graves of all the innocents who have lost their lives on account of this mindless war."

Together, they carried out their duties in silence for the remainder of the night. When they were relieved of their posts, darkness still hung in the sky, though the cobalt blue of dawn on the horizon promised the sun would soon rise. After Davy headed for his bunk, James skirted along the inner bailey wall until he reached the postern tower. And as he neared, he sensed

Lady Ailish's presence as if her soul were a beacon calling to him.

He'd kept his distance until now. First, he'd needed to learn the inner workings of the Carlisle guards as well as earn the trust of the others—though truly ingraining himself among them would take far longer than time allowed. No matter how fast he made friends, he and Davy were still looked upon as outcasts. But the Lord Warden's man-at-arms had been impressed with James' fighting prowess, which he prayed purchased enough goodwill to find a way to rescue Ailish.

As he passed a chicken house, a cock crowed. And after checking over his shoulder to ensure he hadn't been followed, he pushed through the tower's entry. It wasn't a residence like a keep. On the ground floor, an army of men slept on pallets in front of a hearth, its coals nearly burned to cinders. On the balls of his feet, James soundlessly hastened for the stairwell and climbed up two flights of uneven stone steps.

Before he stepped out into the passageway, he fingered his dirk, yearning to wrap his hand around the hilt yet knowing he should not. Instead, he forced a grin—one that made him look like an affable, goodly man. Which he was not. He'd sooner slit this varlet's throat than extend the hand of friendship. In truth, withholding his wrath was one of the most difficult things he'd ever done.

Not yet.

"Hello the tower," he said walking forward.

Propped on a stool and leaning against the wall, the guard sputtered and shook himself awake. "Jimmy? What the blazes are you doing here?"

"My patrol just ended. Thought you might want to join me for a pint afore we head for our pallets."

The lauds bell rang and, just as James expected, footsteps resounded from the stairwell, followed by the stirrings of the men below.

The guard grinned. "Don't mind if I do."

James pointed down the corridor. "I heard you're guarding a princess."

"Hardly. The first night the woman carried on like a shrew. Now she refuses to utter a bloody word."

James' fingers twitched. If only he could wrap them around the disrespectful lout's throat. Instead he moved to the entrance of the passageway. Aye, it would be easy enough to take the lass out of the cell, but then there were a thousand men to contend with once they left the tower. "How many prisoners are under your guard?"

"Just the one at the moment."

"What does His Lordship aim to do with her?"

"Dunno. He sent word to the king. The woman's uncle as well. Truth be told, I'm surprised Caerlaverock hasn't shown his face by now."

"Mayhap he does not want to claim her," James said.

"I would not," the guard replied with a smirk as his replacement stepped into the chamber. They swarmed around this place like flies.

James drummed his fingers on the hilt of his sword. It would be so easy to gut them both and take the keys. In no time, he'd be holding Lady Ailish in his arms.

But another five guards filed into the chamber.

Fie!

"How about that pint?" asked the guard. "I assume you're putting forth the coin."

AILISH HADN'T SEEN HIDE NOR HAIR OF JAMES SINCE SHE'D seen him sparring in the courtyard a sennight ago. Where was he now? Had he left Carlisle? Was she now on her own?

After all, if what the Lord Warden had said was true, the postern tower was as impenetrable as the Tower of London. No one ever escaped and not even the Black Douglas could spirit her away.

I refuse to believe he has abandoned me!

Ailish would go to her grave before she named James Douglas or any of the men as her accomplices.

The door clicked. "You've a visitor," announced the guard.

Her heart raced. Had her knight in shining armor come at last? Did he have a plan? Had he found Harris? She did her best to smooth out her veil, then stood expectantly with her hands clasped.

As soon as her uncle sauntered into the cell, her spirits sank to her toes.

"Well, well," he said, his lips disappearing into a thin line, his shark-like eyes accusing. "It seems I cannot be rid of you. I never should have left you alive. You and that insolent brother of yours."

Ailish tightened her grip, making her knuckles white. "What have you done with Harris?"

"Humph." Herbert raised a kerchief to his nose and moved to the window. "It wreaks in here."

While he had his back turned, she stooped and slipped the dagger from her hiding place. "I agree. The odor has grown quite obnoxious given the present company."

"You always did have a barbed tongue."

"Oh? I hear it runs in the family, dear uncle." She took a step closer, her heart hammering. James had taught her how to wield a knife, but his warnings whispered at the back of her mind. If she failed, she may very well meet her end.

"Why did you not kill Harris if you hate us so much?" she asked, sliding even nearer.

Herbert turned and examined his fingernails as if she posed no threat whatsoever. "The boy is young. Edward thinks he can change him—make him a vassal of the English crown. But I reckon he's wasting his time."

"Is he in London?"

"Edward?"

"Harris."

"I think not. The brat will be fostered and not by me."

"Because you're a Scot?"

Herbert smirked. "Because I am unwilling."

"But you have no heir," she ventured.

By the flash of ire in her uncle's eyes, she'd hit a nerve. And his silence confirmed it.

Behind her back, she turned the dagger, gripping it like an iron pick, the way James had taught her. "That's why you need him."

"I do not need anyone."

"Please." Perhaps a little pleading might help. "I only want to know he is safe and being well-cared for."

"That I can confirm." He shifted his gaze her way, his grey eyes raking down her body. "Now you must tell me something."

"Oh?" she asked, watching the pulse at the base of his neck. *Just a few inches closer.*

"The Lord Warden tells me you've persistently insisted you traveled to Carlisle alone."

She dared to take a step, the knife slipping with perspiration from her fingers. "Is that so difficult to believe?"

"For you?" He snorted. "Not really. You may have inherited your mother's beauty, but unlike her, you always were too headstrong for your own good."

He grabbed her chin with one hand, his fingers digging into her face. "The prioress told me you've been gone for some time, though she did confirm you took a horse and left alone." A haughty chuckle rumbled in his chest. "Might I tell you your carelessness has ruined any feeble marriage prospects you may have had, no matter how despicable the swine. Nonetheless, my guess is you are stupid enough to believe you could ride into Carlisle and demand to see the lad."

"Is he here?"

"Shut it, wench." He sneered, his teeth yellow and his breath rank. "The lad is no longer your concern. You will never again see the light of day. Mark me, I have seen to it you *will* suffer a long and terrible death."

He drew back his hand as if to deliver a slap.

Ailish flinched, but rather than shy away, she lunged in, gnashed her teeth and thrust the knife into the pulsing vein.

As he recoiled, she skirted away. A look of shock and utter disbelief filled the man's eyes as he grappled for the hilt, his only sound a choking croak.

Ailish cringed, her stomach heaving as he dropped to his knees and fell on his face.

Merciful Father, what have I done?

Her gaze shot to the viewing panel. By the grace of God, no guard attended the door.

Clapping a trembling hand over her mouth, she gaped down. "Herbert?" she whispered.

By the blood spreading across the stone floor, he was well and truly dead. If they found her standing over him, she'd be sent to the gallows before the noon bell tolled.

As fast as she could, Ailish retrieved her dagger and slid it into her hiding place. Then she snatched the dirk from her uncle's belt, hissing as she made a small cut on her own throat. Blood seeped down her chest while she wrapped the weapon in his fist.

"Guard!" she shrieked, smearing a swath of red across her throat. "He, he, he tried to *murder* me!"

22

Receiving a slap across the face, James startled awake. "What the blazes?" he asked, lashing out with backhand of his own.

"Not here," Davy clipped in a sharp whisper while he rubbed his jaw.

Blinking the fog of sleep out of his eyes, James sprang to his feet and dressed quickly.

"Follow me."

As James belted on his sword, Davy led him to the rear of the alehouse where they'd spent the first night.

Caelan stepped from the shadows.

"What's happened?" James asked. "Are the men well?"

"'Tisn't the men. They're still hiding. But I followed the Lord of Caerlaverock through the city gates and then, whilst I spent half the day looking for you pair, it seems Lady Ailish slit his throat."

A rock the size of a cannonball sank to the pit of James' gut. "My God."

"Word is the Lord Warden is planning to take her to London to stand trial. His Lordship's man-at-arms is assembling the retinue now."

James scratched the stubble on his chin, itchy from a week's growth. "Why London? Why not pass sentence here?"

"She claims she was defending herself."

"Seems likely. And I'll wager Edward would be elated to assume control of a highborn maid who is as bonny as Lady Ailish." James scratched the itching stubble along his jaw. "But how did she overpower the scoundrel?"

Caelan shrugged. "I'm in no position to ask. I reckon doing so would only draw more attention than we need."

"This could be the opportunity we've been waiting for," said Davy.

"Agreed." Shaking off the last remnants of sleep, a plan began to take root in James' mind. "I want the pair of you to take the men and ride ahead. Set an ambush a good distance from Carlisle—far enough away to prevent someone from easily riding for reinforcements. And ensure you have the high ground."

Caelan grinned, running his fingers along the string of the bow secured across his shoulder. "Aye, sir."

"And you?" asked Davy. "Where will you be?"

"With luck, I'll be riding beside Her Ladyship."

"Luck?" The naysayer shook his head. "Since when has luck ever been on our side?"

"'Tis time for the tides to change, is it not, my friend?" He gave Davy's shoulder a reassuring clap. "If I am denied, I will follow as closely as possible without drawing attention. Now go."

After racing back to his pallet, James collected his gear, then headed to the stables to saddle his horse.

When he rode beneath the archway leading into the courtyard, two sentries crossed their pikes in front of him. "Halt!"

"Allow me to pass."

"Stand down." The man-at-arms who had hired him marched forward. "You ought to be on your pallet, Jimmy. You are needed on the ramparts tonight."

James placed his hands on his horse's withers and leaned

forward. "I'm told you are leading the Lord Warden's army southward with a dangerous prisoner."

"If we are, it is no concern of yours."

"But what if I want to make it my concern, sir?"

"I've already assembled my men—soldiers who have served His Lordship for years, mind you. I need trustworthy men who know how to soldier."

"But I am your best sword. There is no one who can better protect a prisoner than me. Besides, I have no intention of remaining a night watchman for the rest of my days."

The man-at-arms glanced over his shoulder, then squinted his way. "Take up the rear. But if you make one questionable move, I will personally see you hanged."

"Aye, sir. You can count on me, sir," James said, though doing so nearly killed him. And he didn't wait for the man to entertain a change of heart. He immediately turned his mount and headed for the end of the retinue.

Only a dozen soldiers were in formation, sitting side by side on their horses. And James made the thirteenth.

"What are we waiting for?" he asked the guard in front of him.

"They're bringing out the prisoner."

James gulped as he shifted his gaze to the postern tower.

Ailish stepped into the courtyard flanked by two guards, her hands in manacles. Beneath the tie of her cloak, a swath of dried blood stained her throat.

Ye Gods, the bastard truly had tried to kill her. Perhaps that's why the Lord Warden hadn't sent her directly to the gallows.

As she swept her gaze across the scene, James pulled his hood lower on his brow. If she recognized him and it showed on her face, all might be lost. As he dipped his chin, he watched her through the fan of his eyelashes.

The sennight she'd spent in prison had not been kind. But even though she was thinner, her hair matted, and her clothing soiled, the woman walked with her head held high.

By God, she was as regal as a queen. Who knew what horrors she'd endured? Clearly, His Lordship's hospitality had been cruel and unpleasant.

Guilt crept up James' nape. He should have risked everything and attacked before it came to this. But he'd been so hell-bent on slipping her out and avoid being killed in the process—it would have slayed him if she had been harmed in a botched escape attempt. Ferreting her out of the cell was the easy part. Escaping Carlisle alive was quite a different matter. The loss of his kin in Douglas had played too heavily on his conscience. This was war. In war, there were casualties. If any man was afraid to die, afraid to take risks, then he was already dead.

After Her Ladyship climbed a mounting block and was sitting on a horse, he looked to the skies and prayed for no harm to come to Her Ladyship—now flanked two-deep by soldiers.

Though an attack on a small retinue would be far easier than escaping this fortress, once they rode out of the city gates, there were no guarantees. There would be bloodshed, of that he was absolutely certain.

"I WOULD PREFER A MODICUM OF PRIVACY, IF YOU PLEASE," said Ailish, marching into the brush. "I do not need an audience of rank guards supervising as I attend my *personal* needs."

"Form a perimeter," said one.

Ailish groaned under her breath. The Lord Warden's soldiers were insufferable but there was no chance she'd let one of them watch. She stopped behind an enormous clump of yellow gorse and turned full circle to ensure she was out of sight.

Thank the good Lord for small mercies.

After she'd taken care of her needs, she stood and brushed out her skirts when a bannock-sized rock caught her eye. Etched in charcoal was, "*Black D +*." Her heart hammered as she quickly dipped down, rubbed off the writing, and turned the stone over. "James?" she whispered.

The whistle of a warbler came from the brush.

Smart of him. It was too dangerous to talk with so many armed men standing guard.

"My Lady," bellowed one of the guards. "You've had quite long enough."

"Not to worry." Good heavens, her voice sounded far too chirpy. She cleared her throat and she continued, "I am coming out now."

Ailish pursed her lips, affecting an expression of annoyance as she stepped into the clearing. A guard grabbed her manacles and tugged her toward a fallen log. "Sit here. I'll fetch you a bit of bread."

Saying nothing, she did as told while her gaze flicked across the faces of each soldier. Where was James? Was he following? Would he attack? When?

For the love of everything holy, she would do anything to flee from the Lord Warden.

The guard returned with a large serving of bread—more than she'd eaten in any one day since being locked in the postern tower. "I suggest you eat your fill. With the longer days, it will most likely be quite a while before the next meal."

"Thank you," she said, accepting the food and taking an enormous bite. Her mouth watered as if she'd just filled it with nectar. Good heavens, the bread wasn't even stale.

As she ate, she continued to search until she spotted James by the horses. He was larger than anyone else, broader in the shoulders as well. She recognized his two-handed sword at his waist, his dirk and armor. He wore a cloak, but he'd pushed the hood back, revealing a shadow of black hair upon his head. Had he decided to grow it back?

"Jimmy," hollered the man-at-arms, who was standing beside the Lord Warden.

James responded to the call and joined the men. Ailish smiled to herself. Her knight had not been following. He'd been in their midst since they'd set out. But why hadn't she noticed him before?

And why had he not shown himself to me straightaway?

No matter how much she wanted to be angry with him for his ruse, her insides bubbled. Quickly, she glanced across the faces again. Hmm, none of his other men were in the retinue, not even Davy.

She accepted a cup of water and watched James from behind it. What was he planning? If only she could have talked to him when she was in the gorse.

By the time the horses had been rested and she'd been given a leg-up to remount, James still had not even glanced her way. Had he any idea how infuriating it was to have him so close yet suffer his disregard?

Ailish let out a long breath. *He is here, is he not?* The Black Douglas had not forsaken her. The king's champion. A hardened warrior who left nothing to chance. Indeed, he hadn't immediately ridden after Harris, but sent out a scout to gather information so they would be successful on their quest.

Yet things had not exactly proceeded swimmingly.

Things had gone rather badly.

Had he found Harris? Is that why the others were not here?

After they'd been riding for a time, she pretended to admire the scenery. Northern England was much the same as the south of Scotland with sheep and cattle dotting her rolling hills. Ever so subtly, she glanced over her shoulder and examined the five guards at the rear, her gaze halting when it connected with James' dark stare.

Thrice he tapped the hilt of his sword while giving a nod.

She returned the gesture and resumed her forward-facing posture. But now, gooseflesh rose across her skin. Of course, James had a plan. And she must be ready for anything.

Ailish flexed her foot in the stirrup. Her dagger was still

lashed to her leg, though it would be difficult to reach the blade with her hands bound with only a length of chain between them. But not impossible.

As time wore on, she watched the hills for any flicker of movement, any sign of what was to come.

23

James shoved his heels downward, taking in everything through his squint. He assessed the soldiers in front of him and the weapons they bore, calculating which to target first. Every man was hand-picked, deadly, and must not be underestimated.

By the saints, he was dog tired. He'd barely fallen asleep when he'd been awakened early this morn and he was bone weary. Nonetheless, they'd traveled far enough away from the city for Davy to have set up an ambush. If they didn't attack soon, the retinue would be stopping for the night and, if he knew the Lord Warden, he would ensure his prisoner was safely behind the barbican walls of an English fortress.

And there were plenty within a day's ride from which to choose.

The hair on the back of James' neck stood on end as they approached what appeared to be a Roman ruin, consisting of a crumbling tower, crenellated at the top. At least the top third. The rest of the building was all but destroyed.

James sat straighter as he searched the tower for movement. With his next blink, Caelan appeared in a crenel, his bow loaded and aimed at the lead man. Without hesitation, he fired his arrow. Two more archers sprang into view, joining the siege. As the arrows hit their marks, three soldiers shrieked, falling from their mounts with mortal wounds.

"We're under attack!" bellowed the man-at-arms.

'Tis about bloody time!

As his sword hissed through its scabbard, the thunder of horses came from around a bend, announcing Davy's approach with a calvary of James' men.

Acting with haste, he cued his horse to move between the pair of guards he'd been flanking as they grappled for their weapons. Taking advantage of their confusion, James ruthlessly dispatched them with two swings of his blade.

"Retreat!" Bellowed the Lord Warden, his horse spinning on its haunches as he kicked his heels and fled.

Deflecting a strike, James let His Lordship escape before he slammed the pommel of his sword in his attacker's temple. The sentry grunted as he toppled to the ground with a sickly thud.

Ahead, a guard grabbed Ailish's reins and jerked the horse around. She shrieked as she tottered in her saddle. The horse reared in the man's panic to chase after His Lordship.

With a kick of his heels, James skidded beside the cur. "Not so bloody fast," he growled, aiming for a kill to the throat.

Ailish slipped sideways, dipping low and grunting.

"Are you hurt?" James asked, cuing his horse for a sideways approach to help calm her terrified mount.

She straightened, holding up a dagger. "Just reaching for this."

He grinned, giving her a wink just as a blade sliced into his shoulder. James countered in time to deflect the next strike. Thrusting his dirk, he went for the kill, but Davy felled the bastard first.

Thank God, the rest of the Lord Warden's men were either killed or fleeing. The Douglas man grinned, his face splattered with blood. "What took ye so long?"

"Ye ken, we were at the mercy of the bloody English." James

smirked and glanced at the others as the archers from the ruins rode alongside them. "Is anyone injured?"

"Not here," said Caelan.

James arched against the sting of his shoulder. "Then we ride east."

"East?" asked Ailish. "But Harris is north."

"The only thing we've learned about your brother is he's not in Carlisle. I've sent Torquil to Caerlaverock with orders to find out exactly where they've taken him."

"But Caerlaverock is even farther north. Why would we ride east?"

"Because the Lord Warden just headed for home. Now that he's been attacked, he'll pull together his entire army and I do not want to be anywhere near Carlisle when he does."

"Do you think he'll ride after us?" Ailish asked.

"'Tis a certainty." James inclined his head toward her manacles. "I'll knock those off once we stop to rest the horses."

Ailish gave a nod before she gasped. "You've been wounded."

He sheathed his sword. "'Tis but a battle scar. It will heal like the others."

Davy rode alongside him. "Nay, you're bleeding like a stuck pig."

"'Tis not the first time." James tapped his heels, cuing the horse for a trot. "We ride."

"How far do you think we can go before the horses need rest?" Ailish asked.

"They must endure until we reach the border."

"Riding east?" asked Caelan.

"We'll turn north at the River Eden, then skirt through Kielder Forest."

"I'm glad someone kens where we're headed," said Davy.

AILISH CLENCHED HER CLOAK CLOSED AT HER THROAT, THOUGH it did nothing to shield her from the driving rain. She was already soaked clean through, her teeth chattering and now night had fallen upon them. Worse, James had been hunched over his horse's withers for ages. The man was clearly exhausted and yet he refused to stop. "If we do not find shelter soon, we'll all catch our death," she insisted.

In the lead, Davy pointed. "I see a burn ahead. 'Tis the border, for certain."

"S-should be a chapel 'bout a mile on," said James, his speech garbled and slow. "Keep a watchful eye. Edward's men have infested these lands like rodents."

As they came to the edge of the forest, Davy held up his hand, cueing them to halt.

"'Tis too dark and wet to see a damned thing," said Caelan.

Ailish slapped her reins, driving her horse forward. They had to be close. "The darkness is in our favor. Haste. We've no time to spare."

Before nightfall, she'd been watching a trail of blood as it spilled down the shoulder of James' horse, a clear sign his wound needed to be tended. And by his posture, he was injured far worse than he'd let on.

Just as James had said, they arrived at a chapel in no time. But as the big man dismounted, his legs buckled beneath him.

"James!" Ailish shouted, hopping from her horse and dropping to her knees beside him.

His eyes rolled back. "Sleep," he mumbled.

Davy pounded on the thick oaken door. "Open at once!"

After a great deal of pounding, the door was finally opened by a tall, gaunt priest. "May I help you?"

"My friend has been injured," said Davy. "Please, we need sanctuary."

The priest stood back and held the door. "Carry him to my quarters. The door on the left as you enter the vestibule."

Davy and Caelan managed to hoist James up and sling his

arms over their shoulders. But his feet dragged as they moved inside.

Ailish followed with the priest right behind. "Thank you, Father...?"

"Clive."

"We need bandages and water to tend his wound. Have you any leeches?"

"None here. Mayhap we can ride to Hermitage Castle come morn. Sir Ralph de Neville keeps a healer within."

"Nay!" James bellowed, and Ailish knew why. Neville was one of Edward's vassals.

"Are ye in some sort of trouble?" asked Father Clive.

"We are looking for my brother," Ailish explained, avoiding the question. "He was taken from Lincluden Priory not long ago. We were set upon by bandits in the forest."

The priest held the door. "Lincluden? How did you end up here?"

"'Tis a long story."

Inside, the chamber was spacious, a bed on the far wall, a warm fire burning in the hearth across. "Set him on the bed," said Ailish, turning to the priest. "Please, I hate to burden you, but we need the water and bandages."

"Yes, of course." The priest picked up a pail. "There's a well out back. I'll be but a moment."

Davy gave her a look while James grunted, settling face down. "Say no more to him. He may be a spy."

She nodded. "You look nearly as ragged as he does."

"Both of us were on watch last night and barely had a wink of sleep."

"Then quickly remove his mail and shirt. The sooner we set him to rights, the sooner both of you can rest."

Father Clive returned and set the pail beside the bed.

"Have you a cloth?" Ailish asked.

He plucked a folded bit of linen from a shelf. "Here."

"My thanks." She cringed as James bellowed while the men

removed his garments. "I'm sorry to be a bother."

"Not to worry. This is the most excitement I've seen at this wee chapel for ages."

"Is it usually quiet?" she asked.

"For the most part, except on Sunday mornings."

"Does Sir Ralph attend mass?"

"Heavens no. He employs a priest from London within his walls. Says he cannot withstand the Scots tongue."

"Well, I'm certain you are of far greater service to the local kin than you would be to a knight who is hardly ever home."

"I daresay you are right."

Davy set the mail and shirt aside, his expression grim.

Ailish stepped to the bedside and clapped a hand over her mouth to smother a gasp. A jagged cut with the impression of the links of his mail ran from his shoulder to the top of his flank. "Good heavens, he's been flayed."

"He'd be dead if it weren't for his armor." Davy examined the minced flesh. "I've no choice but to cauterize it."

James growled. "I'll be fine."

Ailish lightly patted the cloth around the seeping wound. "I'm afraid Davy is right."

The Black Douglas muttered a shocking string of curses while Father Clive crossed himself, muttering Hail Marys.

"Can the men bed down in the nave?" Ailish asked, drawing the priest's attention away while Davy set a poker in the fire. "Have you any food to spare?"

"A bit of bread and cheese."

"Perfect." She strode to the door and beckoned one of the men. "Please help Father Clive serve the meal."

By the time Ailish had cleaned the wound as best she could, everyone had eaten, the poker had grown red hot and James was sound asleep.

"I'll need all of you to hold him down," said Davy, retrieving the rod from the fire. "And stay clear of this iron unless you want a branding."

Ailish moved to the head of the bed, ready to hold down a shoulder.

"You'd best stand back, m'lady."

"But I want to help."

Davy eyed her. "He'll need you after."

Standing against the wall, Ailish gripped the cloth between her fists, wanting to look away, but unable to do so.

"I'll make this quick," said Davy as James bucked.

"You bloody backstabbing, pustule-sucking maggot!" the big man shrieked as the poker singed his flesh, the stench of the smoke burning Ailish's nostrils. He thrashed so violently, three of the men lost their grips. "Damn ye and your filthy spawn! Every last one of ye!"

Bellowing like a bull in the castrating pen, he dropped to the mattress, his breath ragged.

Davy stood back. "That went well, I'd reckon."

"You cannot be serious." Ailish moved to the bedside and examined the damage. "He's half-dead. Far worse than he was afore you branded him."

"Aye, but he'll be much better off, in a day or two," said Davy. "Come men, we'd best head for our pallets."

Ailish moved a chair beside James' unmoving form. "I'm staying here."

Father Clive tiptoed forward and bent over the wound. "The bleeding has ebbed."

"Thank heavens for small mercies."

"I'll make up a pallet for myself in the sacristy."

She nodded.

"Is there anything else you need, m'lady?"

Though she hadn't told him she was highborn, Davy had used the courtesy. She grasped the priest's hand. "It is of utmost importance that you tell no one of our presence here. Understood?"

He offered a kindly smile. "I believe that is why it is called sanctuary. Your need for shelter is as sacred as your confession."

24

Searing pain gnawed at James' shoulder as he tried to roll to his side. With a grunt, he decided it might be best to remain where he lay on his belly.

Beside him, Ailish slept in a chair, her arms folded on the bed, cradling her head. The amber glow of the fire danced on her face, making her look like an angel. Her lips slightly parted, the fan of dark lashes contrasting against her ivory skin. He brushed an errant lock of silky hair away from her cheek.

James would suffer a hundred brands with a fire poker if it meant keeping this woman safe from harm.

Stirring, Ailish opened her eyes. "You're awake?"

He tried not to grimace. "For the moment."

"How are you feeling?"

"Like I've done battle with the devil and lost."

"What can I do to help?"

"Stay right where you are, lass." He raised his head enough to glance about the chamber. "Where are the others?"

"Father Clive is in the sacristy and the rest have made up pallets in the nave."

"Good."

"Davy's worried the priest will notify Sir Ralph of our presence."

"Nay. We can trust him."

"I thought so, too. But how can you be so certain?"

"I've been here before. With Lamberton. I reckon I was about seventeen years of age."

"He's for the Bruce, then?"

"He's for Scotland. He and many other Scottish priests on the borders have been usurped."

"He mentioned as much." Ailish brushed cool fingers across James' forehead. "Davy told me the pair of you went without sleep."

"Did he?"

"Thank you for riding to my rescue. I almost feared—" Shaking her head, Ailish glanced away.

"What did you fear?"

"Being locked away in a cell for days on end with but a bit of bread and water muddles one's mind. When I heard no word from you, I was afraid you may have forgotten me."

"Never."

"Then why...?"

"Hmm?"

She cupped his cheek. "It can wait until you are feeling better."

"Nay, speak your mind. What is it you want to know?"

"I felt hopeless—as if you left me in the prison to rot."

"I assure you I did not."

"But I heard no word from you for an entire sennight."

"Because I was doing everything in my power to wheedle my way into the Lord Warden's defenses. It would have been a great deal easier to break you out of a town gaol and not a fortified tower protected by five hundred soldiers or more."

"What would you have done if the Lord Warden had not decided to take me to London?"

"I had a plan. Davy and I were hired on as night watchmen. It was only a matter of time afore I convinced the man-at-arms to allow me to guard you."

"But that could have taken months."

"Perhaps." James swallowed the thick goo in his mouth. "Water."

When Ailish brought a cup, he moved just enough to take a drink.

"What happened with your uncle?" James asked.

"He threatened to preside over my very long and painful death." She shook her head, wiping a hand across her brow. "I struck the vein at the base of his throat with my dagger just as you showed me. Every time I close my eyes, I see his gruesome face. 'Tis awful."

James grasped her hand and squeezed. "You defended yourself."

She wiped away a tear. "I'll spend an eternity in purgatory for my sins."

"Nay, lass," he whispered gently. "The man was evil. And in war, we must kill or be killed."

Pursing her lips, Ailish gave a definitive nod as if she were trying to come to terms with the horror of her ordeal. "He refused to tell me where he sent Harris. But said the boy was to be fostered."

"We will find him." James grasped her hand, tightly closed his eyes, and kissed it. His heart squeezed as the warmth of her skin, the thrum of her pulse met his lips. He would do anything for this woman. "On that you have my solemn vow."

NO MATTER HOW MUCH AILISH TRIED TO CONVINCE JAMES that he needed respite, the following day he insisted they continue their journey to Fail Monastery. They traveled the byways through bogs and forests thick with briars while the wind blew, and spats of rain slowed their progress. And though the Black Douglas rode in silence, he grew paler and weaker by the hour.

When at last they reached the monastery, every single one of them was coughing and sneezing. Ailish's throat burned, but she said nothing. Her misery held not a candle to that of James'.

And thank heavens the monks welcomed them, albeit with wary and solemn eyes. They had all taken vows of silence. "Are you under Bishop Lamberton's protection?" she asked an ancient monk with all but a ring of grey hair shaved from his pate.

He nodded over his shoulder as he led them across the courtyard. Davy and Caelan each supported one of James' arms, dragging him as they'd done at the border church.

She'd already ascertained that Torquil had not yet arrived. She coughed, irritating her raw throat. Perhaps it was for the best that the Cunningham heir was not there to greet them. James needed time to rest.

The monk used an enormous key to unlock a door and gestured into a chamber containing only a narrow bed with a cross on the wall above, a stool and a washstand.

As the lads took James inside, Ailish curtseyed to the monk. "Thank you for your kindness."

He gave a brief bow and left while she ventured inside. "This feels as if it is a repeat of our stop at the chapel."

"You were right," said Davy. "We should have stayed there long enough for James to build his strength."

"Rest." James coughed repeatedly, then gasped for air. "H-here."

Ailish pressed the back of her hand against his forehead. "He's afire. I need a cup of willow bark tea. And if the monks have a salve or oil of avens, bring it straightaway."

"Aye, m'lady." Davy sniffed and pulled Caelan toward the door. "Is there anything else you require?"

Neatly folded beneath the washstand were cloths and an ewer of water. "Perhaps some broth. You and the men need to rest. We are all on the verge of succumbing to fever."

"Do not concern yourself with us. I'll fetch the items you need and then we'll take our rest in the stable's loft."

"Very good. And please notify me as soon as Torquil arrives."

NIGHT HAD FALLEN AND AILISH CONTINUED HER VIGIL AT James' bedside, no matter how much he grumbled. "Just a bit more salve," she said, applying the concoction provided by the monks.

Laying on his side, the big knight blindly lashed out with an arm, only to jerk it back and grimace in pain.

"You'll not do yourself a whit of good by fighting me." She set the pot of salve on the washstand, picked up the cup of willow bark tea, and stirred it with the wooden spoon. "You are still fevered."

But James did not hear. His eyes closed, his chapped lips parted, he slept fitfully on his side, shivering now and again.

Ailish coughed into her elbow. By the saints, she was exhausted. "You must drink a bit more tea," she said loudly.

His eyelashes didn't even twitch. She tilted his chin upward and held the spoon to his mouth and ladled in a bit. His Adam's apple bobbed, followed by a cacophony of coughing. No matter how much she wanted to set the cup aside and let him sleep, she persisted until he'd swallowed four spoons.

"If that doesn't set you to rights, there's no hope for you." As soon as the words left her mouth, Ailish wished she could take them back. He'd risked his life for her more than once. He even shaved his head to disguise his thick black hair—hair that identified him as the Black Douglas.

She sat on the stool and swirled her fingers through the soft bristles that had grown in. "You look more menacing with your hair shorn," she whispered. In her eyes, he was as braw as the first time she'd seen him standing atop Moot Hill behind the Bruce. "And the shadow of beard on your cheeks and chin makes ye look like a pirate come to take your plunder."

She kissed his overwarm temple. "But you'd never attack without cause. Just as I would not."

She sat for a time, mulling over all that had transpired since the coronation.

"Have I ever told you about my da?" Though her eyelids were heavy, she smiled while warmth spread through her. "He was a fierce man, but fair. And he ardently supported King Alexander and his heir, the Maid of Norway. Though he kent it was a sham when Balliol took the throne. Your own father paid with his life for that mistake."

As her voice trailed off, Ailish resumed swirling her fingers around James' crown. "Da always told me I would marry into a noble family—told me it was my duty. That I was born of fourteen generations of Maxwells, owners of lands on both sides of the border."

She sighed. "So many families did—still do. And those who opposed Edward have lost all, those who have joined him have become more powerful. I just wonder when it will end. I'm told Longshanks' son is as ruthless and bloodthirsty as his father."

Ailish brushed her lips across James' temple. "I believe in Robert the Bruce with all my soul, but how will we rise above the armies Edward has amassed along the border? Just like Caerlaverock, your keep, Berwick, Edinburgh, Roxburgh, Hermitage, Dunbar...good heavens, there are so many castles taken over by the English, I cannot possibly name them all. Even the Bruce's lands at Annandale have been taken."

Her heart grew so very heavy. "And now the king is in hiding. Certainly, your army is growing, but how will we retake what is ours so that Scotland may return to the peace she enjoyed when Alexander was on the throne?"

"Fight like Wallace?" he asked.

Ailish's breath caught as she leaned over James' face. "Are you listening?"

He said nothing, as if the words had come from above and not from his lips.

"I ken you're listening," she whispered, though he seemed to alternate between wakefulness and nothingness.

Overcome with weariness herself, she closed her eyes and rested her head on the edge of the mattress. Suffering a sore throat and a stuffy nose, she needed a bit of rest to keep the sickness at bay.

It took only to close her eyes and she drifted into a deep dreamless sleep.

When morning came, a ray of light shining through the window bid Ailish to open her eyes. "James, are you awake?"

He shivered as if he'd been out in a snowstorm for hours without a cloak.

"James?" she asked, running her hand over his forehead. Drenched in sweat, his skin was burning.

She picked up the cup and tried to spoon it into his mouth. He thrashed, knocking the vessel out of her hands, it shattered on the stone floor. "You have the fever."

Quickly, she doused a cloth and draped it over his searing skin.

"Argh!" he bellowed, shaking it off.

"You must!" she cried, rolling the linen and wiping his forehead, only to receive a smack between the eyes for her efforts.

But that did not dissuade her. She doused a cloth and then another. "Lie still," she commanded while she rubbed down his entire body.

"C-cold."

She didn't stop. If only he knew how encouraging his one word was. "I ken."

"M'lady," came Davy's voice with a rap on the door.

"Come," she said, standing and straightening her skirts.

Davy's gaze immediately snapped to James. "He's fevered?"

"Aye. We need more willow bark tea."

"I'll see to it, but first you must come with me."

"Have you news?"

"Aye. Torquil has arrived."

25

After the night's sleep, Ailish felt a bit better as she followed Davy into the courtyard. Ahead, Torquil stood at the well, guzzling a ladle of water.

"Please tell me you have something good to report," she said, hastening toward him.

His back heaving with a deep breath, he replaced the ladle in the bucket and turned. But he didn't appear anything like the cocksure Torquil she'd come to know. His face was filthy and purple bruises swelled beneath his eyes.

"What happened? You look as if you've been wallowing in a bog whilst being bludgeoned."

"Mayhap that's because I have been."

She grasped his wrist and tugged him toward a bench. "Sit and tell me everything. Do not leave out a single detail." She sat beside him, while Davy stood with his arms crossed. "Have you located Harris?"

"At least I ken where Lord Caerlaverock took him —Lochmaben."

Ailish's mouth fell open. "But that's so nearby."

"That tidbit of information nearly sent me to an early grave."

"I'm surprised you weren't waiting for us when we arrived," said Davy. "What happened?"

"Firstly, the folk in Galloway are all afraid for their lives. They go about their affairs with their heads down, looking over their shoulders all the while."

Her stomach twisted in a knot. "'Tis on account of Uncle Herbert's cruelty."

"His Lordship and the commander of Dumfries Castle—Sir Richard Girard."

"Girard?" Ailish drummed her fingers on her chin. "I'm not familiar with that name."

"Mayhap because you've been sheltered for the past six years, m'lady," said Davy. "He's one of Edward's henchmen—a murderous tyrant."

Torquil removed his helm and raked his fingers through his wiry hair. "Aye, and after news arrived of Caerlaverock's death, the cur started rounding up every suspect, including all travelers who happened past. I barely escaped with my life."

"Then how did you find out where they took Harris?" asked Ailish.

"When I first arrived, the townsfolk were just chilly, unapproachable, if you ken what I mean."

Ailish nodded, though it twisted her heart to do so. Before the wars, the kin around Caerlaverock and Dumfries were kind and hospitable.

"For eight days, I minded my own affairs—sat in the alehouse and watched the comings and goings. Listened, as well." Torquil glanced up to Davy. "A cleric came in every evening after vespers. Always sat alone, drank one pint and left."

Gooseflesh rose across Ailish's skin. "Alfred?"

"Do you know him?" asked Torquil.

"He was one of my father's most trusted. Alfred was the one who helped us escape—had a skiff waiting at the Firth of Solway."

"Then my news is most likely valid."

"He's the one who told you Uncle Herbert took Harris to Lochmaben?"

"Aye, and then I didn't see him again after the Lord Warden rode into town and announced you had escaped."

"Oh, dear."

"'Tis dangerous beyond these walls. His Lordship has combined armies with Sir Richard and they are plundering all of Galloway, offering a reward to anyone who leads them to you and your accomplices."

"Did you say anything to Alfred about Sir James or Lady Ailish?"

"Not exactly." Torquil rapped his knuckles atop his helm. "But after we talked a bit, I needed to tell him something to earn his trust."

"Of course you did," said Ailish, dryly.

Davy picked up a smooth stone and rubbed it between his fingers. "What kind of something?"

"I told him that I understood on undeniable authority that the new King of Scotland had recognized Harris as the Earl of Caerlaverock."

"Then he told you where the usurper took the lad?"

"That was basically the whole of it. I might have said I kent a man who would do anything to keep the lad from falling into Edward's hands...but nothing too incriminating."

Davy tossed the stone at the well. "How did you end up running for your life, exactly?"

Ailish leaned forward. "I would not think Alfred would reveal your confidences."

"Perhaps he did not, but the Lord Warden was giving coin to anyone who gave them information—especially newcomers. Yesterday, a mob of the scoundrels was waiting for me in the alehouse."

"Did anyone follow you here?"

"They beat me until I decided to play dead, then the blackguards tossed my body into a bog." Torquil grinned—his cocksure smile returning. "No one kent I left."

"Then I doubt they'll search for us here," said Davy "We're far enough off the beaten path. Mayhap sixty miles from Lochmaben. Dumfries as well."

"We may be safe for now, but what of my brother?" asked Ailish, her insides twisted tighter than ever. "The Lord Warden kens I'm looking for him. He'll retaliate, mark me."

Davy covered a cough with his hand. "I say we remain here until James regains his wits."

"Can we not send a scout to Lochmaben?" Ailish asked. "Surely there is someone in the camp from Annandale. 'Tis no secret that Edward is building his grand fortress there on the Bruce's lands."

"She has a valid point," said Torquil quite surprisingly.

"I do." Ailish pushed to her feet and thrust her fists onto her hips. She was a lady, the daughter of an earl, and she would be obeyed. "As far as we are aware, no one is searching for Caelan. Have him make haste to Selkirk Forest and find a man who hails from Annandale. See what he can uncover about my brother. And I want him to report back here in a sennight. James will be fit and ready to fight by then, mark me."

Not waiting for anyone to voice opposition, she headed for James' cell, praying for his swift recovery.

COMING AWAKE, THE FOG IN JAMES' MIND WAS THICKER THAN the mist hovering on the Saint Andrews shore after a midwinter's storm. The last clear thought he'd had was when riding toward Fail Monastery. Above him hung an iron cross, an indication they had arrived at their destination, though he had no recollection of it.

When he shifted his hand to his brow, someone moved.

"Are you awake?"

Ah yes, he recognized her angelic voice.

Slowly, James shifted his gaze to Ailish. Though weariness was etched upon the smooth mantle of her face, she was still the bonniest creature he had ever seen. "A man could grow accustomed to waking to such beauty," he said, his voice gravelly as if he hadn't used it in days.

A bit of color sprang in her cheeks while she leaned over and pressed the back of her hand to his forehead. "The fever has broken."

Now he remembered. A bit, anyway. He'd been abed for some time. And she had remained by his side through it all, spooning water and tea into his mouth. But what he remembered most of all was how soothing her voice had been as was her touch.

By the grace of God, she would make a fine wife.

For someone.

"What are you thinking?"

"I was wondering how long I've been abed," he fibbed.

She daintily blew her nose into a kerchief. "Three days."

"Are you ill?"

"We've all had a bit of a sniffle, but I think we're through the worst of it now."

He took her hand and drew it to his lips. Closing his eyes, he thanked the stars for this woman's selflessness. "You weren't feeling well, yet you remained by my side."

"I would be nowhere else."

"Has Torquil returned?"

"Aye with news. Evidently Uncle Herbert took Harris to Lochmaben."

James sat up, the motion making his head swim. "Unbelievable. He's been right under our noses all this time?"

"I had Caelan ride to Selkirk to find someone from Annandale who would not be suspected if he returned home."

"Smart lass." James reached for a cup of water and drank. "When do you expect them to report back?"

"A few days. Hopefully long enough for you to regain your strength."

He held the cup aloft. "Bring me something stronger than this and a plate of food, and I'll be back to myself by the day's end."

She snatched it out of his hand and planted a wee kiss on his forehead. "I'll believe that when I see you spar like the devil."

26

It wasn't exactly the day's end, but the following morn James marched into the sheep's paddock and found a solid oak fencepost standing like a lone Pictish stone. He walked around it, testing the wood for stability.

This will do.

Glancing toward the grounds, he spotted a few monks going about their chores, but none of his men were in sight. Nor was Ailish.

Raising his great sword above his head, he addressed the post and slowly lowered the blade until it touched the wood. His arms trembled with his weakness, but James bore down and clenched his forearms until the trembling stopped. Closing his eyes, he blocked all pain from his mind. He intended to massacre this bloody post if it killed him.

Bellowing the Douglas war cry, he spun in place and slammed the blade into the column with every sinew of strength in his body. Pain shot through his shoulders while the force of the strike reverberated all the way up to his eyeballs, rattling in his head until he saw stars.

Again, James glanced behind. Thank the good Lord no one had seen him make an arse of himself. He'd been daft to think he could best the post in one deathly swing. He should have begun with a sparring pattern before he tried to smash the devil out of a solid oak pole most likely driven six feet into the ground. For all James knew, it had been there so long it had petrified.

After drawing in a few deep breaths, James again addressed his unforgiving opponent. With both hands, he struck the column from side to side, chipping away the wood. Initially, his muscles burned, but James gritted his teeth and worked through the pain. Bested by a piece of wood?

Not this day.

Not ever.

Still, as he fought, his legs trembled like a weak old man.

Ailish came into view in his periphery, toting an armful of hay. She tossed it on the ground and whistled. "Come, sheep!" she called as the flock headed her way with happy bleats at the prospect of a meal. And knowing Ailish, she was most likely giving the beasts far more than the monks did.

James' heart skipped a beat when she looked at him.

But rather than smile, he quickly addressed the post and lunged, striking with his most deadly "kill" maneuver. Nearly blinded by the pain from his recent branding, James tightened his abdominals to keep his hands from shaking. Out of the corner of his eye, he watched her retreat as he reverted to the warm-up routine.

Nonetheless, he sensed her eyes on him. With a heightened sense of awareness, he put everything he could muster into murdering the post—reaching high, chopping his blade downward while dropping to one knee. James gnashed his teeth and brutally attacked. Damnation, the piece of oak didn't stand a chance.

He imagined himself in the midst of a battlefield, fighting for his life, swallowing down bile as his wound tortured him. Ailish was watching and he'd not be bested by a mere post. He swung his blade from side to side. He darted and spun, wielding the weapon with expert finesse as he'd been trained. And as he worked, he grew stronger and more self-assured. James planted his foot. Holding the sword low, he spun with an upward slice. The tip of the post sailed through the air.

He stopped and chuckled, turning the hilt in his hands. Wiping the sweat from his brow on his sleeve, he glanced back. There she stood, giving him a wee wave and a smile.

Though his arms grew suddenly heavy, he responded with a lopsided grin. He would regain his strength, if not for himself, for her.

THE DAY AFTER JAMES BEGAN HIS RECOVERY, HE AND DAVY began riding on twice-daily patrols. He'd told Ailish they were scouting the lands around the monastery to ensure the Lord Warden's men were not tracking them and, though he hadn't lied, his main purpose was to intercept Caelan and the Annandale man. Twice, Ailish had acted against his orders and, though he knew she meant well, he mustn't allow her to do so again.

"Look yonder," said Davy as they crested a hill to the south. "And not a day too soon."

James cued his mount for a canter and met them at the crossing of a trickling burn. "Hello, men, we've been expecting you."

Caelan reined his steed to a stop. "Och, you're looking a mite better than the last time I saw ye."

James rubbed his shoulder, just above the tenderness. "I wouldn't mind living out the rest of my days without succumbing to a firebrand again."

"I reckon it saved ye," said Davy.

James nodded to Lachlan. "So, you hail from Annandale?"

"Aye, sir. I was a castle guard for Robert the Bruce until the Prince of Wales laid siege to her walls."

"We'll win her back. Mayhap not today, but soon." James gave his horse's neck a pat. "What have you found?"

"Lochmaben is crawling with English. I reckon there's five thousand men or more."

A tic twitched at the back of James' jaw. "'Tis worse than I thought."

"They're brewing a plan to coax the king out of hiding."

"What plan?" James asked.

"The only men privy to their scheme are the knights," said Lachlan. "Definitely not a lowly pikeman like me."

James nodded. In truth, he hadn't expected the man to bring back much information about the enemy's future plans. "And the lad. Have you seen him?"

"Sir Henry Percy has taken Lord Harris under his wing as a squire," said Caelan, patting his horse's shoulder.

James took a quick look at Davy. Was this destiny? "Percy, did you say?"

"Aye."

Not only would he retrieve the boy, he'd have retribution for the attack on the Douglas crofts. "The lad is not in chains and locked in the gaol?"

"Nay. But His Lordship is never out of Percy's sight."

"Is he fostering the lad?"

"Aye—weapons, horsemanship, and who kens what else."

"Fie." James reined his horse toward the monastery and beckoned the men to follow. Most likely, the boy was enjoying his time away from the priory. His sister may have taught him his letters, numbers, and a bit of Latin, but Ailish was not a swordswoman.

"Did you ever speak to him?" he asked over his shoulder.

"His Lordship?" Lachlan snorted. "I'm a pikeman, ye ken."

James didn't like the odds. Thousands of men, and one of Edward's most trusted knights had taken Lord Harris under his wing—a knight James thirsted to best. Was there a chance? "You mentioned Sir Henry is teaching the lad horsemanship?"

"I reckon so." Lachlan's horse tried to nip at Davy's mount, so the young sentry maneuvered the gelding beside James. "I camped on Castle Loch for nearly a sennight and every morn they rode to the water, then continued around the shore."

"How far around the loch did they venture? All the way?"

"Nay. Sir Henry is too savvy to risk riding too far from the fortress. I never saw them ride any farther than the copse of trees on the other side."

"Is there an encampment over there?"

"No, sir. All the men camp either in the fortress or nearby," said Caelan.

"What sort of horse does Percy ride?" asked James. "A warhorse?"

"A mammoth of a beast," said Lachlan.

"And Lord Harris?"

"A pony, of course. A wee lad would not be able to handle a destrier or palfry."

"Agreed." James looked to Davy. "No matter how much I'd relish a fight, I reckon this is a task for one man."

"I'll go," said the Douglas man, the pain on his face showing too well what he had in mind.

James picked up his reins. "Nay, you'll return to the monastery and tell Lady Ailish I'll return on the morrow."

A pinch formed between Davy's eyebrows. "Where should I tell her you've gone?"

"I didn't say, did I?" James turned to the others. "Return to Selkirk. I do not want Her Ladyship to ken you've been here."

Lachlan rubbed his palms together. "The men are itching for a fight, sir."

"Believe me, they'll have it. But for the time being, we must all stay the course."

27

It was late afternoon when James examined the tracks on the southwest side of Castle Loch. True to Lachlan's word, there were several sets of prints, but they had been made by only two beasts—a pony and a warhorse. And they led into a copse of trees.

Not far inside was an ancient standing stone and that's where the tracks ended. A bit of blue thread was caught in a crag of the rock. James tugged it away and twirled it between his fingers. "Does this belong to you, Lord Harris? Or is it from the blue caparison of Sir Henry's mount?"

The answer mattered not.

Across the loch, smoke belched from the men's fires, the largest smokestack most likely coming from a smithy shack. Timber walls surrounded the fort, hiding what lay behind them.

James set his trap, careful to remain out of sight. He camped beneath a thicket where the ground was soggy, the midges feasting on his flesh. Before dawn, he rose, readied his horse, and waited.

And waited.

The camp across the loch had long been bustling with

sentries tending their chores when two riders appeared on the far side of the loch. In the still air, a child's laughter echoed across the water as he skirted the shore, cantering with a knight riding a destrier behind him.

James moved to a crouch, tightening his fist around the rope.

"You'd best kick harder, else I'll overtake you, lad!" bellowed Sir Henry as if he were a kindly man, and not a vile butcher of Scottish subjects.

James' chest burned. How dare the murderer of Hew's wife take the lad and pretend to be his mentor? He wanted to smash his fist in Sir Henry's face. Challenge him man to man.

But such bravado would bring on the English army.

As Harris entered the copse, the lad slowed his mount, threw out his hand, and touched the standing stone, reining his horse into a turn. Two lengths behind, Sir Henry's eyes widened as he caught sight of James snapping the rope taut.

Percy's mouth flew open, but he made no sound as he galloped into the trap, the thick cord slicing into his throat. The knight's head snapped backward as he flew off his horse and smashed into the ground with a bone-crunching thud.

"Harris!" James boomed.

The lad's horse skidded as he stopped, his eyes as round as coins. "Sir James?"

"Haste!" he shouted, snapping a lead line onto the pony's bridle. Kicking his heels, James demanded a gallop. "There's no time to explain."

As they sped away, he caught sight of Sir Henry, flat on the ground and motionless. God willing, the strike had made a clean kill and there was one less tyrant in Edward's arsenal.

After James' recovery, Ailish busied herself by helping in any way she could, and today they'd set her to task, kneading bread in the kitchens. The monastery wasn't as large as an abbey, but fifty-or-so Trinitarian monks resided there, quietly tending to their daily worship and chores which meant the bread oven was never idle.

It was easy to take out her ire on the dough, thrashing, and kneading as if it were Sir James' face. Of course, she would never try to pummel the knight, but that did not allay the fact that she was fit to be tied. Yesterday, he had ridden off without so much as a goodbye and all Davy would say was that the knight had something of grave importance to attend and he'd return this day.

Where had he gone, and why had he not trusted her enough to tell her? After sitting by his sickbed for days, had she not proved her loyalty?

How could he have ridden off without saying a word after being at death's door? What if the fever returned and James was now lying unconscious by the wayside?

Moreover, remaining at Fail was far worse than residing behind the walls of Lincluden Priory. At least the nuns hadn't taken vows of silence. And at the nunnery, she could see Florrie and Coira. And she had her friend Sister Louisa with whom she shared confidences.

Ailish slapped her dough into a ball and draped a piece of linen over it.

"Sister!" cried an unmistakable voice from the direction of the door.

Not believing her ears, she whipped around. "Harris?"

The lad dashed across the floor. No matter how much her hands were caked with flour, she wrapped him in a tight embrace and twirled him in a circle. "How did you find me?"

"'Twas Sir James. He found me."

The Black Douglas stood in the doorway with an enormous grin on his face. "He has become quite a horseman."

Ailish didn't know what to say. On one hand, she was still

angry with the man, and even more so because he hadn't told her he'd set out to rescue her brother. Then again, at last the Earl of Caerlaverock was in her arms. Still staring at James, she set Harris on his feet. "You went to Lochmaben alone?"

"Ah..." His gaze shifted as he tugged on his earlobe. "After I received word from Caelan that the lad took daily rides with Sir Henry, I felt our best chance to recover the lad was to slip in quietly and set a trap."

"And you did not see fit to tell me your plan?"

The corners of James' mouth tightened. And there was no question as to why. In his eyes, she had twice disobeyed his orders. He no longer trusted her. And after all she'd done to help him recover. Even after suffering in the Lord Warden's prison, he was too bull-headed to realize she was one of the few people in all of Christendom whom he *could* trust.

But her rift with James mattered not at the moment. Harris had been returned and, for that, the man deserved a hero's praise. "Thank you, sir," she said, curtsying deeply, while her stomach sank to her toes. It seemed the end of their romance had come. "I am truly grateful for my brother's return."

James gave her a questioning look as if he suddenly had no idea what she was on about. "I should leave you to reunite." He bowed. "I'll go stable the horses."

"Are you hungry?" Ailish asked, giving Harris' shoulder a pat.

"Famished."

"The evening meal will be served soon, but how about a slice of bread and honey to tide you over?"

Never one to refuse a sweet, the lad licked his lips. "Yes, please."

She quickly sliced a bit of bread and drizzled on the honey. "You must be beside yourself with shock after your ordeal."

Harris moved to the table and sat on a bench. "Mayhap I was at first."

"Only at first?"

"Aye, Uncle Herbert was terribly mean. He made me sleep at the bottom of a windowless turret and said he wanted to feed me to the sharks, but since he had no heir, King Edward refused to allow him to do so."

Cringing at the sound of the English king's name, Ailish set the plate in front of the boy, then joined him on the bench. "At least we no longer need to concern ourselves with our vile uncle."

"Because you killed him?"

"How did you know?"

"Sir Henry told me."

"Sir Henry?"

"Percy. One of King Edward's most esteemed knights." Harris took a big bite of his bread, then continued to speak with his mouth full, "He was training me to be his squire. Said I was the earl now, and his duty was to foster me."

Ailish shuddered. Henry Percy not only pillaged the Douglas crofts, he was renowned for his merciless attacks on unarmed Scottish folk. It seemed her brother may have not been rescued soon enough. She brushed a bit of flour off his cheek, only managing to smudge it. "I shall write to King Robert and ask him to appoint a Scottish knight to foster you."

Harris' eyes grew wide with an expression of utter disbelief. "But the Bruce is an imposter."

"I am afraid you have been sorely led astray. Sir Henry was only being kind to you because the King of England wants you to do his bidding. He was trying to turn your loyalties just as he turned Uncle Herbert."

Harris stopped midchew, his face going through a myriad of emotions from disbelief, to deep concern, to realization. "You mean Sir Henry meant to make me as evil as our uncle?"

Ailish hated to oversimplify it, but the boy well knew the devious and despicable nature of their uncle, and that Herbert had not only robbed Harris of his birthright but that he'd joined with Edward to take Caerlaverock Castle and murder their father. "Make no bones about it, the King of England will stop at nothing to annex Scotland to his wicked empire, and cares not who he may hurt."

Harris pushed the plate away, his bottom lip quivering. "But what you're saying cannot be true. At least not the part about Sir Henry. He liked me. He was fun, and he rode with me every morning...l-let me groom the horses, too!"

A tear slipped from the lad's eye, making Ailish's heart twist in a knot. She pulled him into her embrace. "I'm so sorry about what happened to you. But before you were sent to Sir Henry, he burned and pillaged the Douglas—killed many of the families who supported Sir James."

"Not Sir Henry. He would never do such a thing."

"If there is anyone in all of Christendom you can believe, it is me. I have done everything to try to protect you, have I not?"

"Aye."

"And I agree. You must become a squire and learn the ways of knighthood. I will see to it you are trained by one of King Robert's best."

"But...he's a bad person," Harris whispered.

"Nay, he is the only good thing that has happened to Scotland in a very long time." Ailish squeezed her brother's shoulders. "Do you not remember when I went to the king's coronation to plead that he recognize you as the true earl?"

Harris gave a sorrowful nod.

"He gave me his word that he will fight to reinstate you to Caerlaverock and rid Scotland of Edward's men."

"But they're everywhere. And they hate Robert. They're riding to Kildrummy to set the castle to fire and sword and take the Bruce's wife."

Ailish's throat closed so tightly, she felt strangled. "Did you mention this to Sir James?"

"N-nay."

"Do you ken when they're planning to ride?"

The lad shook his head. "I only overheard Sir Henry speak of it two days past when he was outside the stables with his men."

"Did anyone see you there?"

"I do not think so."

"Come." She grasped his hand and pulled him toward the door. "We must inform Sir James straightaway."

28

James draped the horses' bridles over a nail where the tack was stowed at the rear of the stables. Ailish had been so happy to see her brother, he couldn't bring himself to tell her it was time to part ways. The time had come for him to take Her Ladyship and Harris to a safe haven and return to his men. The first place that came to mind was Flanders in France but he had already wasted too much precious time. Unless Bishop Lamberton offered to escort the Maxwells across the channel.

And though his first choice was to head for Saint Andrews, there were many options—the isles seemed to be at relative peace. And Robert had sent his wife and daughter to the north which was also an option. However, traveling to Saint Andrews and gaining an audience with the bishop would be the swiftest.

Weary from hard riding and hungry, James thumped his saddle as he started to leave.

"Sir James!" Ailish rushed toward him with her wide-eyed brother in her wake. He would have preferred it if she'd come alone. He might steal a kiss. But on second thought, stealing kisses would only lead to more heartbreak when he told her it was time to go their separate ways. They both knew as long as the kingdom was in upheaval, they had no hope of marrying.

He stopped and propped his hands on his hips. "Is something amiss?"

"My oath, it is." She tugged her brother beside her. "Harris tells me the English army kens the queen is at Kildrummy and they're making plans to sack the castle and take not only Her Grace, but the Bruce's daughter, Marjorie."

James knelt to be eye-level with the lad. "Did Sir Henry tell you this?"

"I heard him speaking with his men."

"Do you ken when they're planning this raid?"

Harris shook his head. "But they did talk about waiting on the transport of a new siege engine called the Warwulf."

"Will it be delivered to Lochmaben?" asked Ailish.

The lad shrugged. "I couldn't hear all that well."

James patted His Lordship's shoulder. "You've been very helpful." His prior thoughts forgotten, he rose and looked Ailish in the eyes. "We must inform the king at once. We'll leave at first light."

"To see His Grace?"

"Aye," James gave a quick reply, not daring to admit he had just been trying to decide where to take her. But seeking out Robert would not only rightfully put the decision on where to place the Maxwells in the king's hands, James would be able to deliver the news about the English invasion himself and discuss their strategy for keeping the queen safe.

"Should we not send a missive and await his reply?"

"It is no longer safe to remain here. Once Sir Henry's men find he's been slain, they will be champing at the bit for revenge. Our trail might be difficult to follow, but they'll come. Mark me, sooner or later they will come."

"Very well." Ailish clasped her hands tightly. "Can we send someone to Lincluden to fetch Florrie and Coira? We've been apart so long, I'm certain they're sick with worry."

James shook his head. "I'm sorry, but it is a risk we cannot take. Lincluden has already been compromised. It is the first place they'll look."

"Then I ought to write a letter."

"Absolutely not." James waved his finger under her saucy nose. "I ken how important it is to be reunited with your sister but, presently, the best thing you can do for her and your maid is to remain at large. I mean it. Do not disobey me on this."

"I wouldn't think of—"

"Oh no? Like you didn't think when you told the Carlisle guard you were with child. That may have not gone awry, but thinking you knew better and posing as a washerwoman greatly delayed our chances to find Harris. Worse, if we had failed to rescue you from the grips of the Lord Warden, you might very well be at the mercy of Edward's whims."

Ailish glared and crossed her arms. "This is what you think of me? Have you forgotten my arrows hit their marks at the border or the fact that I sat at your bedside for days on end?" She stamped her foot. "I'll wager you cannot wait to be rid of me!"

She grabbed her brother's hand. "Come, Harris, else we'll be late for the evening meal."

James raked his fingers through his hair as the woman stormed out of the barn without a backward glance.

I reckon I deserved that.

Nonetheless, a stone of lead dropped to the pit of his stomach. Aye, Ailish was still the sable-haired lass who'd stolen his heart at the coronation, but until the kingdom was securely returned to the hands of the Scots, he must not let his heart muddle his thinking or his decisions. The Bruce would know where to send Her Ladyship and her kin until the war's end.

Rather than take his meal in the hall, James slipped into the kitchens and ate there. Damn it all. Why was it every time he argued with the lass he felt like a heel? And why did she always seem to bring out the raving beast within his chest? Did she not know how precious she was?

Worse, the mere thought of her one day marrying some pompous lord made him want to bury his fist in the nearest face.

AFTER THEY'D RIDDEN TO AYR AND PROCURED A *BIRLINN*, Harris had insisted on sitting at the bow where he could see everything. Ailish joined him no matter how much she would have preferred to sit astern and brood. Over and over, she'd reminded herself that her brother was her only care. She'd known all along James could not fall in love with her, just as she was prohibited from loving him.

But reason did nothing to soothe the ache shredding her heart into hundreds of hopeless pieces.

Several times she had admonished herself for giving her heart to the Black Douglas, a ruthless man who had razed his own keep. But her daft heart continually answered back that the man she was trying to cast from her thoughts was good, courageous, and loyal to his very soul. He put honor and duty ahead of all, which is what she truly respected. Though she tried to convince herself otherwise, she had no regrets about giving herself to the man.

None at all.

If it ruined me, then so be it.

As they approached the southern tip of the Isle of Arran, the wind blew a gale, making the *birlinn* rock from side to side while water lapped over her hull. But after they turned northward into the straits, the seas calmed enough for the boat to swiftly tack up the isle's western shore.

James had given the fisherman a false name and told him to take them to the Caves of Arran. He hadn't uttered a word to her about who they'd meet there. Of course, Ailish guessed it might be the king, but perhaps it was only a place to meet someone who could ferry them to His Grace. Nonetheless, she didn't bother asking. At the moment, it was simply too painful to speak to him.

"The Caves of Arran are ahead," called the fisherman. "I'll sail as near as I can but you'll need to help the lady alight."

Caerlaverock Castle was on the Firth of Solway and Ailish was no stranger to traveling by boat. "I'm perfectly capable of alighting on my own," she said rather sternly. Her hem might end up wet, but she could hardly bear to let James carry her.

And the idea of having him ask one of the men to carry her was too much of an affront.

Contrary to her wishes, as soon as the fisherman dropped anchor, James hopped over the side. Standing knee-deep in the surf, he reached up. "I'd never again be able to call myself a knight if I didn't help you to the shore, m'lady."

Ailish tsked her tongue while Harris had no problem hoisting himself over the side and splashing through the waves as if he were born to be a sailor. "Very well, if you insist."

"I do."

She grasped his hand, swung one leg over his extended arm and then the other.

Ye gods, as soon as she was cradled in his arms, he grinned. The same bone-melting grin that had ensnared her heart in the first place. Did he not know how much his smile affected her? Or the intensity of those obsidian eyes, or the thick black hair that had grown in enough to curl about his crown, making him look like a dastardly plunderer of women.

Plunderer.

The very word made gooseflesh rise across her skin and her nether parts awake with a need she wished she could forget. And why did she find this dangerous man so attractive? Not that she wanted to forget anything about James Douglas, she simply wanted to forget how lustful he made her feel.

"Have you a chill?" he asked, his voice far too soothing as he carried her beyond the rocks to the white sand.

"Nay." She averted her gaze to keep from delving further under his spell. "You may put me down now."

"If that is your wish."

In a heartbeat, she was on her feet. "Where do we go from here?"

"We wait until the *birlinn* has sailed out of sight," James whispered, then waved to the fisherman. "Thank you, friend."

"Look!" Harris dashed to Ailish and held up a large clam shell. "It has the sound of the sea if you hold it against your ear."

She took the shell and pretended to be surprised when she heard the rush. "That is astonishing!"

It didn't take long for the boat to sail away and, once it did, Sir Arthur Campbell and Sir Robert Boyd marched out of one of the four openings of the cave. At least Ailish counted four. They looked like archways sculpted by the sea. Not uniform like arches along a cloister, but similar enough to appear to be carved by the same hand.

"Douglas?" asked Boyd, his hand on his hilt as he neared.

James marched toward the men while Ailish followed. "We've come with news of grave import. Is the king still here?"

"Aye." Arthur's gaze slid her way before he took her hand, bowed, and kissed it. "M'lady, may I say how nice it is to see your lovely face."

"We've no time for pleasantries," growled James, stepping between them. "We must gain an audience with His Grace at once."

Boyd gave Ailish a polite bow, then waved them toward the caves. "Follow me."

"Come, Harris," she said, beckoning her brother who was using his shell to dig in the sand.

"I want to find a chest of treasure."

She snapped her fingers. "Something tells me you'll have a chance to continue your search later."

Ailish fell in step with Sir Arthur who had danced with her at the coronation. "I'm surprised not to see His Grace on the shore. Is he unwell?"

"We retreat into the caves if a ship is spotted," said Sir Robert.

"Ah, yes. I should have thought."

The king stepped into the light just as they reached the arches. "Lady Ailish Maxwell and Sir James? I see you found the young earl, did you not?"

"We did. But I bring unsettling news—" James placed his hands on Harris' shoulders. "His Lordship overheard his captor, none other than Sir Henry Percy, speak of their plans to sack Kildrummy and take Her Grace and Lady Marjorie prisoner."

"My God." The king gripped his fist over his chest as he glanced aside. "They know?"

"Aye, Your Grace," said Harris. "And they're waiting on the arrival of a siege engine they call the Warwulf."

Though the news was terribly grim, Ailish stood a bit taller. Her brother would soon be turning ten years of age and already he'd proven himself invaluable to the king.

Robert mussed the lad's hair as a dark shadow crossed his face. "Have you any idea how soon they will march?"

James shook his head. "Nay—only that they are assembling their army at Lochmaben."

Harris glanced between them, a smudge of sand on his cheek. "And Sir Henry intended to collect conscripts on the journey northward."

"I have three hundred men ready to take up arms," said James.

"Good." The Bruce's gaze swept across the stoic faces of his knights. "We'll need to make haste."

"But I saw no ships," said James. "How will we reach the mainland?"

"I've a *birlinn* hiding within." The king ran his fingers through his beard. "Tell me, why did you bring Lady Ailish and Caerlaverock bearing such grave news?"

"I had no choice, Your Grace." James explained about the fruitless journey to Carlisle and how they ended up at Fail Monastery, as well as Harris' rescue from Lochmaben.

"My lady's maid and sister, Florrie, are still at Lincluden Priory," Ailish added. "They might be captured at any given moment."

"I see," said the king.

James shifted his fists to his hips. "Since the nunnery has been compromised, I need a safe haven for Her Ladyship and her kin. Of course, a monastery full of monks is no place for a lady."

"No." Robert looked northward as if preoccupied with a great many woes. "M'lady, I am certain the chieftain of MacSween will be able to accommodate you and your siblings at Lochranza Castle on the northern tip of this isle. I'll send a cohort to fetch your sister and your maid straightaway."

Ailish curtseyed. It would be a relief for them to be together again. "My thanks."

"And you, m'lord," said the king, addressing Harris. "You have been most brave, have you not?"

"Aye." The lad gave Ailish a dubious glance. "But Sir Henry made me his squire. I was learning so much. I'd hate to be locked away on this isle like I was at the priory. The nuns were kind but taught me nothing about being an earl."

The Bruce's brows arched. "Is that so?"

"Aye," Harris bobbed his head emphatically. "Sir Henry said I would become a great man, but before I can take my place as Earl of Caerlaverock I must be fostered."

Ailish and James exchanged glances. The lad had grown up so much in the time he was away. Had it been all that long ago when she'd comforted him in her arms as they fled?

"Very true," said the king. "Sir James, you will take on His Lordship as your squire."

The big knight's jaw dropped, and he stood speechless for a moment before he found his tongue. "Your Grace, I'd like nothing better than to take Caerlaverock under my wing, but we are riding into battle."

"And there is no better place for him to learn about war and strategy than in the midst of conflict." Robert looked to Ailish. "Not to worry, m'lady. Your brother will not be taking up arms until his beard grows in, but make no bones about it, everything the wee earl just said is the brutish truth."

She curtseyed, while her heart twisted in dozens of knots. Perhaps she knew one day Harris would no longer be her charge, but she never expected the day to come so quickly. "Yes, Your Grace."

"I also have not forgotten your beauty or your courage," the king continued. "I will make a match with your hand, and soon."

Heat flared up the back of Ailish's neck. She didn't need to look at James to know how intensely the big knight's dark gaze bored into her.

29

While Ailish took a walk with her brother to say their goodbyes, James followed the king deeper into the cave. It was rocky and damp, though there was a makeshift table, pot of ink, and quill on a table where he assumed the Bruce conducted his affairs. "Why are you staying here in this squalor rather than at Lochranza Castle with MacSween?"

"Edward's fleet patrols these waters. There's naught to be seen here, but they've spent a good deal of time watching MacSween—sail past every day or so."

"Do they suspect you've taken refuge on Arran?"

"We spread word that I had fled to Ireland, but the English are nothing if not cunning." The king sat in a wooden chair—the only seat in the cave. "'Tis why you are one of the few who truly kens where I am."

James bowed his head as his chest swelled. For once in his life, he'd found a place where his name was respected.

"'Tis also why we will be sailing this night after the witching hour."

"Sailing at night is dangerous, is it not?"

"Aye, and that's why the English patrols will not see us. The bastards will be tucked in their beds dreaming about swiving their women."

"I commend your courage, Your Grace."

The king eyed him. "You seem quite protective of the Maxwell lass."

"You assigned me to her care, if you do not recall."

"Of course, I remember. But you were only charged with returning her safely to Lincluden Priory. It appears much has happened since."

"It has, Your Grace."

"And you've grown fond of her?"

"Perhaps, but do not allow any affection I may harbor against me. I ken my duty and it is by your side for as long as you need my sword."

"Yes, it is, though you must also see to it you have heirs."

James swiped a hand across his mouth. "Mayhap one day when we're not riding northward to defend the queen—"

"Indeed." The king pointed to a flagon with two cups beside it fashioned out of bulls' horns. "Will you pour?"

James stepped forward and did as asked. "Wine, Your Grace?"

"'Tis good for the soul." Robert took the cup and drank. "Take Her Ladyship to Duncan MacSween and tell him she and her sister will be staying on until I arrange Lady Ailish's marriage."

"Now?"

"Aye, now. Her Ladyship will be far more comfortable sleeping in a bed, mark me. Fewer midges to fester under her skin as well."

The wine stuck in James' throat, making him force it down. Did he want to marry the lass? Aye, if it weren't likely he'd be killed in battle. Perhaps if she weren't so damned stubborn.

Like me.

"Douglas, I sense you are a hundred miles away."

"Forgive me." James bowed. "I suppose after all this time it will be difficult to say goodbye to the Lady Ailish. Even though..."

"Hmm?"

"Even though she challenges me at every turn."

"Is that not what willful noblewomen are bred to do?"

"I beg your pardon?"

The king sat back and cradled his cup between his hands. "Was your mother not of her own mind?"

James thought back on the tales his father had proudly told about his ma. Indeed, Elizabeth Stewart was a force to be reckoned with. "She was, Your Grace. I recall a servant once saying she was the only woman with backbone enough to stand up to my da."

The king took another drink and wiped his mouth. "Thought as much."

James tugged at his collar and looked outside. Ailish and Harris were approaching. "I'd best take Her Ladyship to Lochranza as you asked."

Ailish walked beside James in silence. She ought to be overjoyed for Harris and not woeful that he was leaving her. Moreover, she ought to be swimming with pride because they were able to deliver such important news to the king. Lord knew she'd prayed time and time again for the queen's safety.

But no matter how she ought to feel, the world seemed to be splintering into shards around her. And those very shards felt as if they were spearing her lungs, taking her breath away.

James glanced over his shoulder, then led her behind an outcropping. "I wanted a word with you before we arrive at the castle."

She stared at her folded hands, refusing to meet his gaze. "I suppose there's nothing left to say. You ken how much Harris means to me. I expect you to guard him with your life."

"I will. I give you my solemn vow to protect him as I have you, m'lady."

In truth, Ailish could imagine no one better to foster her brother, though losing him—seeing the wee lad ride into peril made her hollow inside. She pursed her lips and gave a stiff nod.

"I wanted you to know..."

She dared glance up. His eyes were so intense, as if he were tortured by some deep emotion. "What is wrong?"

His Adam's apple bobbed. "It isn't easy to put into words what I am feeling."

She cupped his cheek, his beard far softer than it looked. "I knew when I gave myself to you that our time was fleeting at best. We are both children of this war and we've naught but to cling to each other and share God's gifts when we are able."

"I want—"

"Sh." She pressed her finger to his lips. "I have no regrets."

He nodded.

"Though I do have one request."

"Which is?"

"Please tell the king I am in no hurry for him to arrange my marriage."

James pursed his lips so hard, they turned white. "Are you not worried that I've taken your maidenhead? Especially after the king spoke so openly about arranging your marriage?"

Ailish sighed and smiled as she gazed into his eyes. "As I recall, I begged you to take it. That worry is mine to bear. Not yours."

"No, it is mine as well. If I live—"

"Wheesht. We will not speak of the future."

His gaze dipped to her lips. "May I kiss you?"

"I was hoping that was why you led me off the path, sir."

As his warm lips caressed hers, Ailish melted into him,

sliding her hands around his sturdy waist. Gladly, she opened her mouth and savored the languid swirls of his tongue, drinking him in, memorizing this moment and how it felt to swoon in her lover's arms. To know the beauty of love. For in her heart, she knew she would never again feel this way about a man.

30

It didn't take long for the Bruce to send out word to assemble the Scottish army but marching northward proved devastating to their numbers. In Perth they were outnumbered and taken by surprise by the Earl of Pembroke's forces. Though James and the men fought valiantly, the king nearly fell under Pembroke's blade. Beaten, they fled for the Highlands, losing three-quarters of their numbers. The defeat left the Scots weakened and vulnerable, the remnants of the kingdom all but destroyed.

And their luck only grew worse. As they reached Strathfillan in the mountains of Argyll, an army one-thousand-man strong led by the Lord of Lorne forced the Bruce's bedraggled warriors into battle. The king fought like a lion, putting himself in mortal harm. At one time, Robert was completely surrounded by his enemies and believed the end was near. But by the grace of God, his sword did not fail him.

Still, only through the efforts of his knights was King Robert able to escape. Plucked from certain death by Sir James Douglas and spirited to Dunaverty Castle, they fled further south than where Ailish hid on the Isle of Arran and leagues away from the queen at Kildrummy.

Without an army, the Scottish forces reduced to a handful of loyal knights, James followed as the king's men stealthily moved northward through the Highlands, skirting about the craggy peaks to avoid Lorne and his savagery.

When at last they reached Kildrummy Castle, they found naught but a burned-out shell and a few bedraggled servants. The king's brother had been executed and hung from the castle walls. The queen and Marjorie were taken by Pembroke and, under Edward's orders, they were now being held as prisoners somewhere deep in England, far from the border.

No matter how devastating the news, there was no time for mourning. Now little more than fugitives on the run, James procured a *birlinn*. They sailed to Rathin Castle where they wintered on a small Irish isle in the North Channel.

Sitting in front of the hearth in the great hall, James sharpened his dirk on a leather strap while Harris sat beside him, polishing every link in James' mail.

Gazing longingly at the blade, Harris harrumphed. "When can I start training with a real blade?"

James stilled his hand. "Mayhap after you've mastered the art of wielding a waster."

"Against the likes of you?" Harris snorted. "That will never happen."

"Never? Och, do ye reckon you will be thirteen hands for the rest of your days?

"Nay, but you are the strongest knight in the entire realm."

"Perhaps, but men grow old and with age comes weakness. 'Tis why we must have sons to follow in our footsteps."

"And I already must take up my father's mantle. I need to be able to ride into battle as you do. How else will I defend my lands?"

"Do not be overanxious. In time, you will have all for which you wish. And then you shall reflect upon your youth with longing."

"But first we must drive the English out of Scotland."

James sighed, thanking the stars the lad had forgotten his time with Sir Henry and was once again a loyal Scottish subject. "Aye."

"And then can I take Ailish and Florrie back to Caerlaverock?"

The mention of Her Ladyship's name made the emptiness in James' chest swell like a fathomless cavern. By God, he missed the lass. Aye, they'd had their differences, but there was something the king said ages ago when they were on the Isle of Arran that James had thought about every day since.

Noble women are bred to challenge their husbands at every turn.

And as the Bruce had pointed out, James' mother was the only woman able to talk sense into his da.

Aye, during their time together, Lady Ailish had challenged him plenty. But rather than listen, he'd treated her like one of the men, he'd expected her to be a good soldier and obey his every word without question. And at every turn, the lass had proved she had a mind of her own.

She never should have been put in danger. James' first mistake had been allowing her to ride on their quest to rescue Harris.

But, then again, her fate would have been sealed had she gone to stay with Hew's wife.

"Sir?" asked Harris. "When will I be able to take Ailish and Florrie to Caerlaverock?"

James resumed sharpening his blade. "That is a question I cannot answer. But you will. Mark me, one day you will."

"Do you think she's bonny?"

"Who?"

"My sister. You seemed fond of her when we traveled to Arran."

"And you ask me this now? After you've been my squire for six months?"

"I've been wondering is all."

The hollowness he'd been feeling in his chest tripled in size. "Aye, she is very bonny."

"Have you kissed her?"

"What sort of question is that? If I'd kissed Her Ladyship, 'tis unlikely I'd tell her wee brother, is it not?"

"Because..." The lad pursed his lips and rubbed the links on the mail.

"If you are to be an earl, ye must learn early on 'tis important to speak your mind." He eyed the lad. "Now tell me what you truly wish to say."

"I think you ought to marry her."

The dirk slipped from James' grasp and clattered to the floor.

Harris looked up, his expression completely earnest. "Ye ken, she's of marriageable age."

Why the hell had he told Harris to speak his bloody mind? "Enough."

"And you pair seem to be agreeable."

James grabbed his weapon and sliced it through the air making a hiss. "I do not need a lad of ten telling me whom I should marry."

His wee Lordship stood and examined his work. "I think your mail shines like never before," he said as if he hadn't just issued James with a verbal slap that made his head spin. "May I go to the kitchens? I'm a bit hungry."

James was only too happy to be alone. "Go on, off with ye, then."

As the boy skipped away, James sheathed the dirk and stared at the fire smoldering in the hearth. Harris wanted to wield a blade? Hell, if the young earl had any clue how close he'd come to slaying James with his tongue, he'd forget about sword fighting altogether.

Marry Lady Ailish Maxwell?

Him?

Certainly, the Bruce had spoken about finding her a match. A fact he'd desperately tried to block from his thoughts.

As a spark in the fire popped and landed at James' feet, so too did an epiphany spark before his eyes.

He stood and marched up the stairs to the solar King Robert was using to plot his next battle.

"Ah, Sir James." The king pressed his finger on the map near Ayr. "Before winter's end I will return to Turnberry—my mother's ancestral lands."

"Do you think that wise, Your Grace?"

"There is one thing that is unwise and that is rotting on this frigid isle and waiting for Edward's men to find me."

"I cannot argue with you there."

James stood for a time, pretending to examine the map while shifting from foot to foot.

The king straightened. "Was there something you wished to discuss?"

"There is, sire."

"Come, I cannot have my champion knight tongue-tied. Out with it."

"I have proved myself in battle, and you will not find a more loyal subject."

"Agreed." The king nodded. "If you had not dragged me from Dalrigh, I would have fallen to Lorne and his army of vipers."

James barely registered the king's words and continued to make his point, "I am the son of William, Lord of Douglas, and Elizabeth Stewart, daughter of the fourth High Steward of Scotland."

The king narrowed his eyes as if he weren't certain where James was heading. "Aye."

"My family has served Scotland for generations."

"I do not believe that was ever in question."

James heaved an enormous breath. Why the devil was this so difficult? "I'd like to ask your permission to marry Lady Ailish Maxwell, Your Grace."

"But she's the daughter of an—" The king shut his mouth

and looked toward the ceiling. "Why did you not come forward sooner?"

"I would have, but matters have been dire, making the idea of marriage..." James searched for the right word. "Unobtainable, and perhaps unfair to the lady."

"Sir James, we are wintering in an Irish keep. Our...*your* situation is not exactly secure."

"But when will it be? This is war and in war one must adapt."

"True." The king placed his finger on Douglas lands. "But your castle is in ruins. If I give you my blessing, have you a home in mind for a lady of her station, preferably one with an outer as well as an inner bailey?"

"I received word two days past that my clansmen have built a new roof over my keep."

"A roof, aye?"

"Indeed, and if I ken anyone who can turn that pile of rubble into a castle fit for a queen, 'tis Lady Ailish."

"Have you a ring?"

"No, sire."

Robert tugged a silver band from his smallest finger. "Then take this along with my blessing."

James accepted the gift and bowed deeply. "Thank you."

"Go, wed the lass and plant a bairn in her belly. Then I will meet you at Turnberry on the first of February."

AILISH SAT IN THE LADY'S SOLAR EMBROIDERING WHILE Florrie read aloud. It had been very kind of Lady MacSween to offer the chamber for Florrie's lessons, especially now that the weather had turned particularly nasty. And though there was a thick fur covering the small window and tied down at the sides, there was no warmth within, not even the fire raging in the hearth could allay the chill.

Florrie put a slip of thread in her book to mark her page and set it aside. "Why must winter last so long? I fear it will never end."

"It does seem that way," Ailish agreed. This season was particularly harsh. The wind never stopped. The snow blew sideways. Worse, they'd received no word of Harris who, Ailish prayed, was safely hiding somewhere with James. Of course, Lord MacSween had received report of the Bruce's crippling losses at Methven and Dalrigh, as well as the horrible news that the king had reached Kildrummy too late.

The only heartening news was that James was named among the knights who had protected the king, which meant Harris must be unharmed.

At least that's what Ailish told herself fifty times a day.

As with the dreary weather, all seemed lost and there Ailish sat, further away from her hopes and dreams with no idea where to find her brother, or the dashing knight who had made the lad his squire. Even the man whose coronation she had attended nine months past had seemed to vanish.

Releasing a sigh, she pushed her needle through the linen and pulled the silk out the other side.

Florrie leaned in. "Why did you choose yellow primroses?"

Because they are Sir James' favorite. A lump swelled in her throat as she tried to smile. "Yellow is happy and primroses bloom in spring with the promise of finer days ahead."

"Well, I like them."

"Thank—"

The door opened and Coira popped her head in. "You have a visitor, m'lady."

Ailish looked up. Had she heard correctly? The only people who knew of her whereabouts were presently in hiding, and most likely not even in Scotland. "You're jesting."

Harris burst through the door and threw his arms around Ailish's neck. "She would never jest about me. I'm the Earl of Caerlaverock!"

Hundreds of questions came to the tip of her tongue as she

squeezed her brother with all her strength while Florrie joined them. "Oh, my goodness, it is so good to see you!"

"'Tis storming something awful outside, how did you cross the sea?" asked Florrie.

"There was a matter of some urgency," a self-assured, rather deep voice that was in no way mysterious came from the doorway.

"Sir James!" Ailish cried, releasing her brother and springing to her feet.

The knight strode inside, his hair longer and curled over one eye. His teeth glistened with a grin that made her insides melt into liquid honey. He grasped her hand and kissed it, his lips making gooseflesh shoot all the way up her arm and across the back of her neck. "My word, you are a sight for these war-weary eyes to behold."

Her mind whirred with hundreds of things she wanted to say —like how much she'd missed him, and how much he made her suddenly feel alive when, only moments ago, it was as if all of Christendom had plunged into darkness. But most of all, she wanted to throw her arms around his neck and shower him with endless kisses. "I cannot believe you are here."

His face colored while he stared into her eyes as if they were the only two people in the solar.

Coira cleared her throat. "Harris and Florrie, Lady MacSween has a treat awaiting you in the kitchens."

"And Sir James has something of grave import to discuss with my sister," said Harris as if he were already privy to the king's counsel.

Ailish glanced from her brother back to James, giving him a questioning look. But he said nothing as he stood, holding her hand until they were alone.

"I—"

He dropped to his knee. "Lady Ailish, I would be remiss if I did not tell you I have been tortured in the months since we last embraced."

"I am so very sorry. Were you injured in battle?"

"My suffering has not been of the flesh."

"No?"

"Nay, lass." He kissed her hand again. "It is you who have caused my misery."

"Me?" Whatever had she done to hurt him so?

"Aye, you have held my heart captive and there is only one cure to relieve my torment."

Ailish's own heart began to thrum erratically as James continued, "Marry me, m'lady. Marry me this day in the chapel below stairs, and you will make me the happiest man in Scotland."

Unable to speak, her mouth dropped open as a tear spilled onto her cheek. Ever since they shared their first kiss, she had dreamed of this day. "So soon?" she whispered.

"I cannot bear to live any longer without you in my arms." He tugged her hand over his heart. "I love you. I love everything about you and if you do not say yes, you will slay me from now until eternity."

"Yes." She laughed. "Yes, I will marry you this day!"

31

James had not an iota of remorse for insisting Ailish marry him at once. The last several months had been torture and his patience had run its course. As soon as the king had given his blessing, the only thing James thought about was to have his bonny lass in his arms to cherish for the rest of his days. As soon as he'd stepped ashore at Lochranza Castle, he set MacSween to task, insisting the priest be summoned without delay.

Within an hour, Her Ladyship managed to don a gown of lavender silk and a veil to match. Her beauty took his breath away and he stood transfixed while the priest chanted the order of holy matrimony.

It was a small affair with the lord and lady of the castle in attendance as well as Florrie, Harris, and Coira. After the service, MacSween provided a feast of roast leg of lamb, but there had been no time to arrange for musicians or dancing or any of the pomp that comes with a wedding. And James did not give a fig. He had his strong-willed, quick-tongued, stunningly beautiful Ailish by his side at long last.

All through the meal, he was giddy with anticipation, barely able to wait until they could be alone. Finally, when his bride led him to her chamber above stairs, he followed as if he, the feared Black Douglas, were floating on a cloud.

"I cannot believe this day," Ailish said as she opened the door. "'Tis as if all of my dreams have come true with the snap of my fingers."

"You harbor no regrets that I insisted on a hasty marriage?" he asked, following her inside. The room was small but warmed by a peat fire and lit with an array of candles artfully placed on the mantel. In one corner stood a washstand with an earthen bowl and ewer. There was but one chair, though the round table beside it contained a flagon of wine and two goblets with a note beside it.

"Look at this." Ailish moved to the table and picked up the slip of vellum. "*May the joy that binds you yield fruits of the spirit – MacSween.*"

"He's a good man." James pulled her into his arms, closed his eyes, and kissed her, slowly, deliberately, possessively. "Och," he sighed. "I've never been so happy."

"Nor I."

He glanced to the narrow bed, wedged against a wall. It was a bit small but would do. Hell, the floor would do.

The table.

The window embrasure.

As long as they were in each other's arms, he'd make love to his lady anywhere.

Leaning away, he refused to release her from his arms. "Would you like a wee bit of wine?"

Ailish slowly scraped her teeth over her bottom lip and toyed with the brooch at his shoulder. "First..."

"Hmm?"

"I want you to make love to me."

His knees buckled. It took all the self-control James could muster not to rip the lovely lavender dress from her lithe bones and lay her down. For the past nine months, this woman had consumed his dreams, his thoughts, his hopes.

And now she is mine.

"I've been waiting months to hear you say that," he whispered, nibbling her neck. "I need to be inside you."

Ailish slid the veil from her head. "And when we join, we will be one. Bonded by our love."

Though his hands trembled with his desire to move fast, he untied the bow securing her neckline, slowly tugging the ribbon and spreading the laces of her bodice until the gown whooshed away, dropping about her feet.

Wearing only a thin linen shift, she stepped out of her slippers. Then eyeing him with the intent of a delicious hellcat, she unclasped the brooch at his shoulder and set it on the table. With deft fingers, he unfastened his belt, sending his plaid to the floorboards.

Another tug of a bow and her shift vanished.

His braies vanished.

And in a rush, garters and stockings flew across the chamber.

Their lips fused, their bodies crushed together as in a frenzy while their hands explored, rubbing, caressing. James backed her toward the bed and slid his fingers down her narrow waist, willing himself to regain a modicum of control.

"You are a goddess to be worshiped," he growled, pulling her against his erection. The fervor started again while he sank his fingers into her luscious, soft bottom, his eyes crossing as she rubbed against him. Rocking his hips forward, he bit his lip and pressed harder. Until his thighs shuddered.

Any more and I will spill.

In one motion, he swept her onto the mattress. Exquisite sable hair sprawled across the pillow, her body lithe, naked, and prone to him. Ailish's breasts alone with their gentle mounds and taut nipples arrested his breath. He would do anything for this woman.

James' mouth went completely dry. His wife's beauty enraptured him, seduced him, rendered him at a complete loss for words. Damnation, if his cock met the slightest friction, it would erupt. James' tongue slid to the corner of his mouth as he ached to have his lips on her pert little breasts. He needed her. He needed her now.

Ailish focused a seductive gaze upon him, slowly moving her hands to her breast, her slender belly, and down toward the nest of curls hiding her treasure.

"Holy Mary Mother of God," he growled, climbing over her. Using his knees to spread her legs, he slid his finger along her core. "You have bewitched me and I am under your spell for all eternity."

Rocking back on his haunches, James lapped her. With a feral moan, Ailish thrust her hips forward as he swirled his tongue around her sensitive button.

"Och," she cried, arching into him.

"Och aye," he teased, sliding a finger inside.

"I am the one who has been bewitched, sir knight!"

Chuckling, his cock leaking seed, he slid his finger faster while his tongue relentlessly licked.

Ailish's breathing sped until she gasped. Her body stiffened, then her thighs convulsed with earth-shattering quivers. Crying out, she came undone in his mouth.

Clenching his gut against his urge to release his seed, he continued to lick until her breathing ebbed.

"You are a fiend," she said, laughing as she pushed up on her elbows. "We have not yet joined."

He coaxed her back to the mattress, giving her a devilish grin. "Then we must remedy that at once, Wife."

As she reveled in James' kiss, Ailish's insides quivered with pleasure. "You are the world to me."

"And now you are mine forever," he said, cupping her cheek. "You are an angel come to life."

"You are my warrior king."

"I'm ever so close to spilling my seed," he throatily whispered while the thick column of his manhood jutted between her thighs. The pull of wanting filled her again. But this time, she needed him inside her.

She moved against him, showing James what she wanted. "We have a lifetime ahead of us."

"A lifetime in each other's arms," James echoed.

Slowly, they joined, his breath ragged. He filled and stretched her, caressing the spot that would send her to the stars. And though she knew he was dangling on a ragged edge, he did not rush. Gradually, as they kissed and explored each other, the tempo increased.

Higher their passion mounted. And when Ailish bucked against him, he toppled off the edge into a wild storm of passion. Every inch of her skin craved more until she froze at the pinnacle of ecstasy. In one earth-shattering burst, she came undone around him. With his guttural roar, he thrust deep and spilled within her, his entire body shaking. He panted as if he had run up to the top of Ben Nevis at a sprint.

When at last the frenzy ebbed, he gazed into her eyes and swept the damp locks from her face. "I am yours to command, m'lady."

She? Command the great Black Douglas?

"I promise to be a fair and congenial master, my husband." Giggling, she cupped his face and kissed him. "And this night, you must make love to me over and over again until we are completely and utterly spent."

AUTHOR'S NOTE

Thank you for reading *Highland Warlord.* I've spent a great deal of time crawling around ruined castles in Scotland and have wanted to write a series based on the time of Robert the Bruce for ages.

James Douglas, Lord of Douglas, was also known as Good Sir James and the Black Douglas. He was knighted and one of the king's generals during the Wars of Scottish Independence. Some facts about James' past are represented in this book. Born in 1286 (or so) in Douglas, he was the eldest son of William Douglas. His mother was Elizabeth Stewart, daughter of Alexander Stewart, 4th High Steward of Scotland. She died approximately ten years before the death of James' father, who succumbed to torture in the Tower of London.

After James' father lost Berwick and was sent to the Tower, Lord Clifford was awarded the Douglas lands by King Edward Plantagenet. James, who was about ten or eleven years of age, became an apprentice to Bishop Lamberton who was instrumental in his rise to greatness. As one of the Bruce's generals on the border, James used the cover of Selkirk Forest to stage raids on his enemies. He was relentless and ruthless and did raze Castle Douglas before the Scots were established in Southwest

Scotland, earning the moniker, the Black Douglas. James became the Bruce's closest ally when he saved his king from being mauled by the Lord of Lorne's forces in the Battle of Dalrigh.

There is no record of James' wife, which is common for that period of time. He was father to William, Lord of Douglas, and Archibald the Grim, 3rd Earl of Douglas.

Ailish Maxwell's character is fictional, as were her circumstances. However, Caerlaverock Castle was attacked by Edward in 1300. A garrison of sixty Maxwell men faced an English army three thousand strong. The Maxwell lords were not in residence in the castle at the time and within two days, the men holding the castle surrendered, some of whom were hanged from the castle walls.

Sir James went on to survive Robert the Bruce. Upon his deathbed, the king asked Douglas to carry his heart on crusade to the Holy Land. Though the record is not clear, it is thought that James died in the Battle of Teba (southern Spain) in 1330. He was most likely forty-four years of age. He is buried at St. Bride's Kirk, a partially ruined church in his beloved Douglas.

ALSO BY AMY JARECKI

The King's Outlaws

Highland Warlord

Highland Defender

The Valiant Highlander

The Fearless Highlander

The Highlander's Iron Will

Highland Force:

Captured by the Pirate Laird

The Highland Henchman

Beauty and the Barbarian

Return of the Highland Laird

Guardian of Scotland

Rise of a Legend

In the Kingdom's Name

The Time Traveler's Christmas

Highland Dynasty

Knight in Highland Armor

A Highland Knight's Desire

A Highland Knight to Remember

Highland Knight of Rapture

Highland Knight of Dreams

Devilish Dukes

The Duke's Fallen Angel

The Duke's Untamed Desire

ICE

Hunt for Evil

Body Shot

Mach One

Celtic Fire

Rescued by the Celtic Warrior

Deceived by the Celtic Spy

Lords of the Highlands series:

The Highland Duke

The Highland Commander

The Highland Guardian

The Highland Chieftain

The Highland Renegade

The Highland Earl

The Highland Rogue

The Highland Laird

The Chihuahua Affair

Virtue: A Cruise Dancer Romance

Boy Man Chief

ABOUT THE AUTHOR

Known for her action-packed, passionate historical romances, Amy Jarecki has received reader and critical praise throughout her writing career. She won the prestigious 2018 RT Reviewers' Choice award for *The Highland Duke* and the 2016 RONE award from InD'tale Magazine for Best Time Travel for her novel *Rise of a Legend.* In addition, she hit Amazon's Top 100 Bestseller List, the Apple, Barnes & Noble, and Bookscan Bestseller lists, in addition to earning the designation as an Amazon All Star Author. Readers also chose her Scottish historical romance, *A Highland Knight's Desire,* as the winning title through Amazon's Kindle Scout Program. Amy holds an MBA from Heriot-Watt University in Edinburgh, Scotland and now resides in Southwest Utah with her husband where she writes immersive historical romances. Learn more on Amy's website. Or sign up to receive Amy's newsletter.

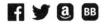